THE BAYOU WITCHES

*The Bayou Hauntings
Book Ten*

Bill Thompson

Published by
Ascendente Books
Dallas, Texas

The Bayou Witches

Published by Ascendente Books
ISBN 979-8-9874247-3-5
Printed in the United States of America

Books by Bill Thompson

<u>Mysterious America</u>
SERPENT
MIDNIGHT PASS

<u>The Bayou Hauntings</u>
CALLIE
FORGOTTEN MEN
THE NURSERY
BILLY WHISTLER
THE EXPERIMENTS
DIE AGAIN
THE PROCTOR HALL HORROR
THE ATONEMENT
DREAD RECKONING
THE BAYOU WITCHES

<u>Brian Sadler Archaeological Mystery Series</u>
THE BETHLEHEM SCROLL
ANCIENT: A SEARCH FOR THE LOST CITY
OF THE MAYAS
THE STRANGEST THING
THE BONES IN THE PIT
ORDER OF SUCCESSION
THE BLACK CROSS
TEMPLE
THE IRON DOOR

<u>Apocalyptic Fiction</u>
THE OUTCASTS

<u>The Crypt Trilogy</u>
THE RELIC OF THE KING
THE CRYPT OF THE ANCIENTS
GHOST TRAIN

<u>Middle Grade Fiction</u>
THE LEGEND OF GUNNERS COVE

THE LAST CHRISTMAS

Here's my latest book set in the Louisiana bayous and dedicated to all my friends in that great state. Special thanks goes to Celeste Landry, who invited me to an author event at the beautiful Southdown Plantation in Houma, Louisiana.

Celeste asked when I was going to write a novel set in Terrebonne Parish. It took a while, Celeste, but here it is!

CHAPTER ONE

The mayoral election was over, and Charity Device had won—of course she had—but the victory came at a dreadful cost to the town. Pendle had lost its only physician, and with him, a small piece of hope.

Dale Staggs, the town's only mechanic, remembered the day Dr. Tom Lester and his wife came to town. Their arrival sparked a rare moment of excitement in what was usually a gloomy place. Pendle wasn't the kind of town where people moved to on purpose. Mostly, its population grew only when couples—against all odds—decided to raise children in this godforsaken corner of the world. But Dr. Lester had come willingly, all the way from Texas, hoping to retire in what he imagined was a quaint, rural village deep in the Louisiana swamps that might welcome a retired, part-time physician.

Why did he choose Pendle? Maybe he didn't notice things at first. On the surface, it looked like any other small town, but beneath that veneer lay something else, something that crept up on newcomers at first, but became frighteningly obvious as time passed.

Dale shuddered at the thought of it. The Lesters had made a grave mistake coming here. There had been a moment, a brief opportunity, when Dale might have warned them. He could have told them to leave and never come back. But fear had choked the words in his throat. What if they casually mentioned his warning to someone? To the grocer? To their Realtor? Or, God forbid, to Miss Device herself? Dale had kept silent, and now Dr. Lester had paid the price. Over in Baton Rouge, he lay dying in a hospital bed from smallpox—a disease eradicated decades ago.

But then again, if there was anywhere in the world where smallpox could reemerge, it was Pendle. Everything about this town defied logic, defied reality.

Dale had dreamed about leaving a thousand times. But leaving Pendle wasn't just difficult—it was impossible. Charity Device made sure of that. She had a way of knowing when someone even thought about leaving. And once she knew, she made sure you never got the chance.

Pendle was Dale's home, the place he had been born, raised, and where he spent his entire life. He'd worked in his father's feed store as a boy, slogged through school, dropped out at sixteen, and taken a job at Harmon's Garage. When Old Man Harmon keeled over dead in 2004, Dale inherited the place and had been eking out a living ever since. It wasn't much, but it was all he needed. His only customers were the residents; it would have been nice to have extra income from people passing through, but that was a pipe dream. Nobody came here on purpose. The town lay far from a highway, down a dirt road, and when you came to Pendle, a sign at the edge of town warned you to stay out.

For years, Dale flew under the radar, keeping his head down and doing what was expected of him. He went to St. Margaret's Church every Sunday, sat at the same table for breakfast every morning at Folger's Café, and would have been the most eligible bachelor in town if not for the grease permanently embedded under his fingernails and the missing front tooth.

But all that changed when Mayor Device died and his daughter, Charity, stepped into his shoes. Suddenly everything was different. For the first time in his life, Dale was scared—truly terrified. Here nobody locked their doors at night, and you could leave your car keys in the ignition and a bicycle in the front yard, and everything would still be there in the morning. But now, that sense of security was gone, replaced by a gnawing, gut-wrenching fear that something terrible loomed ahead. The former mayor had guarded his people and kept them close, but there was something different about his daughter. She had the same powers as her father—all the Device family had special abilities—but he used his power for good, most of the time. Miss Charity Device was evil and cunning—Dale felt it even when she just glanced his way. But he didn't say anything. Never. He didn't dare.

Dale's fear turned to dread when Charity Device announced her candidacy for mayor. That surprised nobody, a Device had been mayor forever, or so they said, and no one in town expected anyone to challenge her. Who would dare? No one except Dr. Lester, who didn't know any better. And look what happened to him.

The election had ended, and the final count was posted on the big elm tree outside city hall. One vote for Dr. Lester—who everyone knew would never live to serve even if he'd won. Four hundred and twenty-seven votes for Charity Device—who was old, but certainly not dead. Probably not, anyway.

Pendle always boasted the highest voter turnout anywhere, because every adult in town voted every time. But there was never a doubt about the outcome of each election. Not a single soul in Pendle would have bet against the Device family and whatever they wanted the town to adopt. Even if Dr. Lester hadn't been lying in an isolation unit in Baton Rouge, dying from a disease that had no business existing in the modern world, no one would have dared to vote against her. But someone had. Dale Staggs decided to take a bold step.

Dale had held his breath as he marked the ballot. He'd known the risk he was taking. Voting was supposed to be secret, but everyone knew there were no secrets in Pendle. You didn't cross the Device family. You didn't play games, and you didn't ask questions.

But Dale was sick of being a puppet. He wanted everyone to know that one of their own had the guts to stand up to Miss Device, even if it was only in a voting booth. Even so, now that the election was over, Dale had to get out of Pendle, and fast. The problem was, how? He dared not tell anyone about his plan. His friends and neighbors would rat him out—they stood loyal to Miss Device because they had to be. She owned everyone, body and soul.

Dale had to plan carefully, without concentrating too hard, because if Charity Device caught wind that he wanted to go and never return, he was as good as dead. Just like Dr. Lester.

CHAPTER TWO

In Landry Drake's French Quarter walk-up apartment, sunlight streamed through the double doors that led to a patio off the bedroom. Landry stretched his hand to the other side of the bed, found it empty, and groggily wondered for a moment where Cate was. Chasing cobwebs from his brain, he opened his eyes and looked across the room at the dog bed on the floor. It was empty as well.

Reality struck hard, and awful memories flooded his brain. *They're both gone. Cate left yesterday and took Simba with her.*

Landry sighed, rubbing his temples. He replayed their last conversation in his mind, Cate's pleading eyes begging him to leave behind the perilous world of paranormal investigation. Her voice, usually so calm and supportive, had cracked with fear and frustration.

"You have to stop, Landry," she told him, her hands trembling as she clutched Simba. "One day, you won't come back. And I can't watch you slowly destroy yourself."

Adventure was in his blood. He couldn't ignore the call of the unknown, the thrill of the hunt. Each ghostly encounter, every whispered secret from beyond, was a puzzle he couldn't resist solving. It wasn't just about the thrill, although there were plenty of those. It was about exploring the mysteries of the supernatural. And to be honest with himself, he never believed she'd actually leave.

He curled into a ball, the weight of her departure crashing down on him like a tidal wave. He glanced around the bedroom, always vibrant with conversation and plans and love, now silent. Simba's absence hurt him almost as much as Cate's, which surprised him. He hadn't considered himself a dog person until Simba came into their lives. The lithe, limber pup brought immense happiness and joy to them both, and loneliness crept like a swirling storm into his head as he wondered why he'd let it come to this.

It's all my fault. I've promised a hundred times not to get into dangerous situations, but I'm a paranormal investigator, for God's sake. How can I do my job and not tempt fate now and then?

Cate had given fair warning she couldn't handle much more—the worry and anguish over the things that got him in trouble, things she called reckless but he viewed as calculated risks. He never imagined his choices would drive her away, but now she was back in Galveston and the safety of family and friends. And Landry was left alone, grappling with the harsh reality of his own shortcomings.

I must change. I have to rein in my daredevil impulses and convince her to come back. Surely she hasn't gone for good...dear God, please don't let her and Simba be gone for good.

With a heavy heart, he arose and opened the doors onto the small third-floor patio. He sat at the outdoor table, looking absently down St. Philip Street toward the Mississippi River, taking in things they loved—the sounds and smells and ambiance of the French Quarter at sunrise. The patio was small and drab, but it was their special place, where he and Cate drank their morning coffees and talked and planned their day. Now, like the rest of their apartment, it was a lonely reminder of what he'd lost. She'd been gone less than twenty-four hours, but it seemed like a lifetime to him.

A trash truck rumbled down the street below, and he watched a barge moving along the river just a few blocks away. This was shaping up as just another normal weekday in New Orleans, unless everything you cared about had suddenly departed the premises.

I'll call her when I get to the office. I'll talk things through with her, try to make her understand.

CHAPTER THREE

Jack Blair was in the middle of a live interview when the call came through that would change everything. As the senior investigative reporter for WCCY-TV Channel Nine in New Orleans, he thought he'd seen it all, but today's shoot with a self-proclaimed exorcist was one for the books. The guest, towering over six feet tall and dressed entirely in black, had smeared dark eye shadow around his eyes in a failed attempt to appear menacing. Instead of invoking fear, he looked more like a caricature—like Tiny Tim, the eccentric sixties singer with a falsetto voice who strummed a ukulele. Jack struggled to take the man seriously.

As the director called a wrap, Jack's focus shifted. An assistant thrust a slip of paper in his hands. It bore only four words and a phone number: *Urgent. Call your sister.*

He stared at the message, an unease settling over him. How long had it been since he last spoke to Melody? At least a year or more. She'd be twenty-four now. She'd left home after he did, and in years, the only calls he got from her came when she needed help. Abusive relationships, scrapes with the law, lack of rent money—one thing after another. He might not have returned the call except the number she left wasn't from a place he expected—the 985 area code was in Louisiana.

He steeled himself for the inevitable conflict. The phone barely rang before she picked up. "Mel?" he began, trying to sound casual despite the growing tension in his chest. "Long time no—"

"Jack," she cut him off, her voice a trembling whisper. "I'm in deep shit. You gotta come help me."

He sighed, familiar frustration bubbling up. "What now, Mel? Lost another job? Robbed by some deadbeat boyfriend? What is it this time?"

Her voice cracked, a mixture of fear and desperation that sent a chill down his spine. "They're gonna kill me, Jack. You have to help me get out of this place."

His skepticism wavered as curiosity and a creeping sense of dread took hold. "Where are you? What the hell have you gotten yourself into?"

"I'm in Pendle, south of Houma. I haven't done anything, I swear! Please, just come get me!"

Before he could ask more, he detected someone in the background—a cold, female voice so eerie that it made his skin crawl. "Who are you calling?" it demanded, sharp and accusatory.

There was a scuffle, the sound of buttons being frantically pressed, and then the same voice, colder now, more menacing. "Jack Blair? You're calling *him*? Are you out of your mind?"

"Help me, Jack!" Melody screamed, her words muffled, as if someone covered her mouth.

Then, with a sickening finality, the call dropped.

Jack stared at his phone, a hollow feeling gnawing at him. He had to help her, and he had to move quickly.

CHAPTER FOUR

Jack tried six times to call her back, but each went to voicemail. Then he called Landry Drake and gave him a brief update. Even with three years of investigative reporting experience at Channel Nine under his belt, Jack wanted to involve his friend and mentor this time. It was his sister—his estranged sibling with whom he had little contact—who was frantically reaching out for help, and he needed someone who could deal with her objectively. God knew he'd never been able to.

Melody had a flair for the dramatic, Jack recalled from the days when he and his sister lived at home in Memphis. Every little thing that happened to her became the biggest issue ever; things were always worse for her than anyone else. He'd last seen her when his mom kicked his drunken ass out of the house and he moved to New Orleans. Years passed, and Melody had left home too on the day she turned eighteen. As time passed and her calls became less frequent, he got his own life back on track and decided that his frustrating sister and her problems no longer concerned him. Now she'd popped back up, and from the sound of her voice, maybe she actually was in trouble this time.

Thirty minutes later, Jack and Landry met at Café Beignet on Royal Street. Jack asked how things were going with their dog, Simba, which caused Landry to have to explain that Cate and Simba went to Galveston. "She's teaching me a lesson," he continued. "She wants me to slow things down on the paranormal side and quit putting myself in dangerous situations. But enough about me."

Jack had just began explaining when his phone rang again, this time another unknown caller in the 985 area code—the area of southeastern Louisiana where Melody said Pendle was situated. Jack took the call, putting the phone on speaker so Landry could listen.

"Mr. Blair, this is Charity Device. I'm the mayor of Pendle, Louisiana." The voice sounded authoritative and cultured, with a trace of an English accent. And cold. Cold as ice. Was it the same voice he'd heard in the background on Mel's call? He didn't know for sure.

Jack gave Landry a shrug as he wondered about this call coming less than an hour after Melody's frantic one from the same area code. He replied while Landry googled the name to see what he could find.

"How can I help, Ms. Device?"

"It's about your sister, Melody. She reached out to you earlier today. I'm calling to advise everything is fine. She suffered a delusional episode, perhaps from medication. Regardless, all is well."

Jack was flummoxed. He stared at the phone for a moment. "I don't understand. Why is the mayor calling about my sister? And how do you know she's fine?"

A mirthless laugh. "It's a small town. We all keep an eye out for each other."

"But how do you know she called me? Were you there with her, the one in the background who yelled at her?"

The response was clipped and even. "I don't know what you're talking about. I'm merely saving you a trip. You haven't seen your sister in years, and she had no business reaching out to you now. She's under a doctor's care, so you needn't worry. I won't take more of your time. Goodbye."

Jack stared at the dead phone, trying to sort out the bizarre call, and Landry read from his phone. "She said her name was Charity Device, but Pendle's mayor is a man with the same last name. There are five hundred and eight people in the town, and it's in Terrebonne Parish, seventy-eight miles from here. By the way, I wasn't aware of a sister. How come you've never mentioned her?"

"Nothing much to mention. My alcoholic, addicted self wasn't much of a brother to her, and she was a teenager when Mom kicked me out and I ended up living on the street here in New Orleans. I haven't seen her in years, and the last time I connected with my mother, she told me Mel had walked out on her eighteenth birthday and there hadn't been a word since. That's been six years."

"Tell me more about the call you got. Do you think she's in trouble or not?"

"Or not would be my initial guess. She's always been flaky as hell. But then again, I haven't heard from her in years. Why would she reach out to me after all this time if something wasn't wrong? And the call from the mayor just doesn't make sense. She mentioned people keep an eye out for each other, but this is way over the top. I think I'll go over there. How about joining me? It'll take your mind off Cate and Simba for a while."

Since they'd left, Landry slogged through the days in a fog. Nothing mattered enough to interest him, and he had a knot in his stomach from the stress. She was teaching him a lesson. He understood that, and part of him wanted to call and say he was ready to do anything she asked, but they weren't married, and they'd never fought over anything except his daredevil escapades in the world of the paranormal. So another part of him—the macho masculine ego-fueled part—told him to resist calling her. Let her reach out when she felt ready to come back.

But a place in the back of his conscience gnawed at him with a thought. *What if she doesn't come back?*

He jerked his head up and returned to the present. Jack sat watching him closely. "It's eating you up, isn't it?" he said. "It's tearing you apart. Do something about it."

"I will," he mumbled. "Soon. I have to. But for now, I'll go with you. First, I want to go to the studio and get my laptop."

Jack said he'd stop by the TV station, pick up a camera, and meet Landry in the parking garage behind the Monteleone Hotel. Shortly, they turned onto I-10, heading out of the city.

CHAPTER FIVE

An hour later, they drove through Houma on Highway 315 and headed south. Jack's GPS guided him to Theriot, then west through pastures and swamps to the shores of Bayou Dularge, where they came upon a faded wooden sign, paint peeling and boards missing. Jack pulled to the shoulder and snapped a picture.

This is Pendle.

Oldest Settlement in Louisiana.

Established 1614.

Residents Only Beyond this Point. NO TRESPASSING!

"1614?" The date surprised Landry. "But how can this place be the oldest if I've never heard of it? I learned in school that Natchitoches is the oldest town in Louisiana." He googled the name and added, "Yep. Natchitoches, settled in 1714. No mention of Pendle at all. I read earlier about its population and location and who the mayor is, but there's nothing online about the town's history."

"Well, I guess we're going to find out." Jack ignored the sign and drove on, rounding a turn that led them into a hamlet nestled in a bend along the bayou. Main Street was a two-lane avenue with mossy oaks along both sides that bathed it in perpetual shade. The trees ended as clapboard houses gave way to a commercial area that ran for a few blocks, lined with ancient brick and frame buildings of varying sizes and heights. Most of the stores were closed; with grimy, cheerless shop windows and faded signage, they appeared to have been untended for some time.

Except for one. In the middle of a block of darkened storefronts stood a welcoming I—a bookstore with paned front windows and black shutters. It stood out like a beacon, a place one could browse and become immersed in the latest novel. And even more surprising was the Open sign beside the wide-open front door.

"Only one store open? That's strange," Landry commented as Jack drove past the little shop. "Let's check it out before we leave."

A few blocks along, the street ran around a town square, where a seedy, once-majestic three-story stone building stood amidst more ancient oaks. It was a picturesque scene that might have graced a postcard back in the day, when the structure had been well maintained and the trees trimmed. At present, it looked like it belonged in a horror movie.

Jack had tried his sister's cellphone several more times during their trip, with no success. Not knowing where to find her, Landry suggested they go to the building in the square, which likely contained offices for the town government. "With five hundred residents, I don't think it's going to be hard to find someone who knows where your sister lives," he added.

They walked up a flight of stone stairs laced with grass that sprouted through cracks in the cement. An urn outside the double glass doors overflowed with cigarette butts, and more lay on the ground where no one had bothered to clean them up. A faded sign above the doors read City Hall.

"Not much civic pride these days," Jack muttered as they entered a long, dark hallway that smelled faintly of urine, stale tobacco and mold. The dim light from one overhead fixture flickered, casting eerie shadows that danced on the cracked, peeling walls.

Panes of frosted glass in the doors that lined the corridor bore faded, painted signs: Department of Sanitation, City Utilities, Office of Public Works. The usual operations of a town, but behind each door, the rooms seemed shrouded in darkness. Landry turned the knob on one—Office of the City Manager, Benjamin T. Haney—and found it unlocked. The door creaked open, revealing a room frozen in time. Gloom enveloped the space, and dust-covered furniture seemed to stand as silent reminders of a forgotten era.

An old-fashioned black rotary-dial telephone and an ashtray adorned each desk, and old metal file cabinets, their surfaces rusted and dented, lined a wall. Papers were strewn about haphazardly as though the staff had just departed, although it was apparent no one had worked in this office for years.

They continued down the long corridor, stopping to listen to a faint rustling in the distance, possibly rats or the building settling. Each step they took stirred up clouds of dust, creating ghostly plumes that floated lazily in the scant light.

The walls bore the scars of neglect, faded posters and notices hung askew, and Landry moved closer to examine a flyer advertising a sheriff's sale on the building's front lawn on July 24, 1973. Further along, a calendar from that same year was tacked to the wall, its pages curled and yellowed, marking time that had ceased to matter in this strange building.

Jack and Landry walked on down the hallway, its oppressive atmosphere weighing on their shoulders. "This place looks abandoned," Jack whispered. "It's giving me the heebie-jeebies."

Landry agreed, wondering aloud why a municipal building would be deserted.

A broad wooden staircase led to the upper floors; on the wall next to it was a directory of offices. Landry noticed one—Archives, Room 200. He made a mental note to see what the archives contained.

Further along, they approached an office that was occupied, the only such one they'd seen. Light filtered through the frosted glass of the door, casting a soft glow into the dim corridor. The words *Marcus Device, Mayor* were painted on the glass, but a page taped beneath declared in scribbled handwriting that Charity Device was the new mayor of Pendle.

Landry tried the door but found it locked. He rapped, and they waited as they heard footsteps approaching from within, and a shadow shifted behind the opaque glass, signaling that someone was on the other side. With a click of a lock, the door swung open to reveal a strikingly tall woman—six feet if she was an inch, Landry speculated— with long, gray hair cascading down her shoulders. Clad head to toe in black, she exuded an air of domination and authority, and when she spoke, her voice was deep and resonant.

"Welcome to Pendle, gentlemen," she said, her dark eyes piercing into theirs. "I see you chose to come despite my assurances Melody Blair is fine."

"How…how do you know who we are?" Jack stammered, the hairs on the back of his neck standing on end. In this tomb of a municipal building, it seemed that ghosts of the past lingered just out of sight, somewhere in the gloom further down the long hallway.

The formidable woman laughed, a harsh sound that echoed throughout the building like the shrill cackle of a raven. "Few visitors come here, and I know every resident by name, so it wasn't difficult. I expected you to defy my order not to come and to ignore our sign that warned you not to trespass."

"Your *order*?" Landry snapped back. "The mayor issues orders to visitors? We took it as a suggestion, but Jack wants to see his sister. He can decide for himself if she's fine or not. Where is she?"

The woman drew a deep breath, turned, and walked into the depths of her office, leaving them at the door. She took a seat behind a massive old desk and said nothing as they approached. The desk, its top completely bare, was one of the strangest things Landry had seen; crafted from dark, ancient wood that seemed to absorb and extinguish the surrounding light, it exuded an unsettling aura. Its surface was scarred with countless nicks and scratches, hinting at a mysterious history.

The legs were the most unsettling feature, twisted and gnarled as if shaped by a malevolent force. They spiraled downward, reminding Landry of the crooked limbs of an old crone, with intricate carvings that could barely be made out in the gloom. To him the markings appeared to be sinister runes and mysterious faces that infused the desk with a palpability, as though it might come alive.

"I have no idea where your sister is at this time," the woman said at last.

Jack replied, "Ms. Device—Madam Mayor—you know everyone in this town. In fact, you seem to keep close tabs on your residents. Just tell us where my sister lives, and we'll be out of your way."

"Get out of my town!" she suddenly screamed, causing Landry and Jack to take a step backwards in surprise. She stood, took a deep breath, and snapped, "You have no business in this place. Everything is fine here, and we have no time and no need for intrusion." She walked around the desk and out into the hall. Stunned for a moment, they followed her, but the dark hallway was empty.

Charity Device was gone.

CHAPTER SIX

They walked the silent corridor of the musty old building, the shadows pressing in on them from every corner. The air was thick, carrying the scent of decay and forgotten times, and each step echoed against the cold, cracked floor. When they emerged into the sunshine, the warmth was almost blinding, a stark contrast to the oppressive gloom inside the building.

"Let's check out the town and see if we can find someone to speak with," Jack suggested, the unease still gnawing at his insides. He drove around the building, following Main Street as it continued into an area they hadn't seen earlier, hoping for a sign of life in this seemingly deserted town.

Here the storefronts were as dark and abandoned as the others had been. Their windows, like dead eyes, stared blankly at the street, revealing nothing but the emptiness inside. After a quick look, they drove back toward the other end of town.

As commercial buildings gave way once again to residences, they saw one business that was open. Harmon's

Garage occupied an old gas station, its faded Texaco star sign a ghostly reminder of a bygone era. An old car was parked in one bay, and a man was working under the hood. As they pulled in and stopped, the man walked outside, wiping his hands on a pair of dirty overalls, his expression wary and tense.

"What do you fellas need?" the man said as he approached their car. "Ain't got gas, if that's what you're wantin'."

"We need directions," Jack replied. "Do you know where Melody Blair lives?"

The man looked away, muttering, "Nope," and retreated to the bay, his shoulders hunched as if expecting a blow.

They both exited the vehicle and followed the man inside. "I'm Landry Drake—"

"Don't matter who you are," the man replied without looking up. "You'd best be heading on out of town now."

"What's your name?"

"Staggs. Dale Staggs. This here's my garage. Now go. It ain't good for me to be seen talking to strangers."

That surprised Landry. "What do you mean? What are you worried about? We just need directions."

The man looked up, his bravado gone and his eyes filled with fear. "Leave me be. Please. You're gonna create a lot of problems..." He stopped, his gaze flicking to the shadows outside as if expecting something—or someone—to emerge.

Landry pushed on. "What are you afraid of? Melody Blair is my friend's sister. She called and begged him to come get her. Why can't you help us?"

Staggs whispered, "There's a trailer park three blocks down Main from here. Her trailer's got a yellow sunflower on the side. Don't tell anybody I helped you. Please!" He went back to work under the hood of the car in his bay, ignoring Landry, who still stood a few feet away, feeling a growing sense of unease.

"Thanks," Landry said, mustering a smile although his insides were twisting with anxiety. "If we need more help, we'll be back."

"Best to get on out of town," Staggs muttered under his breath, his voice trembling. "Just wish I could do the same."

They found the trailer park easily, and although there were perhaps sixty units of various types, sizes and ages parked on concrete slabs, it took little time maneuvering the tight streets to find the rusty one with a sunflower painted on the side. Jack led the way, climbing a set of wooden stairs that led onto a sagging porch. He knocked on the front door, waited a moment, and then knocked again. "Melody?" he yelled. "It's me, Jack. I came to help you." Then he tried the knob, turned it, and went inside.

As he waited in the yard, Landry saw a woman emerge from a trailer next door. He approached her with a smile and said, "Good morning. Do you know if Melody Blair is home?"

Avoiding eye contact, she replied, "None of my business. Yours either," then walked back inside her trailer and shut the door.

"Friendly bunch of folks in this town," Landry muttered as he walked back to Melody's trailer, where he found the door standing open. He called out for Jack and heard a reply from inside, "Come help me look around."

The cluttered rooms nevertheless showed a semblance of order. A stack of magazines on the floor, a collection of salt-and-pepper shakers on a display cabinet, clean plates and bowls stacked on the narrow kitchen counter—

organized chaos was the phrase that came to Landry's mind. He waited while Jack quickly searched the rest of the tiny trailer. No one else was there.

Landry told him about his brief encounter with the woman next door and how she dismissed him with a "none of your business" remark.

From behind him came a voice. "Maybe you should have heeded her advice."

They did a quick about-face and saw Mayor Device standing in the doorway. Her eyes were dark, hollow pools, and a smile played on her lips. "But you've already made it your business," she added as a siren wailed in the distance. "The police are coming to investigate this obvious case of breaking and entering."

Jack and Landry exchanged a glance, realizing they had stumbled upon something more puzzling than they had anticipated. Continuing to block the door, the mayor crossed her arms, her smile widening, and snapped, "Welcome to my town. I hope you enjoy your stay."

CHAPTER SEVEN

An old Dodge police cruiser, worn and battered from years of service, screeched to a halt in front of Melody Blair's trailer. Curious neighbors peeked through their window curtains, eager to see what the commotion was about. The portly, ruddy-faced police chief hoisted himself from the passenger seat, removed his hat, and nodded respectfully to the woman standing in the doorway.

"Good mornin', Madam Mayor. Sounds like you stumbled across some criminal activity," he said as he spat a stream of tobacco juice onto the pavement, narrowly missing his own shoe.

As the other officer, a young man with a scraggly beard, joined the chief, Mayor Device responded, "I caught these men rummaging through this trailer. They entered without permission."

Landry stepped forward and spoke to the chief. "Sir, I'm Landry Drake. This is Jack Blair, Melody's brother. She left a frantic call asking for help to get out of this town. That's why we're here. This lady—the mayor—doesn't know if Jack has permission to enter this trailer or not. We're looking for Melody; do you have any idea where she is?"

The chief chuckled. "My, my, you're pretty uppity for a fella in big trouble, dontcha know?" He turned to the woman. "What do you want me to do with them? Toss 'em in the can for a day or two? Run 'em outta town? Your call, Mayor."

"Mayor," Jack pleaded, "I'd like to find my sister. Everyone in this town seems to be afraid of something..."

She laughed. "Afraid of something? What on earth are you talking about?"

"'None of my business' seems to be the catchphrase around here."

"We're a pretty close-knit group, right, Chief?" she snapped. "We're naturally wary of strangers, and in this case it was a good idea, since you both proceeded to break into this trailer."

"With all respect—" Landry began, but the chief shut him down. "Anythin' you say can be used against you, blah, blah, blah, so you better shut up. Miss Device, you good with me takin' them to jail?"

The mayor turned to Landry. "Mr. Drake, do you think you and your friend can stay out of trouble long enough to get out of town? If so, I'll let you both leave with your reputations and your records untarnished."

Out of options, Landry nodded. "Let's go, Jack."

Jack protested, "But what about my sister? She's in trouble somewhere in this town."

The mayor issued an order to the chief. "Take down Mr. Blair's phone number and start a search for this girl. I'll bet she's not missing at all. She's just causing trouble. But if you get any news, call him."

Just then the police radio in the cruiser crackled to life. "We have her," came the muffled report.

Jack's eyes widened. "Who do they have? Melody?"

"That's police business, mister," the chief snapped. "Now give me your number and get on out of town like the mayor said."

They left on Main, the same way they'd arrived. As they passed the bookstore, they saw the front door was closed and the Open sign had been turned to its counterpart on the reverse.

Once they left the city limits, Jack said, "I'm not done here. Let's have dinner in Houma and come back after dark to see if we can find her."

Landry smiled. "You're getting as bad as I am. I guess we've complied with the letter of the law, if not the intent. We're leaving town, like the mayor told us to. She didn't say we couldn't come back."

This is what Cate would call unnecessary risk-taking, Landry thought, opening his phone to search for restaurants in the nearby town. *But you're not here, Cate. I hope to God you'll be back soon, but without you I have nothing to lose by taking risks.* The realization that the person who loved him wasn't around to warn him about danger saddened Landry.

Thoughts of Cate and Simba took a temporary reprieve when Jack pulled into the parking lot of Boudreau and Thibodeau's Cajun Cookin', a down-home restaurant each of them never missed when they were in Houma. Landry ordered an Abita Amber, and Jack got his usual—a Dr Pepper. Both came in ice-cold mugs. Soon they were feasting on a platter of crawfish and steaming hot bowls of the restaurant's signature dish—"gumbeau" with chicken and sausage—and reminiscing about past supernatural events they'd experienced. There had been plenty of suspense and dangerous situations, some of which they'd barely escaped from. Again he thought of Cate, and when Jack saw his face cloud with sadness, he said, "You miss her a lot, don't you?"

"Yeah, and that crazy little dog too," he said with a rueful laugh. "Not having them with me is eating me up inside."

"That's obvious. For both your sakes, I hope you're together again soon."

CHAPTER EIGHT

They finished dinner, settled their bill, and headed south. At night the highway was a ribbon of blackness, and when they turned west at Theriot and took the narrow, winding road to Pendle, the atmosphere grew even more eerie and sinister. Tall, undulating grass closed in on both sides, and their headlights pierced the night, revealing glimpses of startled rabbits, an elusive bobcat who darted across their path, and a fox, eyes glowing eerily in the beams, who vanished into the underbrush.

As they neared Bayou Dularge, Jack muttered a prayer that the car wouldn't break down way out here in the boondocks. Landry shared his unease; hidden in the grasses were the swamps, where alligators, their predatory eyes ever watchful, lay in the shallow water, poised to strike at anything—human or otherwise—that crossed their path.

They passed the "welcome but no trespassing" sign and rounded the bend into town, only to enter an abyss of darkness. No streetlights, no flickers in the dark windows, no sign of life—just an oppressive black void. The only sign that they had arrived were the looming, shadowy silhouettes of buildings. Jack slowed the car to a crawl as they entered the heart of Pendle.

The scene was unsettling. Only a couple of establishments had been open earlier, but now their darkened hulks stood like sinister, veiled monsters awaiting their prey. Every structure—stores, repair shops, homes—stood cloaked in darkness. It felt as if they had driven into a ghost town, where the only remnants of life were the chilling echoes of the past. The silence was suffocating, and the air was thick with an unseen, ominous presence. It was as though Pendle had been abandoned to the shadows, leaving Landry and Jack stranded in a place where even memories dared not linger.

Landry said, "Let's drive around for a few minutes. I want to see what the churches in this place look like. I googled earlier and got only two hits, Catholic and Anglican. The Anglican makes more sense since these people emigrated from England." They crisscrossed the streets until they found the Catholic one, Church of the Incarnation, in a tiny building next to an overgrown, weed-infested cemetery. At this time of night, it was as dark as the rest of Pendle.

"I'll bet that's the smallest Catholic church in Louisiana," Jack commented. "Doesn't appear to me that many folks in Pendle have need for religion."

They drove on, and two blocks further down they came to an eerie sight. St. Margaret's Anglican Church, a modern wooden structure perhaps twice as large as the Catholic one, stood in the shadows. But this church was far more interesting because just behind the building stood the dark, eerie ruins of a much older stone church. Its ruined arches and walls reached for the sky like silent sentinels. The roof had collapsed long ago, and where stained-glass windows had been, colored shards jutted from empty holes in the walls. Even in its ruined state, the old stone building dwarfed the later church.

Landry saw a single light at the back of the building and wondered if someone inside might answer their questions. They parked and walked to the front door, where they read a sign.

St. Margaret's Anglican Church.
Established 1620.
Struck by lightning and destroyed 1937.
New sanctuary dedicated April 10, 1938.

He knocked on the heavy oak door, the sound echoing through the empty courtyard. For a moment, there was no response. Then they heard a key being inserted into the lock. The door creaked open, revealing the shadowed figure of a priest, his face half hidden in the dim light of the entryway.

"How may I help?" he asked.

"Father, may we talk to you for a minute?" Landry asked, his voice steady but laced with urgency.

The priest stepped out into the dark courtyard. He was an older man, his eyes kind but weary, as if the weight of Pendle's secrets had aged him more than time itself. He gave a faint smile, though there was hesitation behind it. "I'm Father Elias. What do you want here?"

Jack spoke up before Landry could, desperation creeping into his voice. "We're looking for my sister, Melody Blair. She's missing. Any idea where she might be?"

The priest's brow furrowed, and he opened the door a little wider, motioning for them to come inside. "A missing person? Come in, come in. I'll see what I can do."

They stepped inside, the scent of incense heavy in the air, mingling with an eerie dampness. One flickering candle on the altar provided scant light, barely pushing back the shadows. As they walked deeper into the sanctuary, Landry felt a prickling at the back of his neck, a familiar sensation that others were nearby.

Father Elias led them into a side recess, where another single candle burned beside a statue of a saint. He turned to face them, his expression still calm but cautious.

"Now," the priest began, "tell me more about your sister, and perhaps I can—"

"Melody Blair," Jack interrupted. He explained about the call and her plea for help.

As Jack spoke, Father Elias's face grew tight with concern, his eyes flicking to Landry. He opened his mouth to say something, but then paused, his gaze lingering on Landry's face for a long, uncomfortable moment.

Uncomfortable, Landry said, "Is something wrong, Father?"

"Who are you?"

"Landry Drake. We've come over from New Orleans…"

The priest crossed himself, his eyes darting about the room. Then, as if a switch had been flipped, his entire demeanor changed. The warmth in his eyes vanished, replaced by fear. He took a step back, shaking his head. "No, no…I can't help you."

Jack blinked in confusion. "What? But you just said—"

The priest cut him off, his voice suddenly low and urgent. "I didn't realize who you were until now," he muttered, staring at Landry.

Landry frowned. "What does that have to do with anything?"

Elias swallowed hard, beads of sweat now visible on his pale forehead. His voice was a whisper that carried a strange, trembling reverence. "Have you any idea how dangerous it is for you to be here? This town hasn't forgotten you."

Landry asked what he was talking about, but the priest took another step back, his hand gripping the edge of a pew for support. His eyes seemed wild, as if haunted by something unseen. "They're watching. They're always watching. You need to leave."

"Who? What are you talking about?" Landry asked. The poor man seemed disoriented and scared, and his words made no sense.

"You must go. I've said enough. You...you shouldn't have come here."

"What's the deal, Father? Everybody we meet in this town has secrets, and nobody wants to help us find Melody. You're a priest; surely you can help us."

Elias's face turned ashen, and his eyes locked onto Landry as if he were staring at a ghost. "No more questions," he whispered. "I've said too much already. You must leave Pendle before it's too late. They're aware that you're here. They know everything."

"The mayor? Is that who—"

Without another word, Father Elias turned and fled through a door at the back of the sanctuary.

"He's scared of something," Jack said, but Landry focused on the creeping sense of dread clawing its way up his spine. He felt the things Father Elias had mentioned—someone watching and the weight of unseen things pressing on Landry. Something was wrong. And whatever it was involved him.

"Let's go," Landry said, his voice tense as he grabbed Jack's arm and pulled him toward the street. Fat drops of rain began to fall from the thick clouds above, and to Landry it seemed as though the entire town of Pendle crouched in the gloom, waiting for him.

Father Elias had been right. They *were* being watched. No question about it.

And whatever was watching them was very, very close.

You must leave now, a voice in Landry's mind warned. He glanced at Jack, who appeared not to have experienced the same sense of dread.

"Before we leave, I want to go back to that trailer park and look around," Jack said, turning the car further into Pendle rather than on the road that led back to the highway.

Although remaining in Pendle was the last thing Landry wanted to do, he shared Jack's concern over the whereabouts of his sister, so he buried his uneasy thoughts and said nothing.

In the trailer park, a handful of lights burned in windows, a sight that seemed out of place in this dark, eerie town. Jack made some turns, following the route they'd taken earlier, but in a moment he stopped.

He pointed through the window. "Wasn't her trailer there, second one on the right?"

Landry thought so but wondered if they might be on the wrong street. Here, instead of the trailer with the sunflower on the side, a smaller one nothing like Melody's sat in the space.

"Hold on a sec. You're right," Landry said. "That trailer next door's the same—the one the lady came out of. I asked her about Mel, and she said it was none of my business. Let's see if she's home." They walked to her door and knocked. There was no response, but after he rapped harder, he heard muffled noises inside, and at last the door opened. Silhouetted in a frame of light, the same woman stood in the doorway, wearing a bathrobe and slippers, her gray hair wrapped in large, old-fashioned curlers. As he peeked inside, Landry realized why the town was dark; this lady had blackout shades so thick that not a shaft of light got through. Perhaps all the other homes and businesses did too. *Maybe a city ordinance, which would be a really strange thing,* he thought.

"What do you want now?" the woman whispered. "You shouldn't have come back here!"

He pointed to the mobile home next door. "What happened to Melody's trailer? That one wasn't here earlier today. When did she move it?"

The lady glanced from left to right before whispering, "Nobody moved nothing. Now get out. You have no business being here. It's too..." She moved to close the door, but Landry blocked it with his elbow, "She's my friend's sister. We think she's in trouble. Do you know where she is?"

Her eyes showed the fear that gripped her. "Stop it and leave me alone! I can't talk to you anymore. The mayor..." She trailed off, her voice trembling and her gaze darting to the shadows as if expecting someone would emerge. With a final, wary look, she stepped back into her trailer and pulled the door closed behind her. Landry heard the distinct click of a lock.

Frustrated but undeterred, they sat in their vehicle for a few minutes, considering what just happened. The neighbor seemed terrified, and she'd blurted something about the mayor before retreating inside. "Something's wrong here, Jack," Landry said. "Nothing makes any sense, and I'm getting concerned about your sister's safety. No one could have moved her trailer and replaced it with another one in such a short time. That's impossible, so how did it happen?

"Then there's the town itself. It's as though it's designed to appear marginally functional in the daytime, there are a few stores open, but there's none of the usual stuff you'd expect to see. No sales announcements or signs, and the front windows are all empty. The buildings are dirty and grimy too. It's bizarre...this whole place is unreal, like a town built on a film company's back lot—active all day but shuttered and dark at night. It's as though people come here, work here, live here until five o'clock when it's time to lock up the town and go home, wherever that is.

"These people are like actors in some kind of bizarre play. There are exceptions—the neighbor lady who lives by your sister's trailer, for one. She was there at night, although from how quiet things were, I'd bet almost nobody else was in that trailer park. That mechanic too—he seems scared to death. And the mayor—Charity Device— seems real enough, although we didn't see her tonight. The town has no streetlamps, no cars on the street anywhere, and no people in sight."

Jack nodded. "I'm very worried about Mel, but I don't know what else we can do tonight. Hopefully, we can find a clue in the town's archives. Are you up for another charge of breaking and entering?"

Landry, deep in thought, gazed out the car window before replying, "I think we should try, We might learn something. But not breaking in. If we can find an unlocked door or window, then we can go inside. Otherwise we don't. We have enough problems here as it is. Let's go on over there; it's getting late. I'll leave Cate a voicemail to let her know where we are, just in case."

"Is she checking voicemails from you?" Jack asked, and Landry answered with a shrug. "I hope so, I leave them, and that's all I can do."

CHAPTER NINE

They parked on a dark street two blocks from the town square and walked. The moon hung low in the sky, casting long, twisted shadows that seemed to writhe and shift with a life of their own. The town was unnervingly silent, the kind of silence that pressed down on your ears, amplifying every tiny noise until it felt like the darkness itself was alive and listening.

In the oppressive gloom, when one's imagination can run rampant, the municipal building became an enormous, sinister presence--a huge, looming black mass that threatened to engulf Jack and Landry. The sheer size of it felt overwhelming, as if it were a predatory being lying in wait. Involuntary shivers went down their spines as it seemed they were the only two living beings in this godforsaken, ghostly town.

"The archives room is on the second floor," Landry said. "I saw the sign last time we were here. Now we have to find a way in."

"Let's start with the obvious," Jack replied as he approached the main entrance, drawing back in surprise as the door swung open by itself with a groan that echoed down the deserted street.

"What the hell—" Jack cried, but Landry shushed him.

"We should go," Jack said, but Landry whispered they were already here and might as well see what they could find. For now the sensation of being watched had gone, and all that was left was an oppressive gloom.

The moment they stepped inside, the old door slammed shut behind them with a resounding thud. Landry let out a yell as Jack jumped backwards, startled.

As before, the air was stale and heavy, carrying the scent of mold and something that smelled faintly of rot. The only light came from the flashlights they carried, beams cutting through the oppressive gloom as they navigated the wide hallway they'd walked before.

Shadows clung to every corner and crevice, stretching out like dark tendrils that might ensnare them. Their footsteps echoed ominously in the empty corridor, the sound unnaturally loud against the backdrop of silence. Every creak of the floorboards, every distant groan of the old building settling, set their nerves on edge.

Climbing the old wooden stairs, they reached the second floor, where a faded sign caked with layers of grime pointed them to the archives room. The lettering was old and cracked, the paint peeling away like dead skin. A shiver crawled up Landry's spine as he reached out to touch the sign, his fingers coming away coated in dust.

They opened the door and stepped into another room that seemed untouched for decades. The stench of decay was stronger here, and the air was thick with motes that swirled in their flashlight beams. The room was large and had towering shelves that stretched from floor to ceiling. In the shelves were hundreds of boxes that lined the walls like silent sentinels guarding dark secrets. The shelves themselves were ancient, the wood warped and rotting, threatening to collapse under the weight of the years and whatever secrets lay hidden in the boxes.

The thick layer of dust that coated the floor muffled their footsteps. Landry felt something deeply unsettling about the room—that same sense of dread that prickled the hairs on his neck, like they were trespassing in a place where no one should be.

Each box bore a label with a date, many of which stretched back centuries, to the sixteen hundreds, to the time of Pendle's settlement. Landry searched for the oldest boxes and hesitated for a moment before reaching out to one of them, his hand trembling as he pulled it from the shelf.

It was surprisingly light, almost weightless, as if the contents had long since withered away. He lifted the lid and peered inside, only to find it completely empty. Not a scrap of paper, not a trace of what might have once been stored there. Just emptiness, as hollow and cold as the feeling settling in his gut.

"Jack, look at this," Landry whispered, as though speaking any louder would disturb something lurking in the shadows. Jack came over, and together they began pulling down box after box, each marked with dates that should have held the town's records. But each one was the same—despite the year or the century, each was empty, devoid of any archival material, as if someone or something had erased the town's history.

"Why are they all empty?" Jack asked, becoming uneasy. He glanced around the room, his eyes darting to the dark corners where the flashlight beams barely penetrated. "Where are the archives?"

Landry's stomach churned into knots. "I don't know, but this isn't right. We need to get out of here."

As he turned to leave, Landry's flashlight beam swept across the room over a now-empty shelf, and he noticed something—small, hardly noticeable, but there. The light caught faint markings on the shelves, things carved into the wood. He moved closer, squinting at what he realized were symbols etched deep into the rotting wood.

"What's that?" Jack asked, leaning in to get a closer look. Landry had seen some of the symbols in previous work with the paranormal—pentagrams and runes and mystical numbers used to practice black magic. "This isn't just an archive," he whispered. "It's something else entirely."

A sudden gust of wind blew through the windowless room, a seeming impossibility. At once the beams from their flashlights flickered, then went out, plunging the room into darkness.

"Landry!" Jack shouted, but his voice was lost in the rising howl of the wind. Boxes and dust swirled around them, and the shelves creaked ominously as the gale seemed to press in from all sides, like the room itself was alive and aimed to swallow them whole.

And then, just as suddenly as it began, everything stopped. The silence that followed was deafening, oppressive, as if something nearby was holding its breath. Their hearts pounded as their flashlights clicked to life, the beams cutting through the thick, unnatural darkness.

All the boxes, once arranged in rows upon the shelves, now lay scattered across the floor, their lids torn off, their insides still empty. But the symbols carved into the wood all around the room now glowed faintly, pulsing with a sickly green light that made Landry's skin crawl.

"We need to get out of here," Landry yelled, grabbing Jack's arm. But as they turned to leave, the door they had come through slammed shut with a thunderous bang.

Landry rushed to the door, yanking on the handle, but it wouldn't budge. He wondered if the building itself had come alive, trapping them inside its decaying heart. Jack banged on the door, shouting for help, but his cries were useless. No other living soul was in the building.

From somewhere deep within the archives, there came a low, guttural whisper, murmuring words they couldn't understand. An eerie sound slithered through the darkness, curling around them like a cold, invisible serpent. The walls seemed to close in as the symbols on the shelves glowed even brighter, casting an eerie, otherworldly light across the room.

Faint whispers grew louder, more insistent, until they filled Landry's mind with apprehension. The darkness began to pulse with sounds, and Landry sensed something in the room with them, something that might have been waiting in the shadows for centuries. Wispy black shapes formed into blobs that floated in the darkness, drifting toward them.

"Move, now!" Landry shouted. They scrambled away from the door, moving deeper into the room, the voices growing louder with every step they took. As they reached the center of the room, the ground beneath them shifted, and they stumbled, attempting to catch themselves on the edge of a fallen shelf. The floorboards groaned, and with a sickening crack, the floor gave way beneath them.

They fell, the world spinning in a blur of darkness and whispers, and the symbols on the shelves burned fiercely as they plummeted. Below there was nothing but a yawning void filled with nothingness that followed them down, down, down into the depths of Pendle's forgotten history.

CHAPTER TEN

Landry and Jack plummeted through a blur of shadows, but just as the darkness threatened to overwhelm them, the sensation of falling stopped abruptly, their surroundings shifted, and they found themselves standing on solid ground, as if they had simply stepped through a door. The sudden transition left them disoriented and breathless, their minds struggling to comprehend what happened.

Blinking in the dim light, they realized they were standing on the sidewalk in front of the bookstore they had passed earlier that evening. The night air felt cool against their skin, the eerie silence of the deserted town wrapping around them like a heavy blanket. Amid the unsettling stillness, the shop's front door stood wide open, but the soft light from within that cast long, dancing shadows across the sidewalk didn't offer inviting warmth. Instead, the store seemed eerie and mysterious.

They exchanged a look, their eyes wide with shock and confusion. They should have been terrified, questioning how they had gone in seconds from the archives to a store several blocks away. But something about the situation was curious, as if an unseen force had reached into their minds, plucked them from the darkness, and dropped them here with a purpose they couldn't yet understand.

Their bodies moved of their own accord, feet carrying them toward the open door as if drawn by an invisible tether. The closer they got, the stronger the pull became, an insistent force that guided them forward. The rational part of Landry's mind screamed at him to turn back, to run as far away from this place as possible. But his legs refused to obey, and he crossed the threshold into the shop.

Inside, the air was thick with the scent of old books, mingling with the sharp tang of melted wax. Flickering candles lined the shelves, their flames casting an otherworldly glow that bent and twisted the shadows into unnatural shapes. The store was quiet, the only sound the soft crackle of the wicks as they burned down.

The scents of dust and mildew mingled with the faint, acrid tang of something indefinably ancient. Shelves on every wall reached up to the shadowy ceiling, groaning under the weight of countless books, many so old and brittle their titles were barely legible. Tables around the room were piled high with more volumes. Cobwebs clung to the corners, gleaming faintly in the light.

"No best-sellers here," Jack mused as he ran his finger through the dust caked on a mass of old books.

On a high stool behind a dark, worn counter at the far end of the room sat the proprietor. She was a crone, her age immeasurable but certainly ancient. Her hair was a tangled mess of silver and white and framed a face etched with deep lines. Her black, beady eyes glinted with a sharp intelligence as she met Landry's gaze. She wore a long, tattered black dress that hung off her gaunt frame.

As she stood, the candles' flames flickered violently, and the temperature in the room dropped sharply. "Welcome, Mr. Drake," she cackled in a dry, raspy voice so eerie that it gave them chills. "What brings you to my humble shop at such an hour?" The crone beckoned him to come closer, her gnarled hands and twisted fingers looking like the roots of an old tree.

She reminds me of a witch from a fairy tale, he thought as he asked, "How...how do you know who I am?" Thanks to the popularity of his cable TV shows, people recognized Landry everywhere he went, but it seemed illogical that this old woman would have seen him on television.

She ignored the question. "What are you looking for, my dear?"

"How did we get here? We were in the archives room, and the floor collapsed. We ended up on your sidewalk. How did that happen?"

"What does it matter?" the hag croaked. "I asked what you were looking for."

At a loss for words, Landry forgot the questions that raced through his mind—why this single store was open, who she was, and what was happening in the darkened town of Pendle—but he managed to whisper, "Something...old. I'm looking for something old." As the words came, he wondered why he'd said them.

The crone's lips curled into a thin, predatory smile. "Old, you say? My, we have plenty of that here. Come, let us see what secrets the past holds for you." She eased her way around the counter, less frail than she appeared, and motioned for him to follow her deeper into the store. Landry couldn't shake the sensation of having stepped into a place where time was held captive within the pages of the countless books that surrounded him. His heart pounded in his chest as he twisted and turned through a maze of tables, Jack following close behind.

As the woman moved on, Landry turned and whispered to Jack, "Stick close. I'm not sure what she'll do next."

"You got it. Damn creepy place, that's for sure."

Although she couldn't have heard them, the woman turned and said, "You have nothing to fear in my shop, Mr. Drake, but that is not the case once you leave and return to the village streets outside."

Landry's breath caught in his throat. She seemed to know things about him, things a stranger couldn't and shouldn't know. Until now he had been uneasy. Now it was true fear—a sense of impending danger and foreboding.

"You and your friend have many questions," the woman murmured in a tone both mocking and ominous. "This town and its people mystify you, and you seek answers that will alter your life forevermore. Listen to me—" She leaned forward, her face so close he could smell her dank breath. "The more you pry into our secrets, the more danger you will find yourself in."

Her words inflamed the fear that had gnawed at him since he and Jack first came to Pendle. There was something deeply wrong in this town—something hidden beneath its surface that he'd been foolish enough to explore.

"We only came to find—" he began, but she held up her gnarled hand and stopped him. "I know you are looking for this man's sister, but by coming to this town that no one visits, and by asking questions, you have uncovered secrets, and you risk uncovering more. Keep one thing in mind. In the future, I can help you, but you must ask. Do you understand me?"

He nodded dumbly, his mind reeling at the barrage of incomprehensible information she was throwing at him. At last he thought of a question of his own. "We went to the archives room, but every box was empty. Where are the historical records of Pendle kept?"

She cackled. "In the room you visited, of course. Much about Pendle isn't as it appears. There are those who would harm trespassers like you. Especially you, Mr. Drake." She moved aside and beckoned once again. "Follow me. I have something to give you."

Landry paused, wondering whether to obey her or turn and run. At last he joined the crone at a far table. She moved a stack of ancient volumes and pulled out what appeared to be one of the oldest—a small, leather-bound book with an odd pentagram etched into its worn cover—a symbol identical to ones they'd seen carved into the wood shelves of the archives room.

She handed it to him, and he looked at the title.

The First Hundred Years: Pendle, Louisiana, 1614–1714.

"This book," she whispered, "contains the answers you seek. It will explain the most important of our secrets, and with that knowledge, it is possible to learn much more about this town and its people. But beware. Knowledge comes at a steep price, one you may not be able to afford, and some truths are better left buried. Only you can choose whether to open the book and learn things that will cause you to question everything you know about yourself."

Landry's hand trembled as he reached for the book, his mind a whirlwind of fear and curiosity. As he took the volume in his hands, a jolt of cold shot through him as if the book was aware of his presence and what he sought.

Her eyes glittered with amusement. "Remember that the more you learn, the deeper you strive to unravel our secrets, the greater peril you personally will face. Your friend as well, for he will open other dark doors as he searches for his sister. Tread carefully; the ominous shadows of Pendle run deep into the past and are not kind to those who seek to unveil them."

His mouth parched, Landry swallowed hard and stammered a brief thanks. She pointed to the front door, but Jack didn't budge. "What do you know about my sister?" he demanded.

"I know many things," the old woman rasped. "Your sister's situation is not what you think. Searching for her is fruitless. Instead of saving her, you might lose your life."

"Where is she?"

"Listen to me. She is safe, but your interference could change that."

"I don't understand," Jack replied.

"Perhaps in due course you will. Now go."

"One more question—"

"GO!" the woman shouted, gesturing her twisted fingers toward the door. "Leave now, before it's too late!"

Landry said, "C'mon, Jack, let's go. We're going to keep looking for your sister." They turned to maneuver their way back to the entrance. Just then Landry heard it—a soft, raspy whisper that seemed to come from everywhere at once. An ancient voice filled with a malice that sent a shiver down their spines, the words incomprehensible yet carrying a weight of doom that was impossible to ignore.

The whispering voice grew clearer, repeating the same phrase over and over, the words clawing at the edges of their consciousness. The pentagram on the cover of the book Landry held began to glow, and Landry clutched his head, a sharp pain stabbing through his temples as the voice invaded his thoughts, relentless and unyielding.

Suddenly the voice stopped, replaced by a deafening silence that pressed in on him from all sides. The candles flared brightly, their flames shooting toward the ceiling before snuffing out, plunging the store into darkness.

Through the black mist he looked at Jack, who stood waiting in the bookstore. He seemed not to realize what was going on. Could he not see the candles? Did he not feel the malevolence? At last Landry realized this was playing out only in his mind, but to him it was frighteningly real.

For a heartbeat, Landry stood frozen, his breath coming in short, panicked gasps as he strained to see anything in the black void that surrounded him. And then, from the darkness, a pair of glowing eyes appeared from somewhere in the back of the store. The eyes were a sickly yellow, filled with a malevolent intelligence that seemed to pierce straight through them.

A slow, sinister smile formed beneath the eyes, a mouth full of sharp, glistening teeth that gleamed in the dim light. There was nothing more—no body, no mass or form—just a terrifying face that radiated an ancient, dark power.

"Welcome," the face hissed, its voice dripping with malice. "You have returned to your birthright."

Landry's vision blurred, the world spinning around him as the pain in his head reached a crescendo. He sensed Jack's hands gripping his arms, pulling him away, and he heard the figure's voice one last time, whispering directly into his mind.

"The pact is sealed, and the darkness will have its due."

CHAPTER ELEVEN

After escaping from whatever it had been, Landry stood on the sidewalk outside the bookstore, consumed by a whirlwind of emotions. The oppressive fear that had gripped him in the shop still clung to his thoughts, now mingled with a deep, gnawing dread that settled in his chest like a lead weight.

His heart pounded in his ears, each beat echoing the sinister words the creature had whispered into his mind. *"The pact is sealed, and the darkness will have its due."* The phrase repeated over and over in his thoughts, like a mantra of doom he couldn't shake. A cold sweat drenched his skin, and his legs trembled, threatening to give way as the reality of what they'd just encountered sank in.

Landry felt violated, as if the creature's malevolent gaze had peeled back the layers of his soul and seen something dark and hidden within him—something he hadn't known existed. The words *"birthright"* and *"pact"* twisted in his mind, dredging up a deep-seated fear that his connection to Pendle and its horrors ran far deeper than he had ever imagined. It was as if the creature's presence had awoken something dormant within him, something ancient and terrifying.

He tried to focus on the present, on the fact that they had somehow escaped, but the sense of unreality was overwhelming. It made no sense how they had ended up outside the bookstore, and the lack of explanation gnawed at his already frayed nerves. It was as if they had been caught in a nightmare they couldn't wake from, a dark labyrinth where the rules of reality no longer applied.

Jack's grip on his arm was the only thing anchoring him to the moment, but even that felt tenuous, as if they were both teetering on the edge of a precipice. Landry was acutely aware of the weight of the unseen forces at play, the darkness that closed in around them with every step they took. The bookstore's open door had seemed less like an invitation and more like a trap, a threshold they had crossed into a world where the normal laws of existence no longer held sway.

Landry's thoughts raced, trying to piece together what had just happened, but fear and confusion clouded his mind. The creature's parting words had lodged themselves deep in his psyche, leaving him with a profound sense of inevitability. The darkness would have its due. It wasn't just a warning—it sounded like a prophecy, one in which he was now hopelessly entangled.

He struggled to form words. "Jack, tell me. Did you...did you see it? That thing? Did you hear what it said?"

"No, I knew you were in trouble, but everything seemed the same to me. When you looked like you were about to collapse, I grabbed your arm and pulled you away. Let's get to the car, and you can tell me what happened."

The cold night air swirled around them as they hurried to the car and climbed in, locking the doors and pausing a moment to catch their breath. Landry grasped for an explanation about something that defied explanation. They had come to Pendle searching for a girl, but now he wondered if he was a central figure in something else entirely. Escaping Pendle's grip might no longer be an option. The darkness they had encountered and the things that dwelled within it were not just outside forces; they were a shadow that would doggedly pursue Landry until something brought things to a climax.

Landry described what had taken place. It had seemed real but must have been inside his mind, since Jack saw nothing. Jack shook off goosebumps and fumbled with the keys as Landry shoved the book into the glove box.

"How did she do that?" Jack muttered, staring out at the darkened shop with wide eyes. "How did that old woman conjure that evil figure you saw?"

Landry didn't respond, his mind racing as he tried to make sense of what had happened. It was yet another bizarre occurrence in a village that overflowed with them—an eerie place where the normal rules of reality didn't apply. The old bookseller had been unsettling from the moment they'd met her, with her cryptic words and knowing glances. But what had just happened had been downright terrifying.

"I think someone's watching us right now," Landry whispered, casting a glance over his shoulder. He thought he spotted something move in the shadows and strained to see what it was. But whatever had been there—if anything at all—had vanished.

"It's like the whole town is under a spell," Jack whispered.

Landry kept his eyes on the shop, half expecting the lights to suddenly flare back to life or for the crone to emerge from the shadows with that unsettling smile. "I've seen some strange things in my time, but this place...I've never seen anything like it. It's like the village itself is alive, and it doesn't want us here. Do you sense that too?"

Jack nodded, his expression tense. "This place is dangerous, and we've only scratched the surface of what's going on here. You can't come back, Landry, for the sake of your future with Cate, and for your own safety. There's nothing more I can do for Mel tonight, but I promise you I'll be back."

He started the car and pulled away from the curb, both men remaining silent, each lost in his thoughts. The darkness outside seemed thicker, heavier, as if it were closing in around them, and the village—silent and still— watched them go with unseen eyes. The further they drove from the shop, the stronger the sense of unease grew, as if the town's grip on reality was loosening with each passing moment.

They drove down several more blocks past shuttered stores, but when they came to the garage where they had met Dale Staggs, Jack's car stopped dead in the middle of the street—not a problem, since there were no other cars but theirs—and try as he might, Jack couldn't get the ignition to turn over.

"We have plenty of gas," he said. "What the hell's going on?"

At that moment, three floodlights in front of Harmon's Garage blazed to life, startling them. The shadows disappeared, and they saw the mechanic walking toward their car.

"Dale. It's Dale, right? Can you help us? My car died," Jack said through the driver-side window, but instead of a reply, the man stuck his grimy arm into the window toward Landry. "Give it to me, and everything will be fine," he said.

Struggling to come up with something to say, Landry stuttered, "I-I don't know what you're talking about."

"It was wrong for her to give you the book. Hand it over, and you can leave."

Jack had reached his limit in this town. "Just a damn minute. How do you know about that? And she gave it to Landry; it's his, not yours."

The mechanic sighed. "Listen, guys. Don't make this harder than it is. I'm not the enemy here. I'm not one of them; I just got picked...well, nothing. This can go easy, or it can go not so easy. You fellas have no idea what you're doing. The sign at the edge of town warned you. This place is for residents only. Not for strangers or meddlers or investigators or even people looking for other people. Open the glove box and give me the book."

His eyes bored into Landry's, and an eerie sense of disquiet swept over him. Landry did as the man commanded, and as Staggs turned away, the floodlights went dark, and Jack's car roared to life.

They said nothing until they were well out of Pendle and back on the highway to Houma. Now more than ever, Landry realized that before he was done, he must confront it—whatever *it* was—or be consumed by the darkness that hung over the village. This was not just about rescuing Melody Blair. This was about Landry—and for the first time in a long time, he was genuinely afraid.

CHAPTER TWELVE

The minutes dragged by as Jack sped down the lonely highway. At last, Landry said, "I think I'm into something way, way over my head. Something's very different about that town, and if we keep trying to learn about it, we may be in serious trouble."

"Agreed, but my sister's missing. Is she still in Pendle? I won't know until I find her. You don't have to go back; I can find her myself." Jack had never seen his friend like this; Landry was always ready for an adventure, often fearless when facing the unknown, and accustomed to taking more risks than necessary. He continued, "I must find Mel, but you have something to find of your own. You must find Cate again. She warned you against taking more risks, and you can't afford to get involved with whatever is going on in that town. I'll take it from here. No harm, no foul."

Landry disagreed, saying, "I'm going back with you, to protect you if nothing else. You can't fathom the danger you might get into. You didn't see that thing. Perhaps I should give up on this, but I can't stop now. You're right—Cate would be furious. But Cate chose to leave, and we've seen enough of Pendle that I want to find out what's going on. I've been to a lot of creepy places, but nothing like that town. It scares me, to be honest, but all that bookseller's talk about secrets and danger and knowing too much may just be her trying to scare us off, but she also seems to know it won't work. She offered to help, but after what I faced in her bookstore, I don't want to trust her. And how the hell did we end up there when we were in the archives room just before?"

Jack nodded. "So much happened so fast. It was like we were in a horror movie. Scared the hell out of me, frankly. And I'm glad you're staying in, but nothing's more important than convincing Cate to come back. If she comes home, then you must drop this case."

Lost in thought, Landry sat quietly until Jack asked about the book. "What happened with that? You only had it for five minutes; how did that mechanic know we would be driving by and that it was in the car?"

"And why did your car die and then start up again?"

"And what did he mean about being our friend and not one of them? And being the one picked? Picked for what?"

Landry replied, "Who knows? It's nothing but a history book, a chronicle of Pendle's first hundred years. It doesn't sound like something worth protecting. So why did I have to give it up?"

"There are way more questions than answers," Jack agreed. "How about that archives room full of empty boxes? What's that about?"

The same question plagued Landry, and he thought about what might have happened. Someone had removed those records, and it didn't take long for him to piece together who might be responsible.

Charity Device.

There was something very off-putting about Pendle and its citizens, and this act of erasing history was a calculated effort to hide something, to bury the town's past so well that no one could uncover its secrets. The mayor appeared to control Pendle, but her power might run deeper than he'd imagined. And whatever had happened in the archives room had no logical explanation.

The archives should have held detailed records of the settlement, its founders, and the events that shaped its fate and turned it into the dark, enigmatic place it was today. The records might have detailed names, deeds, and the bloodlines of those who had first settled here. But why were they empty? What awful secrets might they have held?

Jack's voice broke the silence, pulling Landry back to the present. "What happened to all the archives?" he asked again, his voice tinged with unease.

"It seems to me someone didn't want the truth about Pendle to be revealed. Those boxes might have been emptied long ago, when someone realized how important it was to keep their history hidden. If the truth came out, it might weaken their hold on the town and maybe even expose them for what they are."

Jack frowned, thinking about that room filled with empty boxes that had flown like papers in a cyclone. "So they just wiped everything out? What was so important?"

"The past. It looks like someone wanted to erase the town's past." Landry suspected it went deeper than just wiping out records. Someone had crafted a reality to manipulate the present and future, but without the burden of a past to answer for.

But there was something else that gnawed at Landry's thoughts. The empty boxes weren't just a precaution—they were a warning. The perpetrators hadn't simply destroyed the archives out of fear; they had done it because they knew someone, someday, would come looking for the truth. Someone like him.

"This wasn't an attempt to rewrite history; they were hiding something specific," Landry said, more to himself than to Jack. As they drove on in the darkness, Landry let his mind wander. Pendle was under some sort of spell, it seemed. And the mayor played a key role in whatever it was. Answers to the questions plaguing them could only be found by resurrecting the town's past, piece by piece, and learning what it took to unearth the truth. The archives might be empty, but somewhere, somehow, the story of Pendle's origins still existed. And Landry was determined to find it.

Reflecting on how quests like the search for Jack's sister might lead to something sinister—but right down his paranormal alley—Landry leaned his head back and fell asleep as Jack drove on in the darkness to New Orleans.

CHAPTER THIRTEEN

The bells of the cathedral struck midnight as Jack turned into St. Philip Street and stopped in front of the building where Landry lived. Jack gave him a gentle nudge and said, "You're home."

Landry stretched and yawned, apologized for falling asleep in the car, and thanked Jack for driving. As the car drove away, Landry stood on the sidewalk and looked up as something high above caught his eye.

The patio door off the bedroom is open, and the lights are on. I don't think I left them that way, and I damn sure didn't leave the door open.

An instant later he understood. *They're back! That's why the house is lit up. Cate and Simba are back!*

He took the steps two at a time, flung open the front door, and rushed into Cate's arms. He hugged and kissed her while Simba whined, wagged his tail furiously, and waited his turn for some attention from his father. When Landry picked him up, the dog nuzzled against Landry's cheek and licked him.

"I'm so glad you're back," he began, but paused when Cate asked where he'd been at such a late hour. He explained in broad terms about going to Pendle while omitting the more eerie and troublesome events.

"Did you find his sister?"

"No, and the people in town don't seem to want to help us."

"So what's next? Are you going to go back there and stir the pot, or could Jack look for his sister on his own? From what you've told me, it doesn't sound like a paranormal investigation. It sounds like you're helping a friend."

That's because I didn't tell you about the bookseller or the mayor or the others. Again he chose his words with care. "The place is different for sure, but yes, I was trying to help Jack."

"Why, Landry? You're not a cop. Let the authorities help Jack find his sister. There's something you're not telling me, and it makes me think you got into trouble in Pendle. I want you to promise me, Landry. No more risky cases. No more causing me worry and anxiety. You can enjoy life running the network and producing shows about the supernatural. I just don't want you going out in the field yourself. I can't bear it any longer."

"I won't go back. I'll do what I can to help Jack until he finds Melody, but I won't go back. I promise." He knelt to pat Simba, and Cate put her hand on his arm.

"I believe you, and that means we're home to stay. I've been so lonely. I love you, Landry Drake."

The honk of a car horn somewhere close jarred Landry awake. He stared groggily into the night and saw the sign up ahead marking the French Quarter exit off Interstate 10. "Did you have a good nap?" Jack asked as Landry realized none of it had been real.

"I...I had a dream. About Cate. And Simba. They were at the apartment when you dropped me off. I promised never to go to Pendle again, and she promised to stay with me."

Jack kept his eyes on the road and didn't reply. Landry fumbled for words. "Nothing's changed. I want to help you. I already said I'm willing to go back—"

"But you can't. You must get her back; that's all that matters. You've taught me well and turned me into a decent paranormal investigator. I can handle it from here."

"Jack, I'm sorry. I want to help you, and it was only a dream."

"More of a premonition, I'd say. Or a wake-up call. Think about it—what if you've had your priorities wrong for a long time, and now you have a chance to tone things down and make amends with someone who means everything to you?"

"I hate to leave you to handle this alone."

"Like I said, I'll be fine, thanks to you. It's not like I haven't done this kind of work before. Unlike you, I'm footloose, and within reason, I can go wherever I want. There's Caryn, of course, but our relationship is nothing like yours and Cate's. She cares deeply for you. That kind of love doesn't come along every day."

"Sounds like you've turned into a relationship counselor," Landry said with a smile. "Just promise me you'll stay in touch and let me know what's going on in Pendle."

As Jack turned onto St. Philip Street, Landry shot a hopeful glance up to the third floor of his building. This time the patio doors were closed and the room behind them dark. Just as he'd left everything.

Landry got out, and Jack said, "Good luck. Put your efforts into the most important project of your life."

CHAPTER FOURTEEN

Landry awoke late the next morning, the events of the past twenty-four hours weighing heavily on him. He sat on the patio with his coffee, breathing in the scent of an approaching storm. The air was heavy with humidity as dark clouds hung over the French Quarter. His mind raced with thoughts he couldn't quite piece together. The supernatural encounter in the Pendle bookstore had affected him deeply, leaving a cold, hollow sensation in the pit of his stomach. It wasn't just the face he had seen—Its glowing eyes and glistening fangs, the way it spoke to him—it was something dark and ancient pulling him back to Pendle, no matter how terrified he was of what he might find there.

Reaching for his phone, Landry pulled up a name from the past—Father Paul Broussard. He needed to talk to someone who understood the gravity of what he was dealing with, who had solved other people's problems, and who might help him sort out his own. It would have been better if he'd been able to talk to Cate, but she wouldn't answer his calls. He had pushed her too far this time, and she needed space, time to process everything that had happened. Landry couldn't blame her for leaving, he had been reckless, obsessed even, and it was costing him the one person he loved most.

He and Paul had worked together on paranormal cases but hadn't spoken in months, not since Paul had left the priesthood and moved from Abbeville to New Orleans. But Paul was still his friend, and more than that, he had seen things—dark things—that few others could understand. He believed in the supernatural, reconciled it with his faith in God, and might be the only person who could help Landry walk through his issues.

Landry's heart pounded in his chest as the phone rang. He didn't know what he was going to say, or even where to begin, but he needed to talk to someone who wouldn't dismiss his fears.

"Landry?" Paul's voice was the same as he remembered, calm and reassuring, with just a hint of the Southern drawl they'd both grown up with. "It's been a while. What's going on?"

"Hey, Paul. Yeah, it's been too long. I was hoping you'd pick up."

"For you, always," Paul replied. "You sound troubled. What's on your mind?"

"It's a lot," Landry began, running a hand through his hair as he struggled to find the right words. "Cate's gone. She left a few days ago—took our dog, too. She couldn't handle it anymore, the way I keep getting sucked into all this crazy stuff I do. There's also a fresh case, something almost beyond imagination. I shouldn't get involved— things like this are why she left—but I can't help myself."

There was a pause on the other end of the line, and Landry could almost picture Paul nodding, understanding. "I'm sorry to hear that, but I'm not surprised. Cate's strong, but she's not immune to fear. You've been walking a dangerous path for a long time now. And to be honest, my friend, you're like an addict. You can't help yourself when you're on the hunt for the paranormal."

"You're right," Landry admitted, his voice cracking. "I've put her through hell. And I promised her I'd be more careful, but I can't. I don't know why, Paul. I can't stop thinking about this place, about what's happening there. It's like the place has a hold on me, something deep in my past. It seems like I'm a part of it somehow, even though that's impossible."

"Are you in town?" Broussard asked, and when Landry said he was, he suggested they meet for lunch. "How about Mr. B's?" he offered, knowing it was one of Cate and Landry's favorites, and at 11:30 that morning, they greeted each other with a hug in front of the popular Royal Street restaurant.

"Father Paul," Landry said, but the former priest put up his hands in mock protest. "Not 'father' anything anymore. You know that. I'm a has-been priest, and any advice you get is worth what it costs—nothing!"

Torn about where to begin, Landry gave Paul his take on Cate's leaving, and he explained how Jack Blair's sister had left a frantic message from a town called Pendle. "They claim it's the oldest town in Louisiana," he continued, "but I never heard of it. Jack and I have been there. It's one of the most unnerving places I've ever been. Nothing about it is right." He glanced up and saw a look of alarm on Paul's face.

"Pendle," Paul said, his voice trembling. "My God, Landry, what are you involved with? I know a good deal about Pendle. I can't tell you how dangerous that place is. It isn't just haunted. It's cursed, tainted by ancient sorcery and blood rites. We studied it in seminary; according to legend, it was founded by witches who fled from England to avoid hanging. They made some kind of deal with the devil. They still live there today. Google Pendle Hill, England. What you find will surprise you."

An icy shiver clawed up Landry's spine, fear coiling in his gut. "What does all that have to do with me? I don't have any connection to that place. So why do I sense a pull, like I'm trapped in its grasp and can't escape?"

Paul exhaled slowly, a mix of pity and horror darkening his gaze. "It's not always about things that are real, Landry. The sins of the past have a way of festering, their echoes reaching through generations, demanding atonement. Your blood might be linked to something in that town—a pact, a betrayal, something unfinished. Or worse, maybe you've become too famous as a paranormal investigator, and now the dark side sees you as a threat."

"I don't want to go back, Paul, but I have to. If I don't, something terrible will happen. Or maybe it's already started. Last night, something filled with evil confronted me. Just a face with glowing eyes and fangs, speaking of my birthright and a pact I never knew about. It was terrifying, to tell the truth."

Silence fell between them, thick and suffocating, as Paul grappled with the gravity of what Landry had shared. At last he spoke, choosing his words carefully. "You're more attuned to the supernatural than anyone I've ever met, and that makes you vulnerable. Of all people, you understand that the beings that lurk in the shadows, they're not elements of good fiction—they're ancient, powerful, and real. If you return to Pendle, you're risking not only your life but also your soul. Whatever is pulling you back isn't something you can fight with logic or brute force. You need to be prepared for what you're facing—prepared for the worst. I wish I could stand beside you, but those days are behind me. All I can offer now is advice and prayers."

Landry swallowed hard as his throat constricted with fear. "I appreciate it, Paul. More than I can say. But what do I do? How do I stop this from ripping my life apart?"

"This is where it gets hard. Above all else, you must make amends with Cate. Whatever you choose to do about Pendle, you can't deal with it alone. Without someone who loves you, who can anchor you to the real world, you'll be at their mercy. And if you do return, go with eyes wide open, armed with everything you can learn about its past. You may learn horrors that threaten to consume you, but I know you; you're strong. I'm begging you not to return to Pendle, but I have no doubt you'll do it anyway. When you do, you must focus on stopping the dark forces."

"I'll try to make things right with Cate. And if I return to Pendle, I'll be careful," Landry promised, though his voice betrayed his uncertainty.

Paul shook his head, his expression grim. "Saying you'll be careful won't cut it. I knew you'd go back. This wasn't about convincing you not to. You want validation, but you won't get it from me. You're putting everything—your life, your soul, Cate—at risk by returning. But I can't stop you."

For the rest of their time together, they spoke of the adventures they'd shared in the past, about Paul's work at the homeless shelter, and about Landry's projects underway at the Paranormal Network. But even as their conversation lightened, the shadow of Pendle hung over every word, a reminder of the peril that loomed.

They sat quietly until Paul said, "I'm surprised you got a dog. Never fancied you a dog lover."

Landry managed a weak smile. "I wasn't, and I resisted at first, but now I can't imagine life without him. He's burrowed his way into my heart."

Paul placed a hand on Landry's shoulder as they prepared to part ways. "Take care of yourself, Landry. Remember, you're not alone. Call me if you need anything."

"I will," Landry replied, his emotions getting the best of him for a moment. "Thanks, Paul. Thanks for everything."

Landry walked back to his studio, considering everything his friend had said. Paul's words confirmed what he had feared all along: Pendle was more than just a haunted town. It was a place where the veil between worlds had worn thin, and his connection to it was stronger and more perilous than he'd ever imagined.

He needed to speak with Cate, to mend things before it was too late. But before that, he had to finish what he had started in Pendle. The town's curse had already started unraveling his life, and he knew it would only tighten its grip the longer he waited. Despite his conversation with Jack about not returning, he had to go back and finish things before Cate came back home.

If Cate came back.

CHAPTER FIFTEEN

The next morning, Jack shot a text to Landry, asking if there had been any word from Cate. He expected a prompt response, he and Landry always stayed in close touch, and no text went unanswered for long. But after a couple of hours, Jack wondered if Landry had already found a new project. He called but got Landry's voicemail.

When Jack left for the day at five, Landry hadn't called, so instead of going home, he walked to Landry's office on Toulouse Street, entered through the carriageway, and took the stairs up to the headquarters of the Paranormal Network.

Henri Duchamp looked up when Jack arrived in the network's spacious second-floor office and waved him over to his cubicle. Jack had known Henri for several years, going back to the days before Henri, Landry and Cate started the Paranormal Network. Today the network's episodes aired on cable TV across the nation, and millions of viewers loved the content. A website and toll-free number linking to the Paranormal Hotline allowed tipsters to alert Landry and his crew to unexplained events, and almost every day they received at least one tip. Most went into the round file, but there had been instances where Landry got a good story idea from a supernatural event reported on the hotline. The most intriguing became episodes on the network's popular *Bayou Hauntings* and *Mysterious America* series.

A man in his early fifties, Henri sat behind his desk, his three-piece suit, bow tie and pocket hankie evidencing his penchant for finery even in the sweltering heat and humidity of a New Orleans summer. "Jack, it's good to see you," he said. "Have a seat. I was about to wrap up; would you care to join me at the Roost for a drink?"

Thanks in no small part to Landry, Jack had conquered alcoholism and gotten his life in order. Henri knew everything about his past, and they both understood that Jack's drink would be a soda and Henri's either a Sazerac or a glass of fine red wine. They walked around the corner to Brennan's, where the maître d' greeted Henri by name and ushered him into the Roost Bar, a dark hideaway tucked deep inside the popular restaurant that tourists didn't know existed. A few locals were at the bar, and Jack followed Henri to his usual quiet table in a back corner.

The savvy bartender waved from across the room, raising a wineglass in one hand and a highball glass in the other. Henri pointed to the cocktail glass and soon the barman brought a Dr Pepper and a Sazerac.

"Mr. Duchamp, Mr. Blair, it's good to have you gentlemen back," he said. "Mr. Blair, I saw your documentary the other night about haunted buildings in the Quarter. You do a great job investigating stuff people enjoy hearing about!"

Jack thanked him, and the bartender said he'd keep an eye out, telling them to signal if they needed another round.

It's nice to be recognized like Landry is every time he's in public, Jack admitted to himself as he settled back in the plush chair. They clinked glasses, and he asked Henri if Landry had mentioned anything about their trip to Terrebonne Parish yesterday.

"Not a word, but in fairness, I haven't seen him today. He called this morning to advise he had some business to tend to and wouldn't be in today. What were you two doing over there?"

Jack explained everything that had happened, including his sister's disappearance and Landry's dream about Cate on the drive back. "I'm worried about him," he confided, and Henri confessed he was concerned as well.

"He's dejected and withdrawn, which isn't like him at all. I know her being gone is tearing him up, and he's left messages for her, but I think he's too proud to get in the car and drive to Galveston to confront her and admit his transgressions. I've always loved the adventurous spirit in Landry, it's what fuels him and keeps him excited, but he must think about Cate's feelings if he truly wants the serious relationship I believe they both do. And it makes things worse that she took the dog!" He chuckled. "In the beginning, Landry didn't want Simba, but now I think he misses that dog almost as much as he does Cate. He needs to fix this, and when I see him next, I plan to tell him so."

Jack spent much of the next hour telling Henri about what had happened in Pendle. It was a tale almost beyond belief, but Henri's years as founder and president of the Louisiana Society for the Paranormal had convinced him their state was filled with mysterious and unexplainable events. To scoff at the occult was to ignore reality, in his opinion.

CHAPTER SIXTEEN

After advising Henri he was taking the day off, Landry took his laptop to Café Du Monde, where he spent the morning drinking strong chicory coffee and googling everything he could find about Pendle Hill, England. He didn't find a lot, and a website called Witch Central turned out to be the most helpful. Landry clicked on a translation of a book written in 1613 called *Witch Trials of Pendle Hill*.

A short but fascinating read, the book purported to be an eyewitness account of a series of trials and executions held in the tiny town of Pendle Hill. Its flowery prose revealed an anonymous author likely more educated than his fellow villagers in this rural setting. Two entries proved especially revealing.

Sunday, August 19

The wind is howling through the trees, carrying whispers of dread through our village on this Lord's Day. The trials began and ended yesterday, and a dark sense of foreboding lingers in the air. Everywhere one turns, there is fear and suspicion, pitting neighbor against neighbor, and accusations against two families have cast a pall over this community.

This unfortunate place we find ourselves in began with claims that the Demdike and Chattox families practiced witchcraft. Young Jennet Device, just nine years old, told the justice of the peace that ten people in those families, including her own mother, brother and sister, were witches. In damning testimony, she swore she had witnessed them engaging in strange rituals, muttering incantations, and casting curses upon their unsuspecting neighbors.

One can imagine the flames of hysteria that arose from the child's words as the town watched ten of their own convicted of practicing witchcraft. Would there be more accusations? Would simple disputes be settled by friend turning against friend, brother against brother, and child against mother? Dear God, we pray not.

Monday, August 20

The townspeople stand in the square around a hastily erected gallows. Now the ten witches, if in truth that is what they be, walk up the stairs single file. I cannot fathom how young Jennet Device can stand at the front of the throng of gawkers knowing that, thanks to her testimony, her closest family members will die.

There are ten nooses. The first is tightened around the neck of Alice Nutter. She says nothing, but as three members of the Device family are readied for execution, the accuser's mother, Elizabeth, noose firmly in place, raises a finger and utters words no one in the crowd can understand. The villagers avert their glances, fearful that a curse may fall upon them, but turn back again in morbid fascination to watch ten convicted witches die. The witch trials are over, and one can hope this will not become the legacy of Pendle Hill, the awful deed for which our town is remembered.

He read other accounts of the accused families, but he saw nothing about a group of people who sailed to the New World. Despite that, there was no question who the settlers of Pendle had been. A name like Device was uncommon, and it was no coincidence that a family group with that name left their homeland to avoid being hanged with the others.

He left the coffee shop, walked to an outdoor café on Jackson Square, and convinced himself having a glass of wine with lunch was fine, since he wasn't going to work anyway. After lunch he spent two hours aimlessly walking the streets of the French Quarter, taking in the familiar sights and smells, remembering one paranormal case after another as he passed landmarks along its ancient streets. He sat for a while in Latrobe Park near the French Market, watching unconcerned people walk by, laughing and smiling, while he had no girlfriend, no dog, and a mystery that involved his own past.

He glanced at his phone, there were several texts from Jack, but he was in no mood to talk to anyone right now. Around five, deciding it was time for a cocktail, he walked over to Muriel's, his favorite watering hole, which occupied a corner spot in Jackson Square only two blocks from his apartment. Unaware that Henri and Jack were chatting over drinks just down the street, Landry wouldn't have joined them even if he'd known. He wanted to be alone, and it was such a rare sensation it brought him close to tears. He made quick work of a dry martini, then another, and asked for a third. Instead of pouring it, Kristine, his favorite bartender, leaned over the bar and whispered, "What's the matter, Landry? I've never seen you ask for a third martini, and I can tell something's eating at you. Want to talk about it?"

He gave her the CliffsNotes version, explaining that Cate had been gone three days and how much it affected him. Kristine lent a listening ear, commiserated with his love of supernatural investigations, but pointed out that it must be hard for Cate, whom she humorously described as an ordinary mortal, to be in a relationship with someone who routinely sought out eerie and dangerous situations. "I love your shows on TV," she added, "but I couldn't be in a relationship with someone who does what you do."

She talked him out of the third martini, and instead he stumbled home, veering side to side to avoid holes in the sidewalk that no one ever fixed. Maneuvering three flights of stairs wasn't easy, but at last he entered his apartment, opened the patio doors in the bedroom to get a night breeze, and fell on the bed in his clothes. He was asleep in seconds.

A ding woke him around eleven. He pawed the nightstand for his phone, saw it on the dresser, and stood to retrieve it. His head spun as a whopper hangover pierced his skull, and he took two ibuprofens before carrying the phone back to his bed.

He'd received a picture, and tears rolled down his cheeks as he stared at it. There was Simba, the little dog he loved so much, sitting in an office Landry recognized as one in Cate's father's psychiatric practice in Galveston. She'd worked there when they met, and he wondered if she was working again. No words accompanied the picture, but the message was clear. It was a tantalizing glimpse of the life he could lose if he didn't change his ways.

She hadn't taken his calls so far, but, encouraged by her texting a picture of their dog, he called her. It went to voicemail, but moments later she sent a text that said, "I'll call you soon. Simba misses you a lot. Me, only a little." And there was a smiley face.

Things just might be moving in the right direction, he thought as he undressed and crawled back into bed. He would dream of Cate and Simba and a joyful reunion but waken to the reality that they were still gone.

CHAPTER SEVENTEEN

Cate sat behind the reception desk at her father's medical practice, substituting for the regular front desk manager, who had taken Cate's job when she left for New Orleans. It was a far cry from the chaotic life she had been living with Landry, a life she had grown to fear more than she cared to admit. She wouldn't stay long, but for now, the steady, predictable routine of her father's practice assuaged her frayed nerves, offering her a sense of peace she hadn't experienced in a long time.

Her dad, renowned psychiatrist Madison John Adams, had welcomed her back without prying into the reasons for her sudden return to Galveston. He was perceptive enough to see the shadows in her eyes, and wise enough to know she would talk when she was ready. He had always liked Landry and enjoyed the tales of his paranormal escapades, but he also recognized the toll Landry's work was taking on Cate. For now, he focused on sharing quiet meals and enjoying simple conversations, without mention of why she and Simba left him.

Cate appreciated her father's understanding, but the silence only amplified her inner turmoil. She was torn between the love she still felt for Landry and the overwhelming fear his investigations into the paranormal had instilled in her. For years she had lived with it and been the supportive partner, but the anxiety and constant worry had become too much to bear. Cate needed space to breathe, to think, and to decide what she truly wanted for her future.

Landry's name flashed on her phone screen again for perhaps the tenth time. She felt a pang of guilt for ignoring him, but she quickly pushed it aside. He needed to understand that his choices had consequences. She wasn't asking him to totally abandon his passion, but she couldn't continue living in a state of perpetual fear. He had to choose between his relentless pursuit of the unknown and a future with her.

Cate sighed and placed her phone face down on the desk, determined not to let it distract her. She had come to Galveston to escape the chaos, to find clarity, and to decide how much of Landry's dangerous lifestyle she could tolerate. She loved him a great deal, but love alone wasn't enough to sustain her anymore. The uncertainty, the sleepless nights, the constant dread—she couldn't go back to that, not unless something changed.

Her father walked into the front office, a warm smile on his face. "How are you holding up, sweetheart?" he asked.

Cate smiled back, though it didn't quite reach her eyes. "I'm fine, Dad. Just trying to figure things out."

He nodded, understanding in his gaze. "Take all the time you need. I'm here for you, no matter what."

"Thanks for that," she replied, her voice soft.

As her father returned to his office, Cate let out a deep breath. She was grateful for the sanctuary her parents provided, but she understood she couldn't stay here forever. Before long, she would have to face Landry, confront the issues that had driven her away, and decide about their future. For now, though, she needed a little more time—time to heal, to reflect, and to find the strength to stand by whatever choice she made. She could only hope that by the time she was ready to talk to him, she would have the answers she needed.

CHAPTER EIGHTEEN

"No one told us we couldn't go back," Landry explained to Henri Duchamp, attempting to justify a return visit to Pendle. Henri had listened as Landry described the enigmatic visit to the remote village and their abrupt order to leave town. Jack had related his version at the bar yesterday, but Landry offered a different perspective. Henri understood why Landry felt driven to return to Pendle, but he said nothing to encourage or discourage his friend. That was Landry's decision to make.

"Before making another trip, why don't you try the archives at the Cabildo?" Henri suggested. That ancient building facing Jackson Square, just a few blocks away, held thousands upon thousands of records, relics and memorabilia, and it was the largest repository of Louisiana historical information. Over the centuries, two fires had destroyed many records, but much had survived, and Henri had spent countless hours with the curator, his dear, late friend Jules Beckman, researching one paranormal project or another.

"Remind me the name of the guy who took Jules's place," Landry said. Less than a year ago, Jules had died at the hands of a monster in a supernatural series of events that had threatened the entire city during Mardi Gras. That story had aired on the Paranormal Network as *Dread Reckoning*, the most recent *Bayou Hauntings* episode.

"Skip Halverson. He's an odd guy—nerdy to the nth degree and to all appearances in the perfect role as a studious curator of musty artifacts. He's also a font of information, as was Jules, who taught Skip everything about the Cabildo. He's been useful in finding things I need for my research. He has a photographic memory, which comes in handy given the thousands upon thousands of documents and relics that remain uncatalogued in that massive old building."

"I'll check with him," Landry replied, "but I'm not sure I'll learn anything. Pendle claims to be the oldest settlement in Louisiana, so how come I've never heard of it? Every schoolkid in Louisiana learned it was Natchitoches. Now out of nowhere, there's a town I never knew about hidden deep in the swamps a little over an hour from here, and it might be even older. Henri, the place is eerie, like people once lived there but just walked away and left things as they were."

Henri said, "I haven't heard of Pendle either, and that surprises me. So are you going to talk to Skip?"

"Might as well see what I can dig up, given that I'm persona non grata in Pendle."

He called the new curator, reminding him they'd met not long after Jules Beckman died. Skip also hadn't heard of Pendle but promised to dig around. Late that afternoon, he called to advise he had information, and asked Landry to stop by. The Cabildo was on Landry's way home, so they agreed he'd be there at six.

Later, as he walked through the Paranormal Network's open-plan office, Landry passed Cate's cubicle, stared at her empty chair and Simba's dog bed on the floor, and felt a wave of nauseating pain. Refusing to consider the chance she might not return, he remained lonely, unable to concentrate on his work and always wondering when Cate would call as she had promised.

Maybe getting involved in a fresh case will help take my mind off her and Simba until she comes back, he thought as he walked along Chartres Street to Jackson Square, then turned on St. Peter, which ran alongside the massive Cabildo. He announced himself to the security guard at a private side entrance and waited until Skip arrived to escort him to the cramped room on the top floor that once served as Jules Beckman's office and now was Skip's.

Skip took a chair, motioning Landry to another that faced a long wooden table occupying most of the room. He adjusted his horn-rimmed glasses and brushed wisps of prematurely gray hair from his face, then pointed to an ancient, worn volume lying on the table. "I think you're going to be surprised. When I came across this book earlier today, I was flabbergasted. Not only is Pendle actually the oldest town in the state, it also has the most unusual history.

"This book contains the earliest records of this area, chronicles of the indigenous peoples who lived in what later became Louisiana, and I found a few entries here and there that mention Pendle."

Skip explained that the bayous and backwaters of Louisiana were home to many settlements, some of which dated back to the 1500s, when Spanish and French explorers "discovered" the Mississippi River and interacted with powerful indigenous tribes in the area. In the mid-1700s, Acadians—later known as Cajuns—migrated from Canada and established communities. Natchitoches, long held to be the oldest, was founded in 1714 by a French-Canadian explorer as Fort St. Jean Baptiste.

Unbeknownst to most historians and scholars, at the time Natchitoches began, another settlement had existed for a century. Two hundred and fifty miles to the south, the town of Pendle sat deep in the swamps near Bayou Dularge. Today it was a remote and difficult place to reach, and it would have been far more so in those days.

"At first glance, it's odd they picked such a location, but after what I learned, I realized it's no mistake that the settlers chose such an inaccessible area to build their town." Skip picked up the old book from the table, opened it to a marked page, and pointed to a passage. "Here's the first notation, and it's brief. I've marked the others. Much of this book is written in Spanish or French, but the parts that deal with the early sixteen hundreds are in old English, which makes things easier. Take your time; I'm going to the basement for a bit. I'll be back shortly."

As he left, Landry's fingers tingled with that anticipatory sensation that swept over him every time he was on a new case. He pulled the old book closer, running his fingers over pages that were brittle and yellowed with age. The ink, faded but still legible, revealed a short but chilling story.

CHAPTER NINETEEN

Migration to the New World. Landry stared at the cover before opening the slim volume and reading. In no time, he realized this book would help answer some of the questions he had from watching the Witch Central blog. Whereas it talked about trials in England, this book told the story of how and why people fled their homeland.

As with most early migrants, those who founded Pendle in 1614 left England for a reason. These weren't opportunists seeking fame or fortune. They weren't zealots persecuted for their religious beliefs or radicals seeking political freedom.

Some on that boat had fled to the New World to avoid facing the gallows. Almost half of the founders of this remote village hidden away on a bayou were accused witches.

He read on, taking copious notes. They named their new town after their home in Lancashire, England, where in 1612, ten people had been hanged for witchcraft. Paranoia had run rampant throughout England at the time, fueled by King James I's book *Demonology* and the monarch's encouragement for citizens to turn in their neighbors and relatives who might be practicing witchcraft.

The most chilling part of the story centered on a group called the Lancashire witches. A nine-year-old girl named Jennet Device accused ten members of her family and another of putting curses on their neighbors. The people she named included her mother Elizabeth, her sister Alizon, and her brother James. Jennet claimed to have seen her sister curse a peddler, causing him to go lame, and she made similar claims against others. All ten were convicted and hanged. Justice came quickly; only three days elapsed between trial and execution.

Landry studied the child's name. *Device. The same last name as that of the current mayor of Pendle.* That could be no coincidence. There must be a familial connection between the English settlers and the current-day mayor of the town in the swamps.

Stupefied, he sat back in his chair and struggled to absorb the significance of this eerie story. The echoes of the past were louder and more insidious than he had ever imagined. The town's dark history and mysterious present cast long shadows, and Mayor Charity Device—almost certainly descended from the Lancashire witches—was at the center of it all. Jack Blair's sister remained unaccounted for, and now it was even more critical that they rescue her from whatever evil enveloped the strange little town.

He scanned the rest of the book, a short tale about settlers founding a new town and a new life in the rugged environs of the bayous. Having gotten all he could use, Landry wrapped up, waiting until Skip returned to say goodbye. When he arrived, his eyes gleamed with expectation. "I'm hoping you found the book useful," Skip said, pausing expectantly.

Landry hesitated, shooting a glance at the man. He'd been doing paranormal investigations for years, and they always included poring through documents and relics in museums like the Cabildo. While a case was in progress, he was tight-lipped about anything he learned and how it might help. In the early days before he learned better, he had shared more than he should have, and it frequently had a bad ending. Some people wanted compensation, in cash or via a cameo role in the TV episode that might result. Others wanted secrets—to be insiders, calling Landry so often for updates that he found it hard to get his work done.

He had met Skip Halverson only once before, and though Skip's boss Jules had been Henri's good friend and had given his life in one of Landry's adventures, he didn't know this curator well enough to open up. Not yet.

"There were some interesting tidbits," Landry replied. "I needed background on Pendle, and I got it." He didn't elaborate, keeping his words vague. Skip picked up on his casual answers and pushed on. "Before you came over, I had a look for myself. What a story! Witches in Louisiana in the sixteen hundreds! Who'd have imagined that? And their town in England has the same name as the one here. Are the witches still in Pendle?"

Skip waited for more, but Landry offered nothing. What he had found was too important to reveal—not just to the curator, but to anyone outside of those already caught in Pendle's web. Everything he'd found so far pointed to something more than witchcraft. There was an oppressive feeling about the village; this little town might prove dangerous for unsuspecting people who wanted to poke around and unearth its secrets.

"I'm sorry," Landry said. "You're right; the story of Pendle's beginning is interesting, and I'm surprised it's not a part of Louisiana history. As to my case, I'm only just getting started. I don't know where things will go from here, or if there's even a story. I don't want to get into speculation. I hope you understand and that you'll call me if you turn up anything else."

"Well, I'm glad it was useful," Skip muttered, disappointed not to have gotten more out of Landry. "I'll keep looking for things."

Landry thanked him and walked to the staircase. He glanced back one last time at Skip, who stood on the landing, watching him with a curious expression. Landry gave a small, tight-lipped smile and waved as he turned the corner and descended to the ground floor. He had found more information today, but all he had were questions with no answers—and a deepening sense of dread about what was waiting for him in Pendle.

CHAPTER TWENTY

Landry was in the shower when his phone rang. He stepped away from the noisy stream and heard the caller announced.

Cate Adams.

He flew out, almost slipping on the tile floor, and raced to the dresser in their bedroom. As water formed puddles on the wood floor around him, he grabbed the phone and answered.

"Cate! Cate, are you there?"

"Hey! You sound like you just ran a marathon! What's going on?"

"I...I was in the shower, but I didn't want to miss your call. God, Cate. It's been six days, but it seems like six years. Please come back. Please. I'll do anything you ask..."

She laughed. "I've missed you too, sweetie. I needed some time to think, to get my bearings and figure out if I'm being too demanding. You are who you are, Landry Drake, and sometimes it tears my heart out when you get into things and I think I may never see you again. But we can talk about all that later. I just wanted to say I'm ready to come back. When I left, I thought you would have to agree to stop all your paranormal fieldwork before I'd come home, but now I'm willing to compromise. We can talk about everything when I get there. I'm leaving at nine; Simba and I will see you sometime late this afternoon."

"I love you, Cate. I love Simba too. I can't wait to see you both again."

Landry walked to work, passing out morning greetings to everyone he saw along the way. He entered his building through the carriageway, bounded up the stairs, and went straight into Henri's office.

"Well, well, you look like someone who's received good news," his friend observed.

"She's coming back late this afternoon, and I can't tell you how happy I am. I'd fix her a gourmet dinner if I knew how to cook, but I think I'll take her to Bayona for an early dinner, and then we can go home and play with Simba."

Henri nodded. "Cate will like that; you can't find a nicer atmosphere or better food in town. But reservations on short notice can be impossible there. I'd work on it as soon as possible."

He called the upscale French Quarter restaurant, left a voicemail with his request and callback information, and picked up his iPhone to check her location. She had insisted they share information during the last dangerous case with which he was involved, and now he could track her progress back to New Orleans. It was half past nine, and she was well on the way to Houston. From there she would go east on I-10 and likely be home in under seven hours.

At 11:30 a manager from Bayona called to confirm his reservation, adding, "We're honored to have you as our guest, Mr. Drake." After the call ended, Landry reflected on how often he became irritated when people recognized him on the street or interrupted him for an autograph in bars.

Today was just the opposite. For once, that recognition had helped.

Unable to keep his mind on anything but the homecoming, Landry piddled around at the office all morning, went across the street to Café Maspero for lunch, and returned, deciding to check Cate's progress one more time. He'd forced himself not to look at the location app every five minutes, and now he saw she was approaching Lafayette, which meant even with a stop for gas and to let Simba get some air, they would be home by four.

Shortly after three, he checked her whereabouts again, and it surprised him that she'd left the interstate at Lafayette, turning south on state highway 90. It would still get her to New Orleans, but it was a longer route and less simple to navigate than the straight shot home. He called her but got a recorded message saying she was driving and couldn't take the call. That was no surprise; Cate often criticized him for using his phone while driving. He recalculated her remaining time and decided she'd be home closer to five. Their reservation at Bayona was for 5:30, so they'd be cutting it close. Quick hellos, maybe a glass of wine and playtime with Simba, then they'd be off for the restaurant on Dauphine Street.

He followed her route past New Iberia and Jeanerette, his hometown. His mind reflected on the supernatural incidents he'd investigated in that area, and he wondered how much more of that she'd really allow him to do. He loved the paranormal, but he'd been in more than one life-threatening jam, and he realized he had to make changes if he was going to keep her in his life. Just how many remained to be hashed out between them.

Landry waved to Henri, left the office around four, and walked home to wait for their arrival. After putting a bottle of white wine in the refrigerator, he turned on the TV, idly flipping channels as he waited.

Half an hour later he checked her location, then grabbed his phone and called her number. Again he got the message, but this time he left a voicemail. "Where are you, Cate? Why did you get off the interstate? And why are you in Houma? You're way, way off track; turn around, go back to highway 90, and follow it east."

Concerned now, Landry turned off the television and called Jack. He explained Cate was on her way back, she'd left Galveston that morning and should be here by now, but he'd been tracking her for the past hour or so. For some reason she had left I-10 at Lafayette, taken highway 90 and then the road to Houma. While he was talking, he looked at the app again and said, "Oh God, Jack. Something's wrong. Something's really wrong. She's headed...she's left Houma, going south on 315. Do you know what that means?"

"You don't know that for sure," Jack answered. "Stay calm. It may be something easily explained. Do you want me to come over there?"

"No. There's no easy explanation for where she is. There's only one. I need to get hold of her. I'll call you back."

He sat in the apartment, staring at the route Cate was driving, and tried to call her again. This time he had no doubt she wouldn't answer, because something had happened along her journey. Instead of coming on the direct route to New Orleans, Cate had turned off. Now she was going in a very, very wrong direction.

For some reason he couldn't fathom, she wasn't coming home. She was going to Pendle.

CHAPTER TWENTY-ONE

Cate awakened early, excited to be going back to Landry and hopeful that her experiment in tough love had caused him to realize what a toll his reckless adventures took on her. She loved him a great deal and intended to spend the rest of her life with him, but for that to happen, he'd have to agree to tone things down a bit. Not so much that it stifled his enthusiasm and zest for adventure, but enough to keep him out of the hospital or the cemetery.

She and Simba got on the road before nine. The traffic between Galveston and Houston was light, and before long she had turned east on Interstate 10, the highway that would take her all the way into New Orleans. She planned to be home before four to allow plenty of time for Landry to see Simba. Then he'd take her out for a nice dinner, and she looked forward to that as well.

Cate stared at the endless stretch of road ahead. The monotony of the interstate highway from Houston to New Orleans was something she had experienced countless times before. Today she would be going home, a comforting thought, and to pass the remaining hours, she turned on an audiobook she'd been listening to.

Simba, her small but spirited dog, lay curled up in the passenger seat, occasionally lifting his head to glance out the window before settling back into a restless sleep. The hum of the tires on the asphalt, usually a calming sound, now seemed somehow amplified, disturbing both of them.

She stopped for food and gas in Lafayette. The brightly lit truck stop she chose seemed like an oasis of normalcy. Simba stretched and sniffed around, wagging his tail as Cate filled up the tank. She grabbed a water, her thoughts already drifting back to Landry. The idea of seeing him again, of finally being home, brought a smile to her face despite the tension that still lingered between them.

Back on the road, Cate again listened to the audiobook. The narrator's voice filled the car, and she became engrossed in the story, the miles slipping away beneath her tires as her mind wandered. The plot twisted and turned, each chapter pulling her deeper into its fictional world.

A flicker of unease crept into her thoughts, barely noticeable at first. She dismissed it, attributing it to her weariness and the emotional turmoil of the past few days. But when she took in her surroundings at last, her heart skipped a beat.

This road wasn't the familiar divided interstate highway she had been driving for hours. The wide lanes had narrowed, and stands of pine trees on either side obscured the afternoon sun. Cate's pulse quickened as she scanned the area, trying to make sense of her surroundings.

She spotted a long-abandoned gas station up ahead and pulled in. The old, faded sign creaked in the wind: Highway 90 Texaco. Confusion washed over her. She knew this road; it would take her home, but it wasn't the faster route she'd chosen. Somehow, she had veered off course without realizing it. She'd have to go south now, through Cajun Country.

"It's okay; I'm still heading to New Orleans," she muttered to herself, trying to shake off the growing sense of unease. "Just a little detour."

Simba stirred, sensing her anxiety, and whimpered. Cate reached over to scratch his ears, offering him a reassuring smile. "We're fine, Simba. We'll be home soon."

Determined to make up for lost time, she got back on the road, resuming the audiobook to distract herself. But no matter how hard she tried to focus, the narrator's voice now seemed distant, almost distorted, as if the words had been spoken through a thick fog.

Then she saw a town up ahead and passed its welcome sign. "Explore Houma: Louisiana's Bayou Country." Cate's heart sank. Miles off course now and heading deeper into the swamps instead of toward New Orleans, she panicked, but beneath the fear, something else festered—a strange, almost magnetic pull that urged her to keep going, as if some unseen force was guiding her, nudging her through Houma, then south, then west.

The road began to deteriorate, the asphalt giving way to gravel and then to dirt. Her car jolted as it hit deep ruts, head-high tallgrass closing in around her. The air grew thick and humid, a scent of wet earth and decaying vegetation seeping into the car. Every instinct screamed at her to turn back, to return to the safety of the main highway, but she couldn't.

Another sign loomed ahead. Dumbstruck, she read the top and bottom lines. "This is Pendle. No Trespassing."

Cate's breath caught in her throat. What the hell was going on? She had never heard of Pendle, yet the name sent a chill down her spine. It was late afternoon, but here the place seemed dark and spooky. Ignoring the warning, she drove past the sign into a small town that seemed to have been forgotten by time, abandoned to the surrounding swamps. Shadows danced on the edges of her vision, and the silence spooked her. Not a voice, not so much as a chirping insect. Nothing.

She sensed she was in trouble. Serious trouble.

Simba growled, a low, rumbling sound that made the hair on the back of Cate's neck stand up. He stared out the window, his eyes wide and alert, sensing something she couldn't see. *I need to tell Landry where I am,* she told herself, her hands shaking as she tried the phone but had no signal. It was eerily still—no birds sang, no insects buzzed. It was as if the bayou itself had cast a pallor of gloom and quiet over the tiny town.

The street ahead led past houses and stores that might have been occupied but looked devoid of life. She wanted to turn around, to head back to the safety of the interstate highway, but the pull remained stronger than ever, as if Pendle had been waiting for her, luring her into its grasp. She shouldn't stay, but somehow leaving wasn't an option.

She drove through the silent town until she came to a tall structure in the middle of a square. An old police car— the first vehicle she'd seen—sat out front, and lights burned in a few first-floor windows. Powerless to resist the siren's call, she pulled into a parking spot, hooked Simba's leash on his collar, and walked with him to the building's entrance. Despite an overpowering sense of dread, something drove Cate to open the door and step into a dark, musty hallway. Simba began to bark, his voice echoing eerily in the empty halls, and he resisted as she pulled him down the corridor past one dark office after another.

Although Cate had never been here, she knew where she was going. She knew whose office she was supposed to visit, although she couldn't imagine why. As she dragged her reluctant dog along, whispers seemed to rise from the recesses of the cavernous building, voices she couldn't quite hear but could feel in the pit of her stomach.

Pendle wasn't just a place, it was a trap, and it held Cate tightly in its web.

CHAPTER TWENTY-TWO

At the end of the hallway, she saw the door to an office standing ajar. This was it—the place she was supposed to go. The light she'd seen from outside came from within. Gathering her courage, she approached the door and pushed it open.

The room was empty except for a single desk with an old rotary phone sitting on it, and a small, well-worn leather-bound book. A flickering desk lamp seemed on the verge of burning out. On the wall, a vintage clock ticked steadily, but the hands stood frozen at midnight.

As Cate stepped closer to the desk, she felt a low, almost imperceptible hum, like the distant drone of a beehive. It seemed to arise from the walls themselves, or perhaps from beneath the floorboards. She reached out to touch the book, her fingers trembling, when without warning the ancient phone rang, its shrill sound piercing the silence and causing her to jump in surprise. She stared at it, wondering what to do as Simba began barking even more, pulling his lips back in a snarl and showing his teeth.

The shrill noise happened again, the old black phone demanding her to answer. Her heart raced as she picked up the receiver and listened.

A voice—male, or so she thought—crackled through the line, distorted and distant. "You shouldn't have come here," it whispered. "Pendle is not a place for the living. Run! Run away, now!"

"I didn't come here on purpose!" she screamed as the voice on the phone faded, leaving behind only an eerie silence. Her breath came in sobbing gasps as she slammed the receiver down and looked around the room, desperate for any sign of life. That was when she heard something— the slow, deliberate click of heels echoing down the hallway.

Until this moment, a sign of life was what she craved, but now a cold sweat broke out on her skin as the footsteps grew louder, each step reverberating like a death knell. The air seemed to grow colder, and a strange smell, like burnt herbs and decay, wafted into the room. Without thinking, she grabbed the small book and stuck it into the waistband of her pants, under her shirt.

The door to the office creaked open further, and Cate's eyes widened in terror as a figure stepped into the doorway. Simba went wild, straining and tugging at the leash to get as far away as possible from the person who now stood in the room. He tucked his tail between his legs, whimpered, and moaned in fear.

Tall and gaunt, the woman had skin as pale as wax and eyes that glittered with a malevolent intelligence. Her hair was a wild tangle of silver streaked with gray, and her mouth twisted into a smile as she surveyed Cate. She wore a floor-length black Victorian gown that rustled like dead leaves as she moved.

"Welcome to Pendle," the woman crooned, her voice dripping with a mocking sweetness. "I am Charity Device, mayor of this quaint little town."

A chill ran down Cate's spine. There was something wrong with this woman—something ancient and evil. Charity's eyes seemed to bore into Cate, seeing right through to her very soul.

"I-I'm just passing through," she stammered, trying to keep her voice steady. "I didn't mean to intrude. I'm not even sure…how I got here."

Charity's smile widened. "Passing through?" she repeated, her tone amused. "Oh, my dear Cate, no one passes through Pendle. Didn't you see the sign? This place is for residents only; we don't take kindly to intruders. You see, this town has a way of keeping those who wander in."

"How…how do you know my name?" she blurted. "Listen, I'm sorry I trespassed. Simba and I will leave and forget we ever came here." Cate moved toward the door, but the old woman moved with unsettling speed, grabbing her wrist in an iron grip. Cate gasped in pain as she was yanked out of the office and into the dimly lit hallway.

"Let me go!" Cate struggled, and Simba nipped and barked furiously, but Miss Device's grip was unbreakable. The mayor's strength was unnatural, and her touch sent a wave of dread through Cate's body.

"Hush, now," Charity whispered, her voice like silk. "There's no need to struggle. Leaving Pendle is impossible. You chose to ignore the warning sign, and now you'll pay the price because you're one of us now. And so is your dog." As she bent toward Simba, he let loose a series of frantic barks that echoed throughout the building.

Her words rang in Cate's mind, the finality of them sinking in like a stone. The woman dragged her down the hallway, past doors that seemed to open and close on their own, revealing glimpses of dark, shadowy figures lurking just out of sight. The walls themselves seemed to pulse, as if the building were alive and breathing.

Just over an hour away at their apartment in New Orleans, Landry checked his iPhone as the dot representing Cate's location flickered on the screen. He had been tracking her route the entire day, and once the signal stopped near Pendle, he watched it, praying she'd turn around and come back. There was nothing in the deserted town for her. But now her signal was moving again, and he knew she had passed the sign and was already into the town itself.

What possessed her to go there? Even as he wondered, he knew she hadn't ended up there on purpose—she'd been lured to Pendle. Something about that eerie town had reeled her in, and he thought he understood why. This was about him—maybe Jack as well, and his sister, Melody—but she'd ended up there because someone in Pendle wanted *him*.

The thought sent a shiver of unease through him, and his instincts screamed that something was terribly wrong. The dot on the map had stopped moving, an indication that Cate was stuck in place. He tried calling her again but got nowhere. Each failed attempt only heightened his panic.

Landry raced down the stairs and to the garage a block away, where he kept his Jeep, his heart pounding in his chest. He had to get to her—Pendle wasn't just some forgotten town in the swamp. In his line of work, places like this had a reputation for being far more than they seemed, and the supernatural always had a way of twisting reality.

He had promised himself to curtail his appetite for the paranormal, to submit to Cate's insistence he take fewer risks, and to stop causing her worry and heartache. Now all those thoughts lay behind him. He had to find Cate and Simba before time ran out.

CHAPTER TWENTY-THREE

Cate struggled to resist as Charity Device forced her up the creaking stairs of city hall, Simba tucked protectively in her arms. The oppressive air of the place seemed to close in on her with every step. Mayor Device gripped her arm, the bony fingers digging into her flesh with a strength that made Cate cry out in pain. This old building felt alive, each groan of the floorboards echoing like a distant cry for help. She had a thought that no one had climbed to the upper floors in years, maybe decades.

When they reached the third floor, Charity dragged Cate down a narrow corridor lined with doors, each one shut tight as if hiding something terrible within. They stopped in front of a heavy iron door at the end of the hall. With a sinister smile, Charity pulled a set of old keys from her pocket and unlocked it to reveal another short corridor with jail cells on each side. With surprising force, she pushed Cate and Simba into the closest one and slammed the barred door shut. Cate stumbled into the room, protecting Simba while straining to maintain her balance and not fall to the concrete floor.

The jail cell was small and suffocating, with rusted iron bars and a single window that overlooked the square. Peeling paint covered the walls, a once-white surface now yellowed with years of neglect. Cate shivered as she stroked her terrified dog. An unpleasant stench filled the air, like someone left this place to rot.

Charity locked the cell door with a loud, finalizing click. "Make yourself comfortable, my dear," she said, her voice dripping with false kindness. "I'll be back when it's time."

Cate stared at her, heart pounding. "Time for what?"

But the mayor only smiled that unnerving smile and turned to leave. "Time for retribution," she said cryptically before walking away, her footsteps echoing down the hallway until Cate no longer heard them.

Cate sat huddled on a narrow, hard cot in a corner, her knees pulled tight to her chest as her heart raced. Simba, her faithful dog, lay pressed against her side, his warm body trembling with a primal instinct Cate had never seen in him before. She fumbled for her phone, praying for a signal, but the screen remained blank—no bars of service and no hope of reaching anyone outside this place. Despair washed over her as she glanced around the dark cell, wondering how long it would be before Landry realized something had happened to her. God, she wished he would come.

But as much as she wanted him to save her, the oppressive weight of dread enveloped her. If Landry came for her, she sensed he'd be stepping into a trap. She believed Charity Device was a deranged and dangerous person, but what was her motive? Against whom did she seek retribution? Landry? If so, why?

The dank stone walls of the cell closed in around them, suffocating her in their ancient silence. She found it hard to breathe. The fear seemed too much. A little light filtered in through the small, barred window, casting eerie shadows that danced on the walls like ghosts. She shivered, wondering how many souls had been locked away in this place before her—how many had never left.

Cate had a terrible sense that the mayor of this eerie town had imprisoned her to lure Landry into Pendle. And she knew that plan would succeed. If he thought of it, Landry would follow her location on his iPhone. If he had pinged her while her phone had service, then he would know her location.

She had no idea Landry and Jack had come to this eerie place just a few days ago, they had met Mayor Device themselves, and Jack's sister had disappeared.

She thought of the voice that had spoken to her on the ancient telephone. "Get out quickly," a man had urged, crackling through the static like a desperate warning. Who had that been? Someone here who might help her, or just another trick, a cruel game played by the mayor herself?

Cate stood and walked to the barred window, peering out at the town square below. Despite the warm weather outdoors, a cold draft blew in through broken panes of glass. The sun sank low in the sky, casting long, ominous shadows across the deserted streets. The buildings looked more decrepit in the fading light, their windows dark and empty. But even as she stared out at what appeared to be an abandoned town, something told her it was far from lifeless. Out there in this frightening little town, someone...or some*thing* watched her every move.

The air outside seemed thick with tension, the type of quiet that precedes a storm. To Cate, it seemed as though the very town itself was alive, pulsing with a dark invisible energy she sensed all around her. The shadows lengthened, crawling up the sides of the buildings like creeping tendrils, and for a moment, she thought she saw something move in the corner of her vision—a flicker of motion just beyond the square. A dark, formless shadow.

She squeezed her eyes shut, willing the vision away, but when she opened them again, the sensation only intensified. Now there were others, dozens of black nebulous blobs moving in the shadows. The town wasn't deserted at all; it teemed with terrifying things, lurking just out of sight, waiting for the sun to dip below the horizon.

Cate backed away from the window, the weight of her situation pressing down on her. The sun was nearly gone, and her imagination ran amok. When the sun set, would the true horrors of Pendle appear, freed at last to claim the town that belonged to them? She didn't know what was coming, but nothing about it would be good.

Simba whimpered softly in her arms, sensing her fear, and Cate held him closer, drawing what little comfort she could from his warmth. She had to get out of here, to warn Landry before he walked into whatever trap this town had set. But how? The cell door was locked tight, and her phone didn't work.

She thought again of that voice—the warning on the other end of the line. It had been real. Someone had warned her. It seemed he wanted to help her, but who was he, and would he realize she was a prisoner now?

Night fell upon the bayou and swamp and the town itself, and Cate had an odd thought, wondering if the jail cell might protect her from what roamed the streets. But what frightened her was the distinct possibility that walls and iron bars wouldn't stop whatever inhabited this town.

As the last rays of sunlight vanished, plunging Pendle into darkness, Cate had little time to find out.

CHAPTER TWENTY-FOUR

Landry's tires screeched as his car skidded around the bend, the ominous silhouette of Pendle looming in the distance. His heart pounded with every mile, the image of Cate's last location burned into his mind. She was in danger—there could be no question about that. The town ahead, shrouded in mist, seemed to beckon him forward, welcoming him back into its dark embrace.

The last tendrils of light played across the western sky as the sun dropped beneath the horizon. He drove along the narrow road into Pendle as a dense fog settled upon the swamps. The further he drove, the thicker the fog became, swallowing the car's headlights. The hairs rose on his neck as he sensed what danger might lie ahead. Every instinct screamed at him to turn back, but he pressed on, driven by his desperate need to find Cate.

Without slowing, he passed the No Trespassing sign and entered the town. As before, the streets stood deserted, but something had changed since his last visit—a sense that evil permeated the shuttered houses and stores. The town seemed alive, pulsing with a malevolent energy.

Heartened to find Cate's car parked outside the old municipal building, he pulled to a stop nearby and looked through the windows of her car. Simba's dog bed lay in the passenger seat, a cooler lay within Cate's reach in the back, and nothing seemed out of the ordinary.

He walked to the building and found the entry door unlocked despite the late hour. *Why? Is the mayor making things easy for me to walk into a trap?*

The hallway looked even more forbidding than it had earlier; a single, naked bulb provided scant light in the wide corridor. His heart pounded in his chest as he walked to the mayor's office and found it locked. He sensed Cate was somewhere in this building, but also other things—things that had no business existing in this world. He had dealt with the supernatural countless times, but rarely did a place emit vibes as wrong as this. The town was a trap with Cate the bait and him the prey.

Landry hesitated for a moment, his mind racing. How would it be possible to fight something he couldn't see? Something that seemed to be woven into the very fabric of the town itself? He had no idea, but he knew one thing: he wouldn't leave without Cate.

The air grew colder as he climbed the wooden stairs and looked around on the second floor. "Cate!" he called out, his voice reverberating off the walls. There was no response, only the oppressive silence that seemed to press in on him from all sides. He turned on his phone's flashlight, its beam cutting through the darkness and the dust motes swirling in the stagnant air.

After giving the floor a cursory look, Landry's mind raced with thoughts of her. She was somewhere nearby in this dank building. An odd heaviness threatened to crush him.

A noise echoed from the darkness ahead—a soft, scraping sound, like nails on stone. Landry froze, his pulse quickening. The beam of his flashlight flickered, casting eerie shadows on the walls. He strained to listen, but the sound had stopped.

He climbed another flight of stairs to the top floor and crept forward, his hand gripping the flashlight like a lifeline. The corridor seemed to stretch on forever, the doors on either side shut tight. With each step, the darkness seemed to cling closer and closer to his skin.

At last he reached a door at the end of the hall, old, heavy, and made of iron. *The old jail,* he thought as he fumbled for the handle, the cold metal sending a chill through his skin. He felt Cate's presence behind that door.

But as he turned the handle, something stopped him. A whisper, barely audible, like a breath on the back of his neck. "Leave…"

Landry spun around, his flashlight sweeping the empty corridor. Nothing. The air was still, the silence deafening. But the voice had been real, and he wasn't alone in this place. Something watched him, waiting for him to make a move.

He turned back to the door, his hand trembling as he gripped the handle. The voice had warned him to leave, but Cate was in there, and he couldn't abandon her. With a deep breath, he pushed the door open, the rusty hinges groaning in protest.

The corridor beyond was dark, the air thick with the smell of decay. Landry's flashlight flickered as he stepped inside, casting an eerie glow on the iron bars of jail cells. And in the first one, huddled on a cot with Simba in her arms, he saw Cate.

"Cate!" he whispered, his voice breaking. He rushed to the cell, his hands gripping the cold iron bars. "Are you okay?"

Cate jumped up, her eyes wide with fear, and Simba raced to her side. "Oh God, Landry. I'm so glad you're here, but something evil is in this place. The mayor—"

Before she finished, a low, guttural growl rumbled from the darkness behind him. Landry turned, his heart stopping as he saw them—dark, shapeless figures emerging from the shadows. The things that had been watching and waiting for his arrival.

Simba raced to the bars, barking incessantly and straining to get into the hallway as the room seemed to warp around Landry, the walls closing in as the figures advanced. His mind raced, searching for a way out, but there was none. The town had him now, just as it had Cate.

As the shadowy figures moved closer, their presence suffocating, the door to Cate's cell flew open, unlocked by an unseen hand. At that moment, Landry realized the truth: somehow the town of Pendle truly was alive, a living, breathing entity that fed on the fear of those it ensnared. And now, along with Jack Blair's sister, Melody, it had captured both of them as well.

But Landry wouldn't give up. Not yet. He would fight—for Cate, for their future—no matter what dark forces stood in his way. Simba raced from the cell to stand by his side with a growl as menacing as a small dog could muster. With a surge of adrenaline, Landry grabbed a rusted iron bar from the ground and faced the encroaching darkness. The bar might not serve as a weapon against these supernatural entities, but it was all he had. "I'm not afraid of you," he muttered as his heart raced.

But the shadows only laughed, a sound that echoed through the vast halls of the building, a sound that promised this was just the beginning of the horrors that lay in store for him.

CHAPTER TWENTY-FIVE

Landry tightened his grip on the iron bar, the cold metal biting into his skin. The shadowy figures halted, their glowing eyes fixated on him. Cate clung to Simba, her breath quickening as the atmosphere thickened with dread. The laughter from the darkness reverberated through the narrow corridor, a haunting melody that sent chills down Landry's spine.

"I'm not afraid of you," he said, his voice shaking.

The shadows seemed to feed on his fear, their forms expanding and contracting with each heartbeat. They moved closer, their presence pressing down on him like an invisible weight. The air grew colder, and the walls seemed to close in, suffocating them.

Cate's eyes met his, desperation and fear mirrored in her gaze. "Landry, we have to get out of here. I can feel it—this place, it's...this sounds crazy, but I think it's hungry."

He nodded, his mind racing. They couldn't just stand there and wait to be consumed by whatever malevolent forces inhabited Pendle. There had to be a way out—a way to escape this living nightmare.

Simba barked again, a frantic, high-pitched sound that echoed off the walls. The dog's usually fearless demeanor morphed into a panicked urgency that spurred Landry into action. He must keep moving, keep fighting, if they were going to survive.

"Cate, stay close to me," he said, his voice low but firm. "We're getting out."

They moved cautiously down the corridor, the flashlight flickering as it cast eerie shadows on the walls. The shadows followed them, whispering words that neither understood but both somehow feared. As they moved, the walls pulsed, as if the building was alive and aware of their presence.

As they reached the end of the corridor, light poured from the open door to the Records Department. Landry found that strange; he was certain it had been dark when he walked down the hallway a few minutes earlier. He paused, turned to Cate and said, "Let me look for a minute," and stepped inside. Unwilling to stay alone in the hall, she followed.

A counter divided the room, and desks behind it marked the places where clerks would have sat. Faded metal signs hung from the ceiling—Deed Recording, Court Clerk, Pay Fines Here, and others. Along the back wall were rows of huge, oversized books—city records, according to the sign. The air inside reeked with the scent of ancient paper.

Behind the counter in the center of the room stood a large wooden table, and on it sat an orb the size of a grapefruit. It was black and appeared to be made of glass. Landry stepped around the counter and picked it up.

Cate grabbed his arm. "Landry, don't—"

Before she finished, the room gave a violent shudder. The orb emitted a bright white light that pulsed like a heartbeat. Now it was opaque, a milky vapor spinning inside, and in seconds he saw a pentagram shape take form inside the ball.

Cate cried out in alarm, and as Landry turned, he saw shadows in the room—wispy things that now became more solid, more threatening. Landry realized the pulsing orb was a trap, a lure to ensnare them even further.

"Destroy it! Use the bar!" Cate shouted, her voice barely audible over the growing cacophony of whispers and unearthly sounds.

Landry raised the iron bar and brought it down on the glass ball with all his strength. The moment the metal made contact, the ball exploded into a thousand pieces that flew about the room, each pulsing with light until it hit the floor and went dark.

The shadows let out a collective moan and disappeared.

Landry took a shaky breath, lowering the bar. "Are you okay?"

Cate nodded, her eyes wide with shock. "I think so. What...what just happened?"

"I don't know, but I think we broke whatever spell was holding this place together. It won't last; we need to get out of here now."

Calm now that the tension was gone, Simba gave a little yip, nudging Cate's leg as if to reassure her. They flew down the stairs and outside into the darkened town. The mayor was nowhere to be seen, and behind them the city hall building lay in total darkness.

"There's no way I can drive," Cate said. "Leave one car; we can come back for it." She got in her car while Landry retrieved everything from his Jeep. He backed out, tires screeching as he tore away from the town square and toward the road that would take them back to reality. But as he came to a familiar spot, he saw Dale standing in the middle of the street, one hand raised to stop him.

"Who's that?" Cate asked, but Landry didn't answer. He kept going full speed, intending to swerve at the last moment and avoid striking Dale Staggs, but just as before, the engine died.

Once again the mechanic approached the vehicle and extended his hand. "Give it to me."

"I don't have it," Landry replied, but Dale pointed at Cate.

"No, but she does. Hand it over, lady."

Cate looked at him blankly. "I...I don't understand..."

"He thinks you have a book."

She pulled the leather-bound volume from under her shirt. "What's going on, Landry?"

He looked at Dale Staggs. "Let me borrow it. I'll bring it back. I'm coming to get my car tomorrow, and I'll bring it to you."

The man paused, considering the request, but shook his head. "It don't work like that. She doesn't want you to have it. Give it to me."

"The mayor? Why does she not want me to have it?"

"Please don't do this. You can't imagine..." He turned and looked around as though someone else was there. "Please, Mr. Drake. Give it to me now."

Landry glanced in the rearview mirror and saw dozens of the black, formless blobs in the darkness, moving in their direction. "Let me go, Dale," he urged the man. "Let me learn from it. I'll bring it back tomorrow. I promise."

He gave a mournful shrug. "Okay, take it, then. You deserve to find out what's going on here, but it's your funeral. Mine too, I guess, but I've stopped caring." As the man walked away, Cate's car roared to life. He floored the car, careening through the dead town toward the familiarity of civilization. Cate looked back to see a mass of black blobs descend upon the mechanic, enveloping him in an ebony drape.

CHAPTER TWENTY-SIX

Even though they were on the way home, Cate found it impossible to shake the lingering terror that had gripped her during her captivity and in the records room. The memory of Charity Device, with her cold, malevolent eyes and aura of unholy power, haunted Cate's every thought. The very air in that town seemed evil, as if the shadows themselves were watching.

Simba had sensed the evil too, whimpering as they huddled in the cold, damp cell. Cate had tried to stay strong for him, but the darkness in Pendle had seeped into her soul, filling her with dread. She could still feel the chill of the cell's stone walls, the way the barred window taunted her with a glimpse of freedom she feared would never come.

As Landry drove toward Houma on the darkened highway, Cate's hands shook in her lap. She heard the rapid pounding of her heart, her pulse racing in her ears as she replayed the events of the past few hours in her mind. Simba lay in her lap, the familiar weight of him grounding her, though it did little to steady her nerves.

They had escaped. She had made it out alive. But even now, sitting beside Landry in the relative safety of the car, her heart refused to believe it. The terror of that jail cell clung to her like a shadow that wouldn't go away. Even now, she felt the cold stone walls pressing in on her, the suffocating silence broken only by the whispers of unseen things lurking in the dark. Those black shapes had been there, watching her. Waiting for her.

She shuddered and pressed a hand to her chest, trying to catch her breath. Her skin was cold, her fingers numb despite the warmth of the car. She glanced at Landry, his face barely visible in the dim light from the dashboard. His hands gripped the steering wheel, knuckles white. He had hardly spoken since they left Pendle, but she sensed the tension radiating off him. She had lived with him long enough to realize that right now his thoughts were far away—back in that cursed town.

"Landry," she whispered, her voice shaky. He didn't respond at first, too lost in whatever thoughts plagued him. She reached over and gently touched his arm. "Landry."

He blinked and glanced at her, his eyes shadowed with exhaustion. "Sorry," he muttered with a smile. "I was so worried about you, Cate. Are you okay?"

Cate looked down at her hands, the weight of his question pressing on her. Was she okay? She wasn't sure what that meant anymore. How could she be okay after what she'd witnessed? After what she had felt in that cell, surrounded by things from another realm?

"Maybe, maybe not," she whispered. Tears formed in the corners of her eyes, but she refused to let them fall. Not now. Not when everything was still so fragile. Landry reached over and squeezed her hand, his touch warm and comforting, but it wasn't enough to chase away the cold that had settled deep inside her. "You're safe now," he said softly. "We're out of Pendle."

Cate let out a shaky breath, her fingers tightening around his. "But for how long?" she whispered, her words hanging in the air like a weight impossible to ignore. "How long before you go back? Because you are going back, aren't you?"

Landry's jaw tightened, and he looked away, his eyes focused on the dark road ahead. She could see the battle in him—the same one that had driven her away a few days ago. He felt compelled to go back. She could feel it in the way his body tensed at the mention of Pendle, in the way his thoughts drifted every time there was silence between them. He wasn't finished with that place. Not yet.

"Landry, you can't go back," Cate snapped, the words rushing out before she could stop them. Her heart clenched as she saw the look of conflict in his eyes when he turned to face her. "You can't."

He opened his mouth to respond, but she cut him off. "I saw what's there, Landry. I *felt* it. Those creatures...those things in the shadows...they were real. They weren't just in my head. They wanted me dead. And it's not even about me. It's about you, isn't it? If you go back..." Her voice broke, and she pressed a hand to her mouth, trying to keep herself from falling apart. "If you go back, they'll kill you."

The car was silent save for the soft hum of the engine and the distant sound of wind against the windows. Cate's heart raced, her pulse pounding in her chest. She searched his face for any sign that he understood—that he would listen.

But Landry's eyes were distant, his gaze fixed on something far beyond the car, beyond the safety they found for the moment. She knew that look. She had seen it so many times before. It was the look he got when he was chasing something bigger than himself, something that made him willing to keep going, no matter the cost.

"I can beat them," he muttered, his voice low and determined.

Cate's breath caught in her throat. She pulled her hand away from his, shaking her head. "How can you be sure?" she whispered. "You don't even know what you're dealing with."

Landry looked at her, his eyes pleading. "Cate, of all people, you should understand. I do this stuff for a living. You and I have dealt with things like this before."

"That's not true," Cate shot back, her voice rising with a sudden surge of emotion. "This isn't like anything you've ever faced. Pendle isn't just some haunted house or a poltergeist you can exorcise. It's something *else*, something darker. You didn't see the things I saw."

"I saw enough," Landry said, keeping from her all the eerie, macabre things he'd witnessed, and the nagging thought that something about the town involved him. "I understand what's at stake, Cate. You think I'm just doing this for the thrill? For the hell of it?"

"No," Cate whispered, her voice breaking. "This is supposed to be about Jack's sister, but Jack can find her on his own. I've seen you do this so many times before. You get involved in something, but then it becomes personal, and you go in headfirst. That town is the creepiest place I've ever been. I believe in the supernatural, and that place is full of it. Landry, all I care about is keeping you safe so we can be a family. That's all."

Landry's face softened at her words, the tension easing from his shoulders. She was right. They weren't even home yet, and already he was trying to push the envelope. He reached out to touch her cheek, his thumb brushing away a tear. "Cate, you're right. You're always right, and I'll do what you say."

More tears slid down her face. "You…you won't go back to Pendle?"

For a long moment, Landry paused. He just looked at her, his hand still resting gently on her cheek. She saw the conflict in him, the push and pull of his need to protect her and his drive to face whatever was still out there in Pendle. He wanted to believe it was possible to do both. He always had.

"If you say no, then I won't do it. I want us together too. These days without you ate me up."

"I can't lose you," Cate whispered, her voice breaking with the weight of her fear. "Please, Landry. I can't."

Landry's hand fell away from her cheek, and he leaned back in his seat, his eyes closing for a moment as if he were trying to find the right words. But when he opened them again, she could see the answer in his face before he even spoke.

She thought about his words—if she told him no, then he wouldn't go back. But that placed the onus on her, and it was a burden she didn't want to accept. She wished for something she couldn't have—Landry's wholehearted acceptance that his life was too risky. He had never been the kind of man to turn his back on something once he had set his sights on it, especially when it involved the paranormal. It was who he was, part of his very core. But that didn't make it any easier to accept. In fact, it made the hurt even worse.

The car felt unbearably small, the space between them suffocating as they sat in silence. Cate could hear every shaky breath she took, every pounding beat of her heart. It was too much—this pain, this fear—it was too much to hold inside. Her chest ached with the weight of it, like she was being torn apart piece by piece. The memory of those dark, twisted shadows in Pendle, the lurking evil that had been watching her, waiting for her, surged up from her core, flooding her mind with terror all over again. She couldn't lose him. She *couldn't*.

Because this time, it wasn't just her life at stake. It was his. And she knew with every fiber of her being that Pendle would take him when the time was right.

"I can't do this," Cate whispered, her voice trembling so violently it barely sounded like her own. She turned back to him, eyes red and swollen, her tear-streaked face a mask of raw emotion. "This can't be my decision. This isn't something I can do for you. It's yours to make. And I have this awful feeling that nothing either of us can do will stop you."

"Cate, I know you're scared—"

"No!" Cate cut him off, her voice desperate. "Don't patronize me. I'm not just scared, Landry, I'm *terrified*. I was trapped in that cell, alone with Simba, and I thought I was going to die. Do you understand that? I thought I was never going to see you again. Now we're free, but will you let us keep things that way? I want to hope so, but I know you too well."

Her voice cracked on the last word, her hands trembling violently as she clenched them into fists in her lap. She couldn't breathe, couldn't think beyond the crushing fear that he would be taken from her forever. And the worst part was that there was nothing she could say that would change his mind. He would go back again. She knew it.

Landry looked away, his eyes fixed on some distant point beyond the windshield, as if he couldn't bear to meet her gaze. Cate's heart clenched painfully at the sight, a fresh wave of grief crashing over her. She could feel him slipping away, slipping into the darkness of Pendle, and she was powerless to stop it.

"I don't want to lose you ever again," he said quietly, his voice low but steady. "You mean more to me than anything."

"But I can't see that!" Cate's voice was sharp with desperation now, her hands gripping the edge of the seat so tightly her knuckles turned white. "Why does it always have to be you? Why can't you just walk away for once? For *me*?" She paused, her chest heaving with ragged breaths, the silence between them thick and heavy. Her next words came out in a broken whisper. "For us?"

Landry finally looked at her, his expression softening, but the resolve was still there, etched in every line of his face. "Cate, you know I love you," he began, his voice thick with emotion. "But I worry about the people in Pendle. They're controlled by witches, and I may be the only person who can stop them."

Cate's breath hitched, her heart breaking all over again. She had always known this about him—his sense of responsibility, his need to protect—but now that sense of duty was tearing them apart. And she didn't know if she could survive it.

"I don't want to talk anymore," she whispered, her voice trembling. "You told me you won't go back if I say so, and I say so right now. If you go back, Landry, I...I can't keep doing this. I must think of myself, my health and my sanity."

The words hung in the air between them, heavy and final. Cate's hands were trembling as she wiped at her tears, her whole body shaking with the enormity of what she had just said. Her chest felt like it was caving in, the pain so sharp and all-consuming that she could barely breathe.

For a long moment, Landry didn't respond. He just stared at her, his eyes wide with shock and hurt. "You...you don't mean that," he said softly, though there was a tremor in his voice. "Cate, please, you can't mean that."

"I do," Cate whispered, her voice broken and raw. She met his gaze, her eyes filled with a pain so deep it felt like it was drowning her. "I love you, Landry. But if you go back to Pendle, I can't stay and wait for you to come home in a body bag. I won't survive it."

Landry's face crumpled, his own eyes glistening with tears. He opened his mouth to speak, but no words came. Cate's heart broke all over again at the sight of him, so strong and determined, yet so completely torn apart by her ultimatum.

"I'm sorry," she whispered, her voice trembling with the weight of her fear and pain. "But I can't let you do this to me anymore."

And with that, she turned away from him, her heart shattering into a thousand pieces.

CHAPTER TWENTY-SEVEN

They arrived back in New Orleans well after midnight. Along the way, Landry left a voicemail for Henri Duchamp, giving him a summary of what had happened in Pendle and that he hoped to see Henri tomorrow at the office. When they reached the apartment, Cate walked into the bedroom without another word, undressed, and took a shower. She crawled into bed and was asleep in minutes. Exhausted too, Simba claimed a spot at the foot of the bed. Although he wasn't allowed on the bed all night, Landry wisely decided not to create more friction, and he let the dog stay.

As he changed into pajamas, Landry's eyes burned with exhaustion, every muscle in his body pleading for rest. Somehow they had left with the old book—the same one the bookseller had given him. Twice he had nearly lost it, and he felt it was important to have a look at it as quickly as possible. Whatever revelations the book might hold needed to be discovered sooner rather than later. But right now, the adrenalin was wearing off, and he felt exhausted.

Cate snored lightly as he tiptoed into the living room. The book lay on an end table beside his chair, its leather cover worn and ancient, whispering promises of secrets long buried. Landry couldn't ignore it. This book, whatever it was, had been too hard to get for him to leave until morning. Something might happen—the book might be snatched from his grasp. And it might hold the key to understanding the malevolent force that controlled Pendle.

Landry sat in silence with the book open in his lap, recalling Cate's harsh words. She was right, of course—he took too many risks, pushed the limit too many times. The truth of it was undeniable; every time he plunged into danger, it strained their relationship and eroded Cate's trust in him. And yet, even as her anger lashed out, the pull he felt toward Pendle was overpowering. Something in that cursed town had taken hold of him, something dark and mysterious that he couldn't just walk away from.

The need to understand, to uncover the secrets that lay hidden in Pendle, burned within him like an obsession. It was dangerous—returning might very well cost him his life. But that didn't stop the questions from gnawing at him, the nagging thought that if he didn't go back, he'd never have peace. There was something about the town that went beyond just the old book, the strange people there, and the menacing presence of Charity Device. It was as if the town itself demanded his return.

But even with that burning desire, he couldn't ignore the guilt that Cate's words stirred within him. He'd promised her so many times that he would slow things down, that he'd put her first, yet here he was, ready to dive headfirst into danger again. The conflict tore at him, the battle between his need to protect the woman he loved and his compulsion to investigate the paranormal. The pain in her eyes, the fear that this time he might not come back, twisted his heart, making him question whether any secret was worth the price he might have to pay.

Landry wanted to reassure her, to say he'd stop, that he'd turn away from Pendle and never look back. But the words caught in his throat. He was walking a fine line, realizing that one more step might be the one that pushed him too far. And yet, the allure of Pendle's mysteries was too strong, pulling him toward a fate he feared but felt powerless to resist.

There would be time later to decide his next move, he assured himself as he opened the ancient book. Although he was weary, he shouldn't let this opportunity slip away, not after what they'd faced earlier tonight. Landry looked at the cover he'd first seen at the bookstore—*The First Hundred Years: Pendle, Louisiana, 1614–1714*—and wondered why an innocuous history book would be so important.

Within the hour he would have his answers.

Sleep tugged at the edges of his consciousness, but Landry fought it. His vision blurred, and for a moment, the words seemed to shift and dance. He blinked, forcing his eyes to focus, determined to push through the haze of exhaustion. The brittle pages rustled as he began to thumb through them. Its text was written in Old English, a language that, though archaic, he deciphered with some effort by sounding out the more challenging words. From the title, he expected a brief history of life and events during the first hundred years of Pendle's existence, and as he read, he found that it delivered on that promise in spine-tingling ways he hadn't anticipated.

Buried among the mundane records of daily life, Landry stumbled upon a macabre account that brought the entire history of Pendle into sharp, terrifying focus. A handful of the settlers made a pact with the devil, trading their souls and the future of their descendants for security for their town and power for themselves. Two powerful families, including the Devices, took control of Pendle. In the book Landry read, the chilling details of the agreement were laid bare, revealing the true cost of the town's success—a cursed lineage bound to darkness, a legacy of evil that would dominate the town forevermore.

This was more than just a historical account; it was a revelation that struck at the core of Landry's own identity. The book didn't just illuminate the town's past—it also uncovered a revelation connected directly to him, a bloodline intertwined with the cursed fate of Pendle. The more he read, the more he realized that everything that had happened to him in Pendle was no accident.

With each page, the weight of that knowledge grew heavier, and now Landry knew that he wasn't just learning about Pendle—he was uncovering an incredible, terrifying history lesson about himself, one that would change everything he thought he understood.

As the minutes ticked by, his eyelids grew heavier, but it was impossible to stop now. The book had taken on a hypnotic pull, each page more revealing than the last. Landry's heart pounded with a mix of anticipation and fear as he read about the town's founding. He had learned the basics from his visit to the Cabildo, but this book explained why the town was malevolent and dangerous, and more importantly, what role he played in all of this.

In 1614, a group of migrants boarded a ship in the dead of night, their faces shadowed by the ominous secrets they carried. But not everyone on that ship was tainted by dark magic. There were many others, including the Drake family—a father, a mother, and their young son, Parson— seeking a fresh start in the untamed wilderness of the New World. Aware of the accusations against their fellow passengers, the Drakes kept to themselves on the voyage, their Innocent dreams starkly contrasted against the witches' whispered incantations.

When the migrants landed on the wild shores of what would become Louisiana and journeyed inland to an isolated spot they found along a bayou, the Drakes distanced themselves from the others, sensing the darkness that clung to some of their fellow travelers. While the others—accused witches and not—formed a new community, the Drakes chose fertile land outside the town and began a peaceful existence farming and raising livestock.

The town of Pendle would never be a place of peace. Intimidated, the innocent townspeople joined the accused, electing one of them, Calvin Device, as their first mayor. He took swift steps to secure the town's prosperity, using means that would bind Pendle to a fate darker than any might imagine. The family of witches were true practitioners of the dark arts, and their escape from England had been a narrow one.

With the aid of his compatriots, Mayor Device forged a pact with the very forces of darkness that had allowed their escape. The terms were cruel—to ensure Pendle's survival and protection, a soul must be sacrificed every fifty years. The cunning witches decreed that the sacrifice would never take one of their own. In 1664, it was time to pay the piper, and the first person chosen to fulfill this dreadful bargain was Isaiah Drake, the ten-year-old grandson of the man who shunned the witches and settled his family on land outside Pendle.

But the Drakes would not be easily conquered. Fiercely independent and unwilling to succumb to the sinister forces at play, young Isaiah's parents fled, leaving behind everything they owned. They journeyed about a hundred miles north, finding refuge among indigenous peoples and eventually blending into a new community of settlers that would later be called Jeanerette, far from the reach of Pendle's darkness. Young Isaiah survived, his bloodline free—but only so long as the witches didn't find him.

Back in Pendle, the pact's unfulfilled terms festered like an open wound. Mayor Device, enraged by the loss of his intended sacrifice, amended the deal with the devil, ensuring that the Drake family would forever be marked for retribution. The pact remained in place, its fulfillment delayed. A Drake would one day return to Pendle, unknowingly drawn back by the pull of fate, and when they did, the debt would be paid in full.

Every fifty years from then on, a child was sacrificed, but the initial pact itself remained unfulfilled, biding its time, waiting patiently for centuries. It was a curse bound to blood, and it would remain unbroken until the day an unsuspecting Drake descendant arrived once more in the cursed town of Pendle, Louisiana.

These are my ancestors, Landry thought. Although his parents had told him almost nothing about his family heritage, he believed in his gut that Isaiah Drake was his grandfather many times removed. He read to the end—the hundredth anniversary of Pendle—and learned that the sacrifice was carried out as agreed in 1714, when a six-year-old girl named Bella Price was hanged in the town square in a celebration that every citizen had attended.

Landry was certain the innocents in Pendle had been forced to attend. Why would they choose to watch a child murdered in public? And what about the condemned girl's parents—were they ordered to watch as well? The book failed to address that question.

At last it was impossible to ignore the fatigue that swept over him like a heavy blanket. His head dipped forward, the book still open in his lap, its secrets now revealed. Even as his eyes closed and sleep crept over him, his hand remained on the book, unwilling to let it go, determined to uncover everything—no matter the cost. He dreamed of hooded figures muttering curses around a fire, black shapes pursuing him through the empty streets of a darkened town, and glimpses of a dark past that was his family's gift to him.

A light touch on his shoulder jolted him awake. He blinked, disoriented, to see Cate standing beside him, her face a mix of concern and curiosity. "Did you stay up all night reading?" she asked softly, her voice breaking through the haze of sleep and fear.

Landry rubbed his eyes, trying to shake off the dreams and to realize why she was here. He took her hand and said, "I'm sorry. I intended to come to bed right after you and Simba fell asleep, but I felt driven to find out what was in it."

"Did you learn anything interesting?" She padded into the kitchen to start the coffee pot.

You cannot imagine. "I...I can't discuss it now," he stammered, his voice hoarse and edged with unease. "It's too chilling, too much to process. I need time to think about what I learned." The weight of the revelations was too much to bear, and he felt as though speaking them aloud would make them even more terrifying.

Cate's gaze shifted to the book and then back to Landry, who asked her, "Why did you decide to take the book? I didn't even know you had it; what made you hide it under your shirt?" The book held answers, and the old bookseller had entrusted it to Landry, only to have it taken away. Implausibly, Cate had found it in the municipal building, but how could she have realized its importance?

Cate looked down, trying to find the right words to explain something that made no sense. "I can't answer that," she admitted, her voice barely above a whisper. "It was as if something commanded me to take it, to bring it to help you learn the past from its pages. You've read it; does what I'm saying make sense?"

"More than I thought possible; it's answered a lot of questions." What he'd read explained why the town affected Landry the way it did, why dark things seemed to be watching his every move while he was there, and what price remained to be paid…by him. At a time when the future he sought demanded he stop taking risks, the biggest challenge of his life waited in a mysterious town that demanded his soul.

Shaken by her imprisonment in the jail cell, Cate desperately wished she could talk it through with Landry, but he seemed distant, lost in whatever he'd read, and he'd spent the night sitting up in a chair. She didn't push for more; she knew something was eating at him and that he'd tell her when he was ready.

While she showered, Landry's mind reeled from lack of sleep and the disturbing realizations. He was certain that under Charity Device's leadership, the town continued to exist only because every fifty years sacrifices had taken place in fulfillment of the pact, but that first unfulfilled promise—Isaiah Drake's soul—festered within the town's heart, a lingering debt that demanded payment. Last night when he'd told Cate the fate of Pendle might rest in his hands, he couldn't have imagined that statement was true.

Centuries after Pendle began, Landry had been born in Jeanerette, the place his ancestors fled to, never knowing his family history was inextricably tied to a tiny village in the swamp. When he and Jack drove there searching for Jack's sister, Landry had awakened the curse placed on the Drake family centuries ago. Landry's fame and reputation as a paranormal investigator drew the attention of Pendle's malevolent forces. Those black shapes—the spirits—had whispered to Charity Device, revealing the truth: Landry Drake was descended from the family who escaped the pact, and he was the key to restoring the town's power and balance.

For the mayor, Landry was both a threat and a means to an end. For her, retribution meant capturing Landry and offering him up to the dark forces as the sacrifice that was long overdue. By doing so, she believed she would restore Pendle's lost glory and solidify her own power with the king of darkness.

But there was more to it than just the curse. Charity Device also harbored a personal vendetta against Landry. Over the years, she had seen the havoc his investigations wrought on other supernatural entities in the region. His successes in battling the unknown weakened the influence of dark forces from the bayous to New Orleans, forces that strengthened her and the others like her. Without knowing Pendle existed, Landry had been eroding the power base that Charity depended on, eventually marking him for extinction.

For her, it was time to settle the ancient score with the Drake family. Landry's return to Pendle would be the final act in a drama that had been unfolding for generations—a chance for Charity to exact her revenge on the man who, without realizing it, threatened her dominion and to fulfill the dark pact that his ancestors had tried to escape.

And yet Landry had to go back. He had no choice, no say in the matter. He'd fought for good against evil many times in the past, but never a battle such as this would be. But how might he explain this compulsion to Cate? Last night in the car, her position could not have been more clear. She refused to accept more of his risk-taking. Was it possible to convince her to allow him one last quest—one last risk, the biggest one of his life? There was only one way to find out.

And if she said no...well, he'd cross that bridge if it became necessary.

CHAPTER TWENTY-EIGHT

When Cate took Simba and left for Galveston, the pain had struck Landry deep in his heart. Then, on the eve of her return to him, he'd helped her escape from the clutches of Charity Device. After that, the revelations in the old book about his own family shook him to the very core. He was conflicted about every aspect of his life; while compelled to return to Pendle, he knew doing so might mean the end of his relationship with Cate Adams.

The distance between them in the hours since her return was impossible for Cate to ignore. She was conflicted too; she hadn't uttered a word to Landry about the harrowing experience of being imprisoned in Pendle, nor, to her chagrin, had he asked. The fear that had gripped her during those dark hours, when she and Simba huddled together in the cold, damp cell, left her with scars that ran deep. Every time she closed her eyes, she sensed the oppressive weight of the iron bars, hearing the echo of her own ragged breath in the silence, and knowing that Charity Device lurked just beyond the walls. But despite the nightmares that haunted her, Cate kept it all buried deep inside, locking it away in a place where even Landry couldn't reach.

Cate watched the man she loved with growing unease, her heart heavy with a mixture of compassion, fear, and guilt. She didn't know what he'd uncovered in the book, but she saw the toll it was taking on him. His eyes, always so full of warmth and love for her and Simba, now seemed distant, shadowed by something dark and consuming. Whatever he'd read gripped him with an intensity that frightened her. It was as if the pages themselves had whispered secrets into his soul, binding him to something he couldn't escape.

The chronicle of Pendle had wholly ensnared Landry. Cate could feel it every time he mentioned the town; it was as though it were a living entity calling him back. She sensed that his connection to Pendle went deeper than she could imagine, and that thought tore at her. If she hadn't taken the book in the first place, maybe none of this would have happened. The thought that she might have helped set something in motion gnawed at her, adding to the growing conflict within her heart. The thought of losing him to that cursed town filled her with a sense of helplessness. It was as if Pendle itself was a rival for his soul, and she was powerless to fight it.

Landry, Cate and Simba walked the few blocks in the French Quarter to the studio. Returning to work at the Paranormal Network brought a sense of normalcy, although it seemed unreal given the chaos that churned beneath the surface. Henri greeted Cate with open arms, his face lighting up as he welcomed her back. "It's good to have you home," he said, his tone warm and sincere. But even as she smiled and reassured him she was fine, a hollow ache nestled within her chest. Henri couldn't have imagined what she had been through, the terror she had faced, or the distance that now yawned between her and Landry. And she thanked God Henri didn't ask about the turmoil he must have seen in her eyes. That was his way; he would wait until one of them was ready to explain what had happened.

As Landry retreated to his office, Cate walked over to her own cubicle, closed the door and sat. She had issued her ultimatum in an attempt to hold on to the life they had built together. She'd staked their future on that one demand: that he not return to Pendle, that he choose her, choose them, over whatever or whoever awaited him there. But now, as she watched him wrestle with his own demons, Cate's resolve wavered. She saw the conflict in his eyes, the pain of being torn between his duty and his love for her. It mirrored her own inner turmoil, and that realization shook her to the core.

Was she being fair? Was it right to force him to choose between her and something he was compelled to confront? Cate's heart ached as she questioned herself, wondering if she should take back her ultimatum. The thought of him returning to Pendle terrified her, but so did the thought of pushing him away, of losing him forever because she didn't try hard enough to understand the depth of his struggle.

Tears welled in her eyes as she wrestled with her emotions. She had always been strong, always stood by Landry's side, but now she felt lost, unsure of what to do. She wanted to protect him, to keep him safe from the horrors that lurked in Pendle, but she also understood that denying him this journey might break something irreparable between them. But then again, what if he never returned? That was her underlying, desperate fear each time he placed himself in danger for the sake of unraveling a supernatural adventure.

What if I'm wrong? What if I lose him either way? The fear of losing Landry—to Pendle, to the dark forces at play, or to her own fear—was almost too much to bear.

She loved him more than anything, but that love was now laced with a fear impossible to ignore. If he chose to go back, could she really leave him? Would her life ever be the same without Landry? Cate wiped away a tear as the weight of her dilemma pressed down on her. She had always believed that love meant protecting each other, but now she wasn't so sure. Perhaps love also meant letting go, allowing him to face the darkness, even if it meant risking everything.

More than anything, she was certain that before long, the time would come for her to deal with this situation. Soon he would come to her and ask forgiveness for having to return to the danger of that cursed town. What would she do?

She simply didn't know.

CHAPTER TWENTY-NINE

Behind the closed door of his office, Landry stared at the phone for a long time before finally calling Jack. His hand trembled slightly as he waited, anxiety gnawing at him. The agony in Jack's voice when he answered the phone was unmistakable, a raw and open wound that matched the turmoil in Landry's own heart. Jack had been on edge for days, getting more and more desperate as he searched for any sign of his sister, Melody. He believed she was somewhere in Pendle—a captive, perhaps, or maybe just trying to survive in hiding from the malevolent forces he and Landry had seen firsthand.

When Landry said he had to go back to retrieve his Jeep, he could hear the sharp intake of breath on the other end of the line. Jack didn't hesitate, his voice firm with determination. "I'll take you," he insisted, his words as much a plea for help as an offer. For Jack, this was one more chance to find Mel and bring her home. He couldn't let it slip away. They agreed to meet in two hours.

As Landry hung up the phone, the weight of what he was about to do settled heavily on his shoulders. He sat deep in thought for over an hour, his mind spiraling with thoughts that threatened to unravel him completely. The sobs he had been holding back for days began to claw their way up, choking him as he tried to swallow them down.

The thought of losing Cate, of watching her walk out of his life for good, tore at him with a force he hadn't anticipated. Could he manage without her? Why would he want to find out? The questions tore at his thoughts. The life they had built together, filled with love, laughter, and the comfort of shared dreams, felt as though it was slipping through his fingers, and he was powerless to stop it. If she left him again, he knew it might be the last time. He could almost picture her standing in the doorway, Simba by her side, turning away and disappearing into a future that didn't include him.

The fear of that future, of a life without Cate, crushed him. It was a pain that felt like it might break him, and for a moment, he wondered why he shouldn't just let it all go, to walk away from Pendle and the darkness that beckoned him. But even as the thought crossed his mind, Landry knew it wasn't a real option. The pull of Pendle's unfinished business was too strong; the need to return and face whatever awaited him there was greater than anything else. His own destiny was intertwined with the town's, and he had to see it through, no matter the cost.

At last Landry forced himself to his feet, his legs heavy as if they were weighed down with lead. He made his way to Cate's office, every step a battle between the love he had for her and the pull of the unknown. As he stood in the doorway, the tension between them was almost tangible, a crackling energy that filled the space like a storm about to break.

Cate looked up at him, her eyes wide with a mix of fear, anger, and sadness. He could see her struggle, the way her chest rose and fell with quick, shallow breaths as she fought to keep her emotions in check. The air between them felt thick, charged with all the words they hadn't said, all the fears they hadn't voiced. Landry's heart pounded in his chest as he finally spoke the words he knew might shatter everything between them.

"I have to go back to Pendle," he mumbled. "To return the book. And get my Jeep."

Cate had known this was coming, yet she'd clung to a fragile hope, desperately wishing he'd choose differently. Her heart raced, the tightness in her chest almost suffocating as her face paled and her eyes blazed with a mixture of disbelief and raw hurt. She swallowed, trying to steady her voice, but it cracked under the weight of her anguish. "Landry, I begged you not to do this," she whispered as a tear rolled down her cheek. "You know what that place did to us—what it did to me. If you go back, I don't think I can stay." Her voice faltered, the unspoken ultimatum lingering in the air like a sharp edge, waiting to cut them both.

Her words felt like a punch to Landry's gut, knocking the breath from his lungs, even though he wasn't surprised. Still, hearing it, seeing the tears glistening in her eyes, made his heart clench in a way that left him feeling hollow. He took a slow step toward her, as if bridging that physical space could somehow erase the chasm growing between them. His gaze locked on hers, and the weight of his guilt pressed down like a storm he couldn't escape. Desperation flickered in his eyes, his voice unsteady and thick with emotion. "Cate, I don't want to lose you," he rasped, each word edged with pleading. "But I can't just walk away from this. I have to finish what I started. Please try to understand, for me. I need you to trust me, even if it's hard."

Cate's heart was breaking, but at last she saw her answer. She knew what she had to do, as much as it tore her heart apart. She simply couldn't allow him to go, because she loved him too much. She had pleaded with him for so long, fought for their love, but now it felt like the ground beneath her was crumbling away, leaving her with nothing but an empty ache. Tears welled up, spilling over, and she hated herself for feeling so powerless.

Looking at him now, the man she had once felt so safe with, she saw someone who was about to walk into a nightmare again—one that might take him from her forever. Her voice trembled, barely more than a whisper. "I can't," she choked, tears streaming down her face. "Not this time, Landry. I can't watch you choose that place over us." The finality of her words broke her, and she felt the threat she had never hoped to use unravel before her.

The finality of her words hung in the air, and for a moment, it felt as though time itself had stopped. Landry stood there, frozen, as the gravity of his decision set in. And so, as a tear rolled down his cheek, Landry nodded, acknowledging the painful truth that lay between them. He stepped closer, reaching out to take her hand, but she pulled away, the hurt too fresh, too raw.

"I understand," he said as he choked back a sob. "I just hope to God you'll be here when I come back."

The silence that followed was deafening, filled with the unspoken fears and doubts that had been building between them since she'd left earlier. As Landry turned and walked away, Cate stared numbly, knowing that this might be the moment when everything they had built together crumbled.

Landry stumbled back to his office, picked up the book, and photocopied each page. Then he walked to the exit, stopping to look back once more, trying to keep this moment in his mind. Cate sat at her desk, staring at nothing, and Simba lay in his dog bed nearby, unaware of what was happening to his mom and dad.

Realizing it was the hardest thing he'd ever done, Landry turned and walked out.

CHAPTER THIRTY

As he and Jack drove to Pendle, Landry explained about Cate's experience there, how they had escaped, and that she had issued an ultimatum.

Jack glanced over at his friend, dumbfounded. "And you're here with me because…"

"Because of what I learned in the old book the bookseller gave me. We got it back last night, thanks to Cate finding it. Dale tried to make us give it up, but finally he said we could take it. I brought it along because I promised to return it to him."

"Landry, what about Cate?"

"Walking out was the hardest thing I've ever done. She's strong-willed, and I can only hope she'll let me finish something I've started. After that, I'll do what she wants. I'll cut back my fieldwork and concentrate on episodes for the Paranormal Network in the studio."

"But what if…"

"I just pray to God she won't leave me. That's all I can do. For the sake of the innocent people in Pendle, and for my own soul, I have to settle this thing."

He changed the subject, sharing everything he'd learned by reading the book. Jack listened intently as Landry explained things that finally made some sense. The town, the pact, his family's involvement, and the reason they wanted Landry back—everything was clearer now, although many questions remained unanswered.

"We have to find Melody," Jack said. "I can't believe she's hiding out; I think they kidnapped her."

They rode on in silence, considering the dangers that lay in wait for them. For Landry, the memory of rescuing Cate from the clutches of Mayor Device and the bizarre visit to the archives that ended at the bookshop still haunted him. Jack, on the other hand, was on a mission to find his sister that so far had been thwarted at every turn.

They came to the edge of town and were struck by a sight that made them question their own eyes. The No Trespassing sign, which had stood like a sentinel at the town's entrance, was now covered with vibrant banners fluttering joyfully in the breeze. Similar banners in vivid colors lined the streets; the gloom that once hung over Pendle had evaporated, replaced by a festive atmosphere. The shops that had been shuttered and cloaked in shadow were now open for business, their windows filled with colorful displays. People who had kept to themselves now bustled about, their laughter and chatter filling the air.

Jack shot a confused glance at Landry. "What the hell happened here?" he asked, disbelief evident in his voice. Landry didn't reply immediately, his mind racing as he tried to reconcile this cheerful, lively town with the eerie ghost town he had fled earlier. A gnawing unease settled in his gut—there was something deeply wrong about this transformation, something that defied logic and reason.

As they drove through the town, people waved at them with bright, welcoming smiles. The warmth in their expressions should have been reassuring, but to Landry, it was anything but. To him it felt like a mask—a veneer hiding secrets underneath.

As bright as everything appeared, things were not right in Pendle. The festivities felt contrived, and the happy, smiling townspeople looked like actors in a play. As they drove, a sense of wrongness grew, like a shadow looming just out of sight. Jack shifted uneasily in his seat, his eyes darting from one cheerful face to another, searching for any sign of his sister. But instead of hope, he felt concern. What if she was a captive somewhere nearby?

The first order of business was to return the book to Dale Staggs as promised, but when they arrived at his mechanic shop, something was wrong. In stark contrast to the festive atmosphere everywhere else in town, the shop was unadorned and dark. They knocked several times, but it appeared Dale wasn't around.

They drove to the bookstore, its bell tinkling as they entered. The old woman was behind the counter, her eyes gleaming with a knowledge that made Landry's skin crawl.

"We're looking for Dale Staggs," Landry said. "We stopped by his garage, but he's not there."

With a smile still affixed, the crone shook her head. "He was a foolish man," she murmured, her voice laced with a dark satisfaction. "He voted wrong, and he talked too much. He paid for his sins."

A shiver ran down Landry's spine. The words were simple, but his blood ran cold. He knew better than to ask what she meant—he could guess well enough. So he pulled the book from his bag and handed it to her.

"I promised to give this back to Dale," he said, trying to keep his voice from trembling. "It's the book you gave me."

"I know what it is." The old woman took the book, her gnarled fingers tracing the pentagram on the cover with a reverence that bordered on madness. She looked up at Landry, her eyes piercing into his own. "What did you learn from reading it?" she asked, a cruel curiosity in her tone.

Landry hesitated, the memories of the night before flashing before his eyes—his family's involvement with the devil's pact, the ancient rites, the blood spilled in the name of dark forces. "I understand what Pendle is about," he finally said, his voice barely above a whisper. "And how I fit into the picture."

"And yet you returned? What a brave man you are. Or foolish, perhaps." A twisted smile crept across her face. "Aren't you afraid you'll be taken by the dark forces? They have been awaiting your arrival for centuries."

Landry forced himself to ask the question that had been gnawing at him since they walked in. "How are you able to talk about all this without the mayor stopping you?"

The old woman's smile widened, a sinister gleam in her eyes. "The mayor has no power over me," she said cryptically, her voice dripping with an ancient malice. "She's family; I'm a Device too. In this town, some of us answer to higher authorities."

"Why did you want me to have the book?"

"Better to approach danger with eyes wide open," she replied with a malicious grin. "Even a condemned man deserves to know the charges against him."

Landry's blood ran cold. He knew that they had been playing a game where the rules were written long before he ever set foot in Pendle. And those who knew the rules—the ones who controlled the town—were the personification of evil. And yet he had deliberately come back in defiance of everything that mattered to him.

"Where's my sister?" Jack asked. He'd gotten an evasive answer last time, but now there was nothing. She stared into his eyes, and he tried but failed to hold her gaze. "Let's go, Jack," Landry said at last. "We'll find her somehow."

They drove to city hall; the building that had once loomed over the town like a grim overseer now appeared almost welcoming. Flowers bloomed in neat beds outside, and the oppressive silence that had once hung over the place was replaced by the hum of everyday activity. In the town square, a brass band played rousing Sousa marches.

There was a basic truth Landry and Jack understood—none of this was real, because it wasn't possible. The town and its inhabitants couldn't have been transformed overnight, so every aspect of the "new" Pendle had been contrived by the dark forces that controlled the town.

As they walked into city hall, Landry was immediately struck by the contrast between the bright, cheerful exterior and the eerie familiarity of the interior, which no one had bothered to spiff up. The shadows seemed to cling to the walls, reluctant to let go of their hold on the place. And there, standing in the hallway with a smile that sent a shiver down Landry's spine, was the mayor. He walked down the corridor, but Jack hung back near the exit, ready to bolt for help if things got problematic.

"Do you like the new look of our town?" she asked Landry, her honey-sweet voice laced with sarcasm.

Landry stared at her, his mind reeling. How could everything change so drastically? How powerful *was* this woman? His thoughts raced as he struggled to find the right words. "Why did you do all this?" he blurted.

Her smile widened, and the malevolence in her eyes deepened. "Because of you, of course," she purred, her tone both triumphant and mocking. "The people can finally celebrate because Landry Drake has come home."

Landry's skin prickled as the weight of the mayor's words settled over him like a suffocating blanket. The shadows that clung to the walls seemed to deepen, the flickering light overhead casting long, twisted shapes that danced eerily down the hallway. He felt the oppressive presence of something unseen, something ancient and powerful, lurking just beyond his perception.

"Celebrate?" Landry echoed, his voice hoarse as he tried to comprehend the meaning behind her cryptic words. "What do you mean, 'celebrate'?"

Charity's smile never wavered. "You're a smart man. You've read the book, so you know that you are the missing piece of Pendle's puzzle. Your return marks the beginning of something monumental, so it is a day of celebration."

Landry's mind raced as he searched for an escape, a way out of this twisted nightmare. But the room seemed to close in around him, the walls themselves conspiring to keep him trapped. The air was thick with the scent of decay, and he felt as if everyone was poised and waiting for him to make the next move.

"This is your family's legacy, Landry," Charity continued, her voice a silky whisper that seemed to seep into his bones. "It's woven into the fabric of this town, into its history, its future. And now that you're here, Pendle can finally fulfill its destiny."

Landry's eyes darted around the room, searching for anything that could give him a clue, a way to break free from whatever grip this place had on him. The shadows, the twisted shapes on the walls—he couldn't shake the feeling that dark shapes stood watching him, waiting for something.

"You see," Charity continued, her voice dropping to a conspiratorial whisper, "Pendle has been waiting for you. For four hundred years, everything has been prepared, just awaiting your return. And now that you're here, we can finally begin."

Landry's breath hitched in his throat. He could feel the weight of something heavy and dark pressing down on him, a force that threatened to pull him under. The shadows on the walls seemed to writhe, coiling like serpents, their movements synchronized with the pounding of his heart.

He knew what they intended to do. He'd read it in the book. He was the fulfillment of destiny. "What comes next?" he asked.

Charity's smile widened, revealing teeth he hadn't seen earlier—teeth that were just a little too sharp, a little too white. "Why, we're going to finish what our ancestors started, of course. The pact must be honored, Landry. The town demands it."

Before he could react, the black blobs surged forward, wrapping around him like tendrils of smoke. The room seemed to spin, the walls melting into a swirling vortex of darkness. Landry struggled, his movements frantic, but the shadows only tightened their grip, pulling him into the shadows.

And as the darkness consumed him, the last thing he heard was Charity's voice echoing in his mind like a sinister lullaby. "Welcome home, Landry. Our town has waited for you for far too long."

That end of the hallway went dark, as if a curtain had been pulled across it.

CHAPTER THIRTY-ONE

Jack stood halfway down the hall, watching everything unfold. As soon as he saw the mayor's sinister smile and heard the chilling exchange between her and Landry, he knew he had to act quickly; once again, Landry was in trouble with the supernatural; and he had to get help in a town that offered nothing but obstacles.

Jack edged closer to the door. His movements were slow and deliberate, every muscle tensed, ready to spring into action. As he reached the exit, he paused for just a moment, his eyes flicking back to Landry. Guilt gnawed at him for leaving his friend behind, but he knew that staying would do neither of them any good.

Pushing the door open just wide enough to slip through, Jack stepped out into bright sunshine. The festivities were in full swing—a man sold cotton candy from a pushcart, another offered hot dogs and sodas, and the band oompahed another rousing march. The townspeople looked happy, but he thought about Landry's idea that perhaps they were merely actors in a play. Could it be true, that they were puppets being manipulated by Charity Device?

Jack's mind raced. Whom could he trust in a town like this? The locals he had encountered so far had been strange, to say the least, their eyes holding secrets they were unwilling to share. But there had to be someone—someone who hadn't been entirely corrupted by whatever force controlled the town. Not the bookseller, who was one of them. Not Dale Staggs, who was nowhere to be found. Nor the lady in the trailer next to his sister's. But those were the only people he and Landry had encountered.

He wandered off down the street, his footsteps echoing off the cobblestones. Rounding a corner, he spotted a small house off the town square. It was the only one in the block without festive ribbons and banners. Maybe, just maybe, the people inside were rebels who refused to celebrate Landry's return. Having nothing to lose, Jack hurried toward the house, praying that whoever was inside might be willing to help.

He reached the door and knocked sharply. After what felt like an eternity, the door opened to reveal an old woman wearing a housedress and apron. She had a kind face, and her eyes held a warmth he'd seen nowhere else in Pendle. She took a step back and beckoned.

"Come on in, Mr. Blair. I'm glad you found me. I've been expecting you."

Jack stood on the doorstep in shock. "How...how do you know who I am? And how could you have been expecting me?"

"I know many things. Come in and have a chat."

Jack stepped over the threshold, presuming this woman had extrasensory powers of her own, but hoping she was different than the rest. It was a gamble, a huge risk that could spell disaster for Landry and for him if things went wrong. But it was all he had.

The faint scent of herbs and old wood filled the air as the woman closed the door behind him and led him into a parlor, her gaze sharp and assessing. A cheery fire crackled in the hearth, pleasantly warming the room despite the summer heat outdoors. "Sit here," she said, motioning to a worn but comfortable-looking armchair. She took another close by.

Jack struggled to gather his thoughts in the urgency of the situation. "My friend Landry," he began, his voice tight with anxiety. "He's at city hall with the mayor. She—she said something about a pact, about sacrifices. He's in trouble."

The woman nodded, her expression grave. "Charity Device," she muttered, almost to herself. "I feared it might come to this. Your friend is Landry Drake, and yes, he is in deep trouble. He should never have come to Pendle."

Surprised, Jack asked, "How did you know his name?"

"I know far more than I wish I did," the woman replied. "The Device family founded this town, as did my own. Charity's ancestors made a pact with the other side and allowed them to control Pendle. It's a pact that demands blood, power, and unwavering loyalty."

Jack's brow furrowed. "I know some of that. The lady at the bookshop gave Landry a book, and he learned about the pact. We went to the town archives, and something happened...something I can't explain. The people we've met all seem subservient to the mayor, like they're bound to her will."

The woman sighed, her eyes flickering with something that looked like both resolve and sorrow. "Most of them are. But not everyone. My name is Lydia Peel, and fate guided you to me. My family were among the others who sailed from England accused of witchcraft, but back home our family wasn't hanged as the Devices were. We've always resisted the darkness and tried to work for good. The women in my family were all healers—witches, to be honest—and they passed down spells to protect us from the dark forces. The magic Charity Device wields doesn't touch us as easily, but sadly there are only two of us left in Pendle, my sister and me."

Jack felt a glimmer of hope. "Are you saying you can help Landry?"

"Possibly, but we must move quickly. Charity is powerful, and once the ritual begins, it will be impossible to stop her. We need to disrupt it." She called out a name. "Rose! Rose, come quickly. We must help Landry Drake!"

A much older woman hobbled into the room on a cane. Her back was bent, but like Lydia, she had a warm face, and her eyes glowed with interest. "Landry Drake, you say? After all these years, they finally lured one of the Drakes back to Pendle? Is this him?"

"No, dear, this is his friend Jack Blair. Jack, meet my sister, Rose. Come help me, dear." She crossed the room to a large wooden chest near the fire, lifting the lid to reveal an array of items: herbs, crystals, vials of various liquids, and several very old, well-used books. She pulled out a small pouch and handed it to Jack. "Hold this for me," she instructed.

"What's this?" he asked, opening the pouch to find a handful of finely ground powder inside.

"A protective mixture," Lydia explained. "It's made from a blend of herbs that my family has used for centuries. Sprinkle it around Landry, and it will create a barrier that Charity's magic can't penetrate—but it's very short-acting.

Maybe an hour at most. It should give us enough time to get him out of town."

Jack stared at the pouch, hope battling with doubt. "And what about Charity? What if she tries to stop us?"

Lydia's expression hardened. "Oh, she will try. You can count on it, but I have a few tricks of my own. The magic that flows through Pendle isn't just darkness. There are ancient protections, wards that my ancestors put in place to safeguard those who resisted. Over the years, her family's power has intensified while ours has waned, but there's plenty I can do to buy us time."

She began gathering a few more items from the chest—candles, a piece of chalk, and a small silver dagger engraved with intricate runes. As she worked, she spoke quickly but calmly, outlining the plan. "When we get to city hall, Rose will draw a ward around the building's entrance to prevent Charity from leaving once she realizes what we're doing. You and I will go in, find Landry, and I'll use the powder. Then we'll get him out. If we can break the ritual before it begins, Charity's power will weaken. But we have no time to spare."

Jack grew excited as he listened to Lydia's plan. It was dangerous, but it was a plan—a real chance to save Landry from whatever horrors Charity had in store for him.

"Why are you helping us?" he asked, realizing he hadn't yet understood her true motivations.

Lydia paused, her hands stilling for a moment as she looked at Jack with an intensity that made his breath catch. "Because I've seen too many good people lost to this town, to the Device family's twisted sense of destiny. My own family paid the price for standing against her. If I can save even one person from that fate—especially Landry Drake, whose sacrifice will make her even more powerful—then it's worth the risk."

With that, Lydia finished her preparations, took the pouch, and handed Jack a small, rough map of the municipal building. "Here," she said, pointing to a spot. "This is where Charity would have taken him. The basement in the heart of the building, where the original foundation stones are laid—it's a place of power. We must get to him before she can start the ritual."

Jack could feel the weight of what lay ahead, but Lydia's calm determination gave him strength. Together, they would face the darkness of Pendle—and with any luck, they would bring Landry back from the brink.

As they stepped out into the sunshine, the festive atmosphere seemed even more contrived than ever, as if the town had been ordered to celebrate the pending demise of Landry Drake. Jack knew it might happen, but with Lydia and Rose on his side, he had hope.

And in a town like Pendle, hope was about the only weapon they could wield.

CHAPTER THIRTY-TWO

Landry awoke to a suffocating silence, his head pounding with the remnants of a nightmare he couldn't quite remember. The darkness around him seemed absolute, pressing in on all sides, so thick and oppressive that he could feel it in his lungs with each shallow breath he took. He tried to move, but his limbs felt heavy, as if they were submerged in a thick, viscous liquid. Panic surged through him as he struggled to remember where he was, how he had ended up here. He was lying on a stone floor, its surface damp and slick.

Landry tried to sit up, his muscles straining with the effort. The darkness was so complete that he couldn't see his hands in front of his face. It seemed he was entombed underground, the air thick with the smell of earth and decay.

As his senses gradually returned, Landry noticed a faint, rhythmic sound in the distance—a slow, steady drip of water, like the ticking of a clock in a forgotten crypt. The sound reverberated through the stone chamber, amplifying the overwhelming sense of isolation. He was alone, completely alone, in a place that seemed to have been forgotten by time itself.

His eyes adjusted, and he realized that the darkness was not absolute. Tendrils of light shone between boards in the ceiling…boards that made up a floor in a room ten feet above.

He stood on shaky, unsteady legs. Breathing in the dank air, he began to feel his way along the walls of the chamber, hoping to find a door or an exit. The stones were rough and jagged, and more than once, he felt something wet and slimy brush against his fingers. Just as he was about to give up hope, his hand brushed against a smooth metal surface. He ran his fingers over its edges and realized it was a door.

Was this some kind of twisted game? Had Charity Device left him here with the means to escape, or would opening this door lead him into even more peril?

As Landry's fingers closed around a knob, he held his breath and turned it. There was a soft click, and the door creaked open with a groan of rusted hinges. He stepped through the door, bracing for whatever awaited him.

The moment he crossed the threshold, the door slammed shut behind him with a deafening clang, plunging him into an even deeper darkness. But in the distance, he could see a faint glimmer of light—just a tiny pinprick, but it was enough to give him hope. He stumbled toward it, his hands outstretched as he felt his way along the stone walls.

The light grew brighter as he approached, revealing the outline of another door at the end of the narrow passageway. As he drew closer, the door swung open with a loud creak, the light flooding out and nearly blinding him. Squinting against the brightness, he stepped through, and what he saw on the other side made his blood run cold.

"Come in, come in," said a tall figure draped in black. Its voice slithered through the air, low and malevolent, like the hiss of a serpent curling around Landry's spine. Landry placed his hands over his ears, realizing the figure hadn't spoken aloud; instead, the words had crawled into his mind, reverberating through his skull in a way that felt both ancient and inhuman. The words were a guttural whisper, but they carried an unsettling power, as though they bypassed his ears entirely and sank straight into his bones.

His eyes grew accustomed to a dim light from a solitary candle, and he looked at the figure. The face that stared back at him was not human, nor had it ever been. The skin was stretched tight over the bones, cracked and peeling like dried parchment, with hollow eye sockets that seemed to bore into Landry's very soul. The mouth was twisted into a grotesque grin, revealing blackened teeth, and as the figure opened it to speak, a voice that sounded like the rustling of dead leaves filled the room.

"We've been waiting for you," the voice continued, its tone a sickening mix of mockery and seduction. Each syllable stretched and coiled, dripping with a sinister glee as if considering a savory treat for dinner.

The voice was the eeriest thing Landry had ever heard—a voice that didn't belong in any world he knew, one that was a part of nightmares. It was both cold and burning, a rasp like rusted metal scraping against stone, yet impossibly smooth, like velvet laced with poison.

"Step closer," it purred, a command laced with venomous pleasure. "Your place is waiting."

The temperature plunged as Landry felt his resolve falter, his instincts demanding he run, yet his legs were frozen in place as the voice dug deeper into his psyche. The figure laughed, a hollow, echoing sound that felt like it came from every shadow, vibrating through the walls and through his very soul. It was the sound of inevitability, a twisted laugh of something that had all the time in the world to enjoy Landry's terror. "You cannot resist. You were always mine."

The figure stepped aside and raised its arm, gesturing for Landry to step further into the room. Other candles sprang to life as if lit by an unseen hand, and now he saw a stone altar—waiting for him. Next to it stood Charity Device.

"Welcome home," she said, her words dripping with malice. "It's been such a long time."

Landry stumbled back, his mind reeling as she began to advance toward him, but the menacing figure loomed behind him, allowing him no place to go. The figure moved closer, its hollow eyes fixed on him, and as it drew nearer, Landry could feel the cold, malevolent energy radiating from it, suffocating him, choking the life from his lungs.

"Your bloodline has unfulfilled promises," the figure whispered, its voice echoing in Landry's mind, filling it with visions of fire and darkness, of ancient rituals and forbidden pacts. "You cannot escape your fate. The pact of the ancestors must be paid in blood."

Landry's heart thundered in his chest, his pulse pounding in his ears as the figure loomed over him, its decayed hands outstretched, the stench of death overwhelming. He felt the walls closing in, the darkness swallowing him whole, and as the figure's icy fingers brushed his skin, he let out a scream that reverberated through the chamber, a scream that no one would hear in this stone room.

Landry was unable to resist. With nothing more than a touch, the figure guided him to the stone altar and commanded him to lie down. One thing became clear to him as his mind began to cloud with an odd numbness.

Charity Device had summoned a truly imposing figure to assist her in the ritual he was to be a part of.

Before he closed his eyes, he looked into the figure's face once more—into the face of the devil itself.

CHAPTER THIRTY-THREE

Jack, Lydia, and Rose resolutely made their way toward city hall, moving among revelers who sang and danced in the street. As they approached the building, Lydia stopped them and turned to her sister. "Rose, this is your moment," Lydia whispered, handing her sister a piece of chalk and one of the candles. "Draw the ward as we discussed. We need to make sure Charity stays inside until we're done."

Rose nodded, her movements slow but precise. Glancing here and there to be sure no one was watching, she knelt by the entrance. It surprised Jack to see how agile she was, given her age. She began to draw a complex pattern on the ground, the chalk scratching against the stone. As she worked, she murmured under her breath, words in a language Jack didn't recognize. The air around them seemed to hum with energy, and Jack felt the hairs on the back of his neck stand up.

Lydia placed a hand on his shoulder. "Stay close to me, Jack. Her spells will protect us, but we need to move quickly."

Jack and Lydia slipped inside the old building. In sharp contrast to everything outside, in here the air was stale, and the hallway was lit by what little sunlight streamed through dirty windows.

"Where is Landry?" Jack whispered, glancing around nervously but seeing no one.

"Downstairs in the heart," Lydia whispered. "I can feel the energy. I believe she has summoned the dark lord himself. That means she wants to move quickly, and Landry is in grave danger."

As they descended a flight of stairs in the middle of the building, Jack felt the temperature drop. His breath misted in the air before him, and a deep, oppressive cold settled into his bones. He tightened his grip on the pouch, his anxiety mounting with each step.

Lydia suddenly stopped and put a finger to her lips. Jack strained to listen, his heart racing. At first, he heard nothing, but then, faintly, the sound of chanting reached his ears—a low, rhythmic murmur that sent a shiver down his spine.

"She's beginning," Lydia hissed. "We have little time left. Follow me. Quickly, now."

Lydia led the way down a stone-lined corridor. They came to a heavy wooden door, where Lydia paused, placing her hand against it as if feeling for something on the other side. Jack could hear the chanting clearly now, the voices harsh and guttural, sending waves of unease crashing over him.

"They're inside," Lydia whispered. "When I open the door, be ready to use the powder. We'll only get one chance."

Jack nodded, his throat dry. He opened the pouch and made ready as Lydia slowly pushed the door open.

The room beyond was dimly lit by flickering candles, their flames casting long shadows across the stone walls. In the center of the room stood Charity Device, her back to them, her hands raised as she chanted in a language that Jack couldn't understand but instinctively knew was ancient and dangerous. Before her, lying on a stone altar in a circle of candles and symbols drawn in blood, was Landry. Jack's heart lurched at the sight of his friend, unconscious and pale, as if all the life had been drained from him. But the most frightening thing of all—the most bone-chilling thing Jack had ever seen—was the black figure standing on the far side of the altar, watching with keen interest as Charity chanted.

Lydia motioned for Jack to stay back as she stepped into the room, her presence seemingly unnoticed by those whose focus was entirely on the ritual. Lydia began to move in a wide arc around the room, her eyes fixed on Charity, who continued to chant, her voice rising and falling in a disturbing rhythm.

Jack watched, his hands trembling, as Lydia reached into her own pouch and began to sprinkle a fine line of powder along the floor. The air seemed to shimmer where the powder fell, and the temperature in the room dropped further, frost forming on the stone beneath their feet.

Lydia nodded to Jack, signaling it was time. He stepped forward, careful to stay outside the circle of candles, and began to sprinkle the protective powder around Landry. The powder seemed to absorb the flickering candlelight, glowing faintly as it settled on the ground.

For a moment, nothing happened. Charity's chanting continued, the air thick with dark energy. But then, the powder around Landry began to glow more brightly, forming a barrier of light around him. Charity's voice faltered, her chant stumbling as she realized something was wrong, and the malevolent creature stepped back, doing nothing.

"No!" Charity hissed, spinning around to face them, her eyes blazing with fury. "You dare to interfere?"

Lydia stepped forward, her voice steady as she began to chant in a language that matched Charity's, but with a tone of defiance. The two women's voices clashed, the air around them crackling with power as their wills battled for control. The dark figure stood in silence, adopting a neutral stance and allowing the humans to do battle in their own fashion.

Jack felt a surge of fear as Charity raised her hands, and the shadows in the room came to life, twisting and writhing toward him. But before they could reach him, the barrier of light flared even higher, forcing the shadows back.

"Jack, get him out of here!" Lydia shouted, her voice strained as she struggled to hold the barrier in place. "Now!"

Without hesitating, Jack rushed forward, grabbing Landry by the shoulders and pulling him toward the door. Landry was heavy, his body limp and unresponsive, but Jack didn't let go. He could feel the resistance in the air, the darkness trying to pull Landry back into the circle.

As they reached the door, Jack felt a cold hand clamp down on his shoulder. He spun around to see Charity, her face twisted with rage, her eyes burning with a malevolent light.

"You will not take him from me!" she snarled, her grip tightening, the darkness swirling around her like a living thing.

But before she could do more, a sudden, blinding light filled the room. Jack shielded his eyes, and when he looked again, Charity was stumbling back, her grip broken, her power disrupted by the light that radiated from the barrier Lydia had created.

"Run, Jack!" Lydia screamed. "Take him and run!"

Jack hauled Landry through the door and stumbled up the stairs. As they moved away from the chamber, Landry awoke, groggy but alert enough to walk on his own. Rose was waiting for them at the top of the stairs. She took Landry's arm, guiding them out of the building and into the square. "To your car—hurry!" Rose screamed. As she jumped into the passenger seat, Jack helped Landry into the back and crossed his fingers the car would start. Luck was with them, and he drove madly to the end of town and roared past the No Trespassing sign.

A mile or so away, Rose directed him to a path that led into the woods. Barely wide enough for his car to maneuver, he made his way to a clearing, where Lydia Peel sat on the ground before a campfire. How she had gotten here ahead of him and managed to build a fire, he had no idea.

By this time Landry had awakened, his mind groggily trying to process what was happening and where he was. Lydia came to the car, opened the back door, and said, "Come with me, Landry Drake. You are still in danger."

CHAPTER THIRTY-FOUR

Landry's head throbbed as Jack helped him walk over to the crackling fire. He collapsed to the ground and mumbled, "I feel like I've been hit by a truck. What happened to me? I can't remember anything."

Lydia knelt beside him and pulled a small, dark bottle from the satchel slung over her shoulder. "Drink this," she said. "It's a potion that will help you recover your strength in no time."

He hesitated, staring first at her, then Rose. "Do I know you? Jack, who are these people? Are they witches?"

"They're witches but not like Charity. If it weren't for their help, you might be dead by now."

Landry's hands trembled as he took the bottle and uncorked it. The liquid inside was thick and dark, with a pungent smell that made him hesitate. But he trusted Jack, and he knew he needed to be at full strength if he was going to find a way out of this nightmare. He tipped the bottle to his lips and drank.

The potion burned as it went down, a fiery warmth spreading through his chest and radiating out to his limbs.

Almost immediately, he felt a surge of energy, and the fog that clouded his mind dissipated. The pain in his body dulled, and the dizziness started to fade.

"Thank you," Landry said. "I don't know how I'll ever repay you."

Lydia smiled, her expression kind but tinged with sadness. "You can't, my dear, but there's no need for repayment. I've lived in Pendle all my life, and I've seen the darkness that envelops our town. My ancestors tried to fight it, but the pact has held this town in its grip for centuries. I couldn't stand by and let another innocent soul be lost to it. Especially you. If a Drake is sacrificed under her watch, Charity will have even greater power."

His thoughts turned to the room where he had almost been sacrificed. "Did you see that figure with Charity? I couldn't resist its power. All it did was lay a finger on my skin, and I obeyed its every command."

"The dark lord," Lydia whispered. "I hesitate to speak his name because I don't want to give him room in my mind. I was taken aback when I saw him there. I've never seen him in person before, and the fact that he came for your ritual demonstrates the importance of sacrificing a Drake to satisfy the pact."

Jack pointed out that the dark lord had stood back, doing nothing while they rescued Landry. "Why didn't he stop us?"

"We were fortunate. The moment I saw him step back, I realized what was unfolding. Charity made certain promises to him, assurances that she has the power to bring you to the altar for your sacrifice. He intends to hold her to those promises without help from him."

"Now that I'm free, how can we break the pact? This will all happen again if they aren't stopped, right?"

"Yes, that's right. And believe me, my ancestors tried to find a way, as have I for my entire life. Now that there's a Drake to become the sacrificial lamb, it must be carried out. Now that you've come to Pendle, if the pact isn't honored, the town will fall into ruin, and the dark forces that work with Charity will demand the lives of every decent person who lives here. She *must* put you to death in order to survive herself. And you must die to save the innocents in this town."

"There has to be something the pact didn't account for, some loophole that can break it without me having to die."

Lydia shook her head. "I'm not aware of one. I've studied the pact and all the records I could find. I've tried every spell, every ritual, every protective charm, but nothing has worked. The pact is too strong, too deeply woven into the fabric of Pendle. I'm sure there's a counter curse; almost every one has a way to undo it. If you are lucky enough to find out a way, I can provide you with all the things you'd need."

Landry was determined to find a solution. Maybe he'd fail, but he had nothing to lose. If he could find some piece of information that had been overlooked, some flaw in the pact that he could exploit, then he might stop Charity and her coven.

"Jack, let's get out of here," he said, determination hardening his voice. "Tomorrow I'll go back to the Cabildo to see if the curator missed anything about Pendle. I have a photocopy of that book the old woman gave me. Maybe I can find something in it that I missed earlier. It's all we have, and it's worth one more try."

Lydia held out no hope, but still she encouraged him. "I'll be here and ready to help if you need me. But be careful, Landry. The dark forces tied to Pendle are powerful and cunning. They'll be watching you, waiting for any sign of weakness. I urge you not to come back unless you're prepared to settle things with Charity."

He thanked the two women for their help. He assured Jack he was fine to drive his Jeep, and he and Jack began the trip back to New Orleans in two cars. As he followed, Landry's thoughts were not concerning the danger he faced in Pendle, but about whether Cate and Simba would still be at the apartment when he returned.

CHAPTER THIRTY-FIVE

Landry raced upstairs to his apartment. His hand hesitated on the doorknob, his heart pounding as if it could break through his chest. The harrowing events in Pendle still lingered in his mind like a dark cloud, but nothing weighed heavier on him than thoughts of Cate. And Simba too. He should—no, he absolutely must—make things right.

If they were still here.

All the way from Pendle, he had struggled to think what he would do if he opened the door and they were gone again, this time for good. Now the wondering was over. Taking a deep breath, he pushed open the door and stepped inside.

The apartment was dimly lit, a single lamp casting a faint glow across the living room. Landry's eyes scanned the space, searching for any sign of Cate. His heart skipped a beat when he saw her curled up on the couch with a blanket wrapped around her. Simba was there too, and he leapt to his feet, tail wagging furiously, and ran to greet Landry.

Cate's eyes fluttered open, and when they met his, Landry felt a rush of emotions. Relief, love, guilt, fear—they all collided in a wave that nearly overwhelmed him. He stood frozen for a moment, unable to speak. "You're…you're still here," he choked. "Thank God."

Cate stood and went to him. For a moment, they simply looked at each other, trying to process the emotions each felt. He put his arms around her and pulled her tight. Finally he spoke. "I was afraid you'd be gone. I'm sorry. I'm really sorry."

"Stop. You don't have to apologize. I know you too well. I know this isn't just a job for you—it's who you are. But that doesn't make it any easier to live with."

"I never wanted to hurt you," he said, his voice raw with emotion. "But I also can't ignore what's happening in Pendle. There's something there that I can't walk away from. People will die—a lot of them—if I can't help them."

"Help them how? By dying yourself? You may not realize that you deal with every paranormal situation you investigate the same way. You jump in headfirst and hope for deep water. And that's what scares me the most."

"I promise you once this is over—once Pendle is finished—I will do everything I can to minimize the danger. I don't want to lose you. I *can't* lose you."

She squeezed his hands, her grip firm and steady. "I love you, Landry. And I know you love me. But love isn't always enough to make things work. You must find a way to stay safe. That's all I need."

He nodded. "I'll find a way. Just let me finish what I've started in Pendle. There's a curse there—a darkness that needs to be put to rest. And I can't do that alone."

"I'll help you. Whatever it takes, I'll be there. But once this is done, we need to talk about the future—about what comes next for us."

Landry felt a surge of hope at her words. "We will. I promise."

They stood in silence for a moment, simply holding each other. The warmth of her presence gave him a peace that overpowered all the horrors of Pendle. For the first time in days, he allowed himself to relax, to let go of the fear and uncertainty that had gripped him for so long.

Finally, Cate pulled back and gave him a sly smile. "You're exhausted. Me too. Let's go to bed."

They got in bed and again allowed Simba to sleep at their feet. Landry stretched, feeling the weight of the past few days beginning to lift now that his biggest concern of all seemed assuaged, at least for now.

Cate leaned up on an elbow and looked over at him. "I hate to tell you, but you look like hell. Want to talk about it?"

"It's better not to. The curse is deeper and more entrenched in the town's history than I realized. And it's tied to my family. I had no idea."

"Well, now we're in this together. I've fought beside you in the past, and we did pretty well as a team."

Her words were like a lifeline. He had been so consumed by the darkness in Pendle that he had almost let go of the thing that mattered most. "I don't deserve you. But I'm so grateful that you're here."

She leaned in, pressing a soft kiss to his cheek. "You're right about not deserving me, but you're not getting rid of me that easily, Landry Drake."

He smiled. "I never want to get rid of you. I want to build a life with you. A life that we can both be happy with."

"Then that's what we have to work on," she replied. "But first, let's deal with Pendle. Once that's behind us, we'll figure out the rest. For now, let's hit the sack."

Landry lay next to her, feeling a renewed sense of purpose. He wasn't out of the woods yet—far from it—but he wasn't alone anymore. Cate was with him, and together, they would face whatever came next.

They awoke early the next morning to a dark, rainy day. He called Henri to advise they'd be in late and told Cate everything that had happened since she and Simba went to Galveston. Landry told her about the horrors he had encountered in Pendle, the revelations about his family's dark past, and the chilling encounters with Charity Device. He didn't sugarcoat anything, knowing that Cate deserved the truth, no matter how dangerous it sounded.

She listened intently, her hand never leaving his. When he finished, she took a deep breath and said, "You're dealing with something far bigger than you could ever have imagined. But I believe in you, Landry. If the curse can be broken, you'll find a way to do it."

"I hope so. It's going to take everything I've got. And I can't promise that I'll come out of this unscathed."

"Just be careful," she said. "We just signed up for a future together. You must be around to do your part!"

"I promise. I'm ready to settle down. I just have to finish—"

She smiled and put a finger to his lips. "No promises just yet. Not only is this paranormal stuff in your blood, it's what you do for a living. I don't want to force you to give up the things you love most. I just want you to start considering your moves with both of us in mind instead of just yourself."

As they sat together in the quiet of the apartment, the darkness of Pendle seemed a little less daunting, the weight of the curse a little less heavy. They still had a long road ahead of them, but for the first time in a long time, Landry felt like he could see a light at the end of the tunnel.

But reaching that light would require everything he could muster to conquer the evil that sought to destroy him.

CHAPTER THIRTY-SIX

Tonight, unlike the one when he had read the book until daybreak, Landry joined Cate and their new bed partner, Simba, and held her close until they fell asleep. By six the next morning they were on the patio, drinking coffee. Landry took Simba for a walk through the French Quarter, shaved and showered, and the three of them walked to the office.

For several hours, Landry closeted himself in his cubicle, poring over his photocopy of the old book and searching for something he might have missed the first time. He read each page carefully, double-checking his earlier translations from old English. He'd hoped to find a clue—something he could use to break the pact, but every page offered only confirmation that the pact could only be broken by a Drake's sacrifice. At last he reached the end, his eyes burning from close reading and concentrating. He leaned back in his chair, stretched, and closed the old book.

His phone rang, and Skip Halverson, the curator at the Cabildo, advised he'd found additional references to Pendle in a box he'd uncovered deep in the archives. "It's another old book," he added, piquing Landry's interest. Within minutes, he was out the door and on his way to Jackson Square, and shortly he was in Skip's office, prepared to look at yet another book.

He knew from his last visit he'd have to give Skip more than vague answers this time. In the first place, the man deserved it. He was working to help Landry. Also, he seemed like a decent guy, a bookish man in what Landry considered a boring job overseeing a museum. He longed for adventure, and that was exactly what Landry had to offer. He told himself he'd be more appreciative today, and he'd give the man some tidbits to chew on.

It took no time to get to the point. As they sat, Skip said, "Before we begin, do you mind if I ask what your interest in Pendle really is? I'm a huge fan of your shows, and I know that book I showed you last time had some interesting tales about witches. I don't want to butt into your business; it just would be exciting if something I turned up helped you solve a mystery. God knows It would be fun to have a little excitement in this musty old museum!"

He briefed Skip on how a friend's missing sister had called for help from Pendle, their visits there, and the strange things that had happened in the remote village in the bayou. He omitted important facts like the ritual from which he'd escaped, the figure Lydia had called the dark lord, an army of black blobs that seemed to do the witches' bidding, and a town filled with people who lived under an ancient spell.

"Of course we know the founders of Pendle were escaping punishment as witches in an English town," he added. "We haven't found the missing sister, and surprisingly I discovered there's a tie to my own ancestors and an ancient curse I'm working on solving."

Astonished, Skip asked a few questions about the curse, and Landry gave him only a little, purposely holding back what he'd learned about his family.

Skip gave Landry a card with his cellphone number, saying he'd be around but he'd let Landry get to work. "Call when you're done," he said, and left.

Landry's fingers traced the spine of this book, another old one, its leather cover cracked and weathered by centuries of neglect. He felt his usual rush of adrenalin as he turned to the first page.

My Wretched Life in Exile, by John Device.

As Landry held the slim volume in his hands, Landry noticed something peculiar. The hard front cover seemed to be thinner than the back. The difference was subtle, but it caught his attention. He turned the book over, studying the back cover more closely. It was thicker, a detail that seemed odd to him.

Curious, Landry gently ran his fingers along the edge of the inside back cover. The yellowed paper there was affixed firmly, but as his fingertips moved across it, he felt a bulge beneath the surface. Something was hidden within the cover.

He had to put his curiosity on hold; although he was anxious to see what was there, he couldn't just take the cover apart without talking to Skip first. This artifact belonged to a museum—the Cabildo—and it must have been in the archives somewhere in the building. But even if it hadn't been on display in a glass case, the cover wasn't his to deface. He left it for later and turned to the volume itself.

It was more than a mere historical record; it was a journal written by a member of the Device family. The writing was filled with scribbling and difficult to decipher, written in archaic English with apparent disregard for rules like spelling and punctuation. The journal's author appeared to have been young, likely a teenager, and the scrawled entries gave insight into the Device family's dark practices.

Many pages contained only a few sentences penned periodically as the year 1614 progressed. As Landry delved deeper into the journal, he became enthralled. The entries provided a rare, personal perspective on the early days of Pendle from a relative who clearly wished to distance himself from the family's traditions. John Device, the writer, detailed his discomfort with the dark rituals he was forced to participate in and his lack of friends, caused in his opinion by the fact his family members—parents included—were witches. His writing was filled with adolescent thoughts and a sense of desperation.

The journal included references to a ritualistic sacrifice planned by John's parents and the new mayor of Pendle, also a family member. The sacrificial lamb wasn't named, but Landry knew from his earlier discovery it had to be Isaiah Drake, his ancestor who was to have been delivered over to the dark forces to solidify the mayor's pact with the devil.

At last Landry called Skip, who was back so quickly Landry wondered if he'd been waiting by the door all this time.

"Anything interesting?" he asked.

Landry looked up, unable to contain the excitement he felt. He needed Skip's permission now, and it was time to tell him what he was anxious to learn.

"I found a lot, actually. This book's a diary, and it's fascinating. I can't wait to read the rest of it. But I want to show you something interesting. Sit here and look at this."

Landry closed the book gently, mindful of its fragile condition. "I think something's hidden inside the back cover." He compared the thicknesses of the front and back covers, and Skip ran his hands over them, the wheels turning in his mind.

"What do you think it is—a piece of paper, maybe? It's so small it's hardly noticeable."

"I was hoping we might open up the cover and find out."

"Ordinarily I'd defer on the side of archival preservation," Skip replied. "But I found this in a box in the basement that clearly had been forgotten. Sadly, we have a lot of those. There are thousands of relics and papers and other stuff crammed into boxes and cabinets all over the place, and from what you just told me about how interesting the book is, I had already decided to let you keep it. So there you go; it's yours to do with as you please. But if you're going to look inside the cover, I want to see what you find!"

Landry opened the back of the book and asked for something to slit the cover. Skip went to his desk and returned with a sharp hobby knife. Landry gently ran his fingers along the back, calculating the size of the small bulge under the paper that was glued to it. His heart began to race with the excitement of a potential discovery. Something was concealed within this centuries-old volume—something he hoped might provide some answers for a change.

He slipped the knife blade under one corner of the paper and ran it along an edge, then up one side, revealing an old, brittle envelope tucked away inside. He took pictures with his phone, then retrieved the envelope and examined it closely. It was yellowed with age, and if it had once been sealed, time had worn away the adhesive. He carefully removed the piece of paper that was inside.

The handwriting had faded, the ink having bled over the centuries. As Landry began to read aloud, his eyes widened in astonishment. The letter, authored by the same John Device who wrote the journal as a teenager, was written in June 1622, eight years after the last entry in the diary. The penmanship, style and choice of words revealed the thoughts of an older and more educated young adult.

The letter, short but filled with revelations, was a confession of sorts. John wrote candidly about his family's true nature. He admitted they were witches, and the powers they wielded had originally been acquired by his ancestors in England. John expressed his disillusionment with this legacy. He did not embrace the dark arts as his relatives did but instead played along, masking his true feelings to avoid suspicion, banishment, and possibly death.

He feared the supernatural forces that his family embraced, speaking of rituals and dark ceremonies that the Device family practiced, controlling and influencing others he referred to as the lucky ones in Pendle—those who weren't bound by debts to the devil. He yearned to break free from this oppressive lineage while being haunted by the knowledge that he was forever tied to its sinister legacy.

Landry read another few lines in silence before pausing. This part was information he'd have preferred to keep to himself, but he felt obliged to repay Skip for his perseverance. If it hadn't been for the curator's diligent searching, Landry wouldn't be holding this old volume in his hands.

"There's more. This boy says there's a secret key that his family brought with them from England. It's kept in hiding by the Device family, and it can somehow break the power of the witches." He read the words that described a safe place within a church where the key had been hidden.

"John Device was determined to find it and break free from his family's dark legacy, but that's all he says about it. From there the rest of his writings are sad, desperate pleas for understanding by others and for freedom from what he views as his fate—to be forced to join them or suffer the consequences."

Skip let him sit in silence for a moment, and then said, "And you want to find that key so you can stop the witches in Pendle, right?"

Landry nodded, and Skip pushed for more. "You said you'd been there a few times. Did you see any churches?"

Unwilling to share details, Landry said they had seen two churches, both small and modern. He didn't mention the ruins that loomed behind the Anglican church—the ancient building that dated to the founding of Pendle.

"What's next?" Skip asked, and Landry said he was going to call Jack Blair and go back to Pendle right away.

"Jack Blair, the TV investigator? I'm a fan of his paranormal shows on Channel Nine. But how's he involved in the Pendle case?"

Landry filled in the blanks he'd left in his earlier explanation, and Skip said, "Well, this has been one of the most interesting mornings of my career. A cursed town populated by witches who fled England! Who'd have known we had something like that in rural Louisiana?"

"I can think of no better place." Landry laughed. "There's no shortage of the supernatural in our state."

Now that he had the letter, Landry asked if Skip wanted to keep the book, but he insisted he take it, adding that if everything all turned out well, Landry might consider donating the book and letter back to the museum, where they could be part of a fascinating display of early Louisiana history. Skip thanked him profusely, promised to keep the information to himself, and wished Landry good luck and safety.

Landry walked down Royal Street toward Channel Nine in hopes he'd find Jack there. He thought of Skip's last comments, and he too hoped that all would turn out well, but for now there was no assurance of that outcome on any front. Jack's sister, his own family curse, the town run by witches—it was almost too bizarre even for Landry's experiences.

The letter contained more information than he had read aloud. Realizing the importance of what he'd found, he had skipped a few paragraphs toward the end. Now Landry was anxious to get to a place where he could study those words, which is why he had fingers crossed Jack would be around. He wanted another set of eyes—another person who had seen Pendle's horrors himself. And once Jack saw what Landry had found, he would be only too willing to help.

CHAPTER THIRTY-SEVEN

When he saw the excitement in Landry's eyes, Jack ushered him into his office and closed the door. Within minutes they were huddled next to each other, poring over the centuries-old letter and trying to understand its meaning.

John Device explained the pact that doomed a Drake family member and attempted to describe what he called a "binding", some kind of paranormal seal that rendered the pact unbreakable. The seal was tied to the blood sacrifice of a child, but there was a "key" that could unlock the seal and free both Pendle and the family from the curse. Considering its power, the key had been safely concealed to protect it from falling into the hands of those who would rid the town of witchcraft. According to young John, his parents kept it in reserve in case of challenge by another family of witches, whose power could be broken by its use.

Landry's heart raced as he read and reread the passage, his mind whirling with possibilities. The text was vague, the words simple yet difficult to interpret, but there was something there, something that hinted at a way to break the pact without a sacrifice.

Jack leaned over the letter, his brow furrowing as he reread the passage. "A key. What does that mean? Is it a literal key, or is it something symbolic?"

"I don't know," Landry admitted as he turned over ideas in his mind. "But this is the first real lead we've had. We have to figure out how to find it, and then we can see if we can make it work."

Jack nodded, determination lighting his eyes. "It's hidden in a church in Pendle. That's where we start, and I'm going back anyway."

Having previously seen two churches in Pendle, they agreed to leave first thing the next morning to check them out. Then Jack hesitantly broached the subject of Cate, asking if Landry felt comfortable going back to Pendle so soon after her return.

"I made a commitment," he replied. "I told her I'd be more cautious, and we promised to stay together from now on."

Jack waited, wondering how a promise like that could include returning to Pendle, but Landry offered nothing more.

Neither could have imagined how soon Landry's promise would be tested, and in what awful ways.

CHAPTER THIRTY-EIGHT

Today when they arrived in Pendle, the church doors were open. Hoping the priest wouldn't run away as he'd done before, they went into the sanctuary and found him dusting the altar pieces. He looked up, recognized them, and said, "Well, well, gentlemen, I must apologize for my abrupt departure last time. It just took me by surprise that Landry Drake was in our town. What brings you back?"

"I've found some information about a key," Landry began. "Supposedly it was hidden in a church in Pendle's early days. We were hoping you might help us."

"If I can," the priest replied. "Who hid it? One of the Device clan?"

Landry nodded and told him about the entries in John Device's seventeenth-century journal.

"I haven't heard of a key, but I'm not surprised the Device family is involved. They're behind everything in this town and always have been. Have you had the pleasure of meeting our mayor yet?"

Landry gave him a brief version of his encounters with Charity Device, and also the bookseller, the Peel sisters, and

Dale, the mechanic. The priest listened closely and said, "When I first met you, I said you were in danger here. You're a Drake, and you know about the pact, yet you've tempted fate by coming back over and over. Do you truly understand the gravity of the pact? This is no small matter; for you—and for your friend as well, I'm afraid—it could mean losing your life."

Landry smiled. "I understand the danger, but I'm a paranormal investigator. If I were afraid of everything that I've experienced, I'd never go anywhere."

Father Elias nodded. "I'm well aware of your work, Mr. Drake. And you can be certain the mayor is too. The people who run this town speak your name often; you might say you're always on their minds. Your past successes in overpowering the supernatural is of great interest to them. They consider you an adversary, one who unravels the same things they spent centuries creating. Not to mention the pact, which affects you personally. If you keep coming back to Pendle, it will one day be the place of your demise, I'm afraid. When they're ready, they'll try to kill you."

Landry thanked the priest for his advice and insight, adding, "There's something else, Father. We mentioned last time that Jack's sister is missing, and you were about to help us when you learned who I was and left. We still haven't located her; do you have any suggestions where to look?"

"A missing person? I wish I could suggest something that might help. You know by now that the usual avenues of assistance—the police or city officials—aren't available to you in this town. Pendle thrives on secrets, as I'm sure you've learned. And sometimes missing persons aren't as they seem. Some disappear on purpose, you know."

"Not Mel," Jack insisted. "She's in trouble."

The priest looked away as if hiding a thought, then changed the subject. "About the ruins of the church behind this one. I've spent a good deal of time within the confines of that old building. There's not much else to do here; only a handful of parishioners come to church. Almost half of the town's population is...well, I'm sure you've heard rumors that people here practice the dark arts."

"Those are no rumors, as far as I'm concerned," Landry replied. "So you're saying the witches in Pendle don't attend Christian church services. That doesn't surprise me, but why wouldn't the other people come?"

"A few of them come, and a handful of others go to the Catholic church, but intimidation keeps most away. Charity frowns on organized religion, and her family has always derided people who attend church as weak and disloyal. So they stay home. But you asked about the old church. It was struck by lightning and burned in 1937. It had been a church since the 1600s. Some of the original founders built the oldest parts, and it served as the only place of worship for Pendle until the early twentieth century, when the Catholics built another."

Landry received permission to poke around in the ruins, and Father Elias escorted them to the back door. The ancient church lay less than fifty yards away, and they entered by walking through a tall, lonely archway into what had been the nave of the church, now just a plot of grass surrounded by stone walls and open to the sky. A once-tall Gothic spire lay toppled in the grass, and Landry considered how imposing the structure would have been in its day.

They could determine where rooms had been only because remnants of stone foundations still existed. Landry was disappointed; this was nothing like he had expected. He had hoped for a hidden crypt or an old, rotting altar or wooden pillars with secret recesses. There was no floor beneath which something might be hidden, no interior walls with places to put a key, and no rooms left to explore. This was a shell of a building that once existed, and anything that might have been hidden here likely was gone forever.

Father Elias had said the founders of Pendle had built the earliest parts of this church, and Landry wondered if that included the Device family. They were no fans of Christianity, but that didn't necessarily rule out their involvement. What if this church had only become Anglican in later years, and in the sixteen hundreds it was something else entirely?

He freed his mind to consider eerie possibilities. He imagined dark rituals and supernatural incantations taking place at an altar draped in black. What if this building had been the very place where the pact with the dark side was agreed? What if Satan and the first Mayor Device sealed the deal on the spot where he stood?

Unable to do more, they walked back and thanked Father Elias. He had doubted they would turn up anything on a cursory walkthrough. Finding a key in the ruins of a building was much like finding a needle in a haystack, he mused aloud.

And he wished them God speed, keeping to himself the plan he was hatching to find the key.

CHAPTER THIRTY-NINE

Charity Device sat pondering a problem in her dimly lit office. She preferred candlelight over modern lights, and tonight the flame from a single taper flickered across the room, casting long shadows on the cracked walls. She closed her eyes for a moment, allowing herself to savor the stillness, the quiet power she wielded over this town. But deep within, a nagging doubt stirred, gnawing at her like a rat chewing through wood.

Her powers were not what they once were.

For centuries, her family had ruled Pendle with an iron grip, controlling the townspeople with whispered threats of dark magic and the forces that lurked in the shadows. The Device family had built their dominion on fear, and Charity kept the tradition alive, leading Pendle's citizens to believe that she could summon the dark forces at will and make them do her bidding. But that was a lie, a carefully constructed illusion she had maintained for as long as she could remember.

The truth was that Charity did not control the dark forces. They came and went as they pleased, appearing as malevolent black blobs that slithered through her town like living shadows. When they manifested, they often sowed terror and destruction, but Charity had no command over their appearances. They were not her creations, nor could she summon them on demand. Countless times she had tried to bind them to her will, to make them her servants. But each attempt had ended in failure.

She opened a book of spells, an ancient book brought from England by her ancestors. The symbols etched into the pages were familiar—runes of power, curses and incantations to draw forth the forces of darkness. She had read these pages a thousand times, each time hoping to unlock the secret to controlling the dark forces, to summoning them when she needed them most. But the spells to control them didn't work for her anymore.

This was Charity's secret. Her father, the previous mayor, had known her powers were more limited than his, because he'd observed her abilities as he taught her spells and incantations. But no one else knew, not even her coven of followers. To them, Charity was a goddess, an all-powerful leader who could summon the darkness with a mere thought. It was this belief that allowed her to keep everything in line and maintain her hold over Pendle. But now, with a Drake heir on the scene, it appeared that the pact made so long ago was nearing fruition. At the same time, Charity's weaknesses were becoming harder to ignore.

The pact. The thought of it filled her with a mixture of dread and excitement. The agreement between her ancestors and the dark forces required a sacrifice, and now the sacrificial lamb had come to them. His bloodline was tied to the founding of Pendle, just as hers was, and his death would cement the bond between her family and the dark forces. There would still be sacrifices every fifty years, but this promise from the earliest days of Pendle would soon be satisfied.

Time was running out, and Charity could feel the pressure building. The forces were restless, impatient. They wanted their prize, and they would stop at nothing to get it.

The problem was, she couldn't catch him.

Charity cursed under her breath. Landry Drake had eluded her for weeks, slipping through her grasp like water through her fingers. He had been to Pendle more than once, she knew that, but she couldn't sense when he was here. For all her power, all her supposed might, she couldn't even tell when Landry was within the town's borders.

Unlike what she had led her followers and the townspeople to believe, she couldn't feel the presence of her enemies unless they were right in front of her. She couldn't stretch her consciousness across Pendle, couldn't use the dark forces to locate those who sought to defy her. She was blind, relying on others to be her eyes and ears. It was infuriating.

"Miss Charity." A voice interrupted her thoughts, and Charity looked up to see a member of her coven standing in the doorway. The woman looked nervous, her hands clasped together as if bracing herself for a rebuke.

"What do you want?" Charity's voice was sharp, impatient. She had no time for hesitation.

"It's about Landry Drake," the young witch stammered. "And Jack Blair. They're here in Pendle."

Charity's eyes flashed with a mixture of relief and anger. Relief because she finally had a lead on Landry, and anger because she couldn't discern his whereabouts herself.

"Where are they?" Charity demanded, rising from her seat. The book lay forgotten on the table as she crossed the room, her long, dark robes sweeping the floor behind her.

"The church. St. Margaret's. They were last spotted on the church grounds, and we can't go on sacred property."

"I know that!" Charity snapped, cutting her off. "Watch their every move. Don't let Landry Drake leave Pendle."

The witch nodded and scurried off to carry out her orders, leaving Charity alone once again. She took a deep breath, trying to steady herself. This was it. The moment she had been waiting for. Landry was within her grasp, and she would see to it that he never escaped again.

But even as she steeled herself for the coming confrontation, a flicker of doubt crept into her mind. The dark forces were unpredictable. They had their own agendas, their own desires, and while they wanted Landry's sacrifice as much as she did, they didn't answer to her. They often operated in tandem with her, sometimes appearing when she needed them, but other times vanishing into the shadows, leaving her vulnerable.

There was a time when Charity had control—control over other witches, over Pendle, over the forces of darkness. But now, as the final moments of the pact approached, things had changed. The dark forces were no longer hers to command. For now they tolerated her because their interests aligned. But once that changed, she had no idea what they might do to her. The thought filled her with a cold dread that she hadn't felt in years.

She had no choice but to rely on her own strength, on the fear she had cultivated in her followers and the townspeople. If they believed she was all-powerful, if they believed she could summon the forces of darkness at will, then they would continue to obey her. She had to maintain the illusion.

As she made her way down the dim hallway, her thoughts raced. Landry and Jack were dangerous. They came and went at will, ignoring the warning not to trespass, and she knew they would be prepared for another confrontation. But she had something they didn't—decades of experience, centuries of dark magic, and a few tricks left up her sleeve.

Her witches were loyal, but not out of love or respect. They feared her, feared the dark forces she claimed to command. That fear was her weapon, and she would use it to the fullest.

By the time she reached the entrance to her building, her plan was set. She would corner Landry and Jack, trapping them like rats. The dark forces would come—they always did, eventually—and they would exact their revenge on Landry. And then the pact would be fulfilled.

And yet, deep down, Charity knew she was playing a dangerous game. She had kept her limitations hidden for decades, but if Landry discovered the truth—that she wasn't the all-powerful witch she claimed to be—her reign over Pendle would crumble. The townspeople would rise against her, and the dark forces might turn on her as well.

She couldn't let that happen.

With a flick of her wrist, she cast a spell, sending a wave of dark energy through the town, alerting her witches to prepare for battle. The air around her crackled with tension as she made her way toward the courthouse, her heart pounding with anticipation.

The final confrontation was coming soon, and this time Landry Drake wouldn't leave Pendle alive. She would see to it. But as she walked the quiet streets to the church, Charity heard voices whispering in her mind.

You don't control this situation. We control you, and we will determine when the final confrontation occurs.

Charity hesitated. The dark forces had always been unpredictable, and today would be no different. She could sense their presence lurking just beyond the veil, waiting, watching. But they wanted to handle Landry their way.

I should back off and let them do it.

She dismissed the thought as quickly as it had formed. She couldn't afford doubt, not now. The pact had to be completed. Landry had to die.

And if the forces of darkness decided to turn on her? Well, she would deal with that when the time came.

For now, she had a town to rule and an ancient debt to collect. Soon there would be a day like none had been since the town was founded in 1614. It would be the day of reckoning.

CHAPTER FORTY

With the departure of the two strangers, the ruins of St. Margaret's Church again stood silent and forlorn, the remnants of its once-majestic presence now overrun with moss and ivy. Father Elias had watched from a window as Landry Drake and his friend scoured the decaying building with its crumbling walls and shattered stained glass. Of course they'd found nothing; if anything of value had existed, he would have found it himself long ago.

Elias had taken a keen interest in the mystery surrounding the old church. The ruins had always been a place of intrigue for him, shrouded in the whispered legends of Pendle's dark past. He believed that the ruins of St. Margaret's might hold secrets, and it was possible the key Landry sought might be there somewhere. From what he had learned about the ruins, he believed that St. Margaret's originally began as a center for pagan rituals. At some point, that had changed. The Device family wouldn't have donated a church to the opposition, so it was more likely the witches had abandoned the building at some point, and the Anglicans had slipped in behind them.

As one of only two men of the cloth in a town filled with witches, Father Elias led a solitary life. But these days he was protected by a ritual of sanctification that had taken place centuries ago. The grounds of the church were impenetrable to people like Charity Device, as was the priest himself...but only when he was on church property. Charity might discern the thoughts and motives of others in Pendle, but what went on in Elias's mind and in his church were his own secrets.

Over time he'd studied the town's history, learned about things passed down from one generation to another, and aside from the Device family, by now he knew more about Pendle's past than anyone. He hadn't heard of the key Landry read about in a diary, and he hadn't pressed him on why he sought it. But if Landry Drake wanted it enough to risk coming back to Pendle, perhaps Elias should look for it as well.

Today he wandered through the ruined church, his thoughts turning to a memory that had surfaced recently. Years ago his predecessor, an elderly priest named Matthew, had mentioned a small wooden chest that had been placed within the stone walls of the old church in the seventeen hundreds. Father Matthew had examined its contents and described it as a time capsule that held information about the church's history and the early days of Pendle. It had been years since that conversation, and Elias had forgotten about it. Now he wondered if it might contain information that would help locate the key.

But had Father Matthew revealed its location? Elias couldn't remember, and as the day turned into evening and he prepared his supper, he kept coming back to the question. He tried to recall their conversation, but too many years had passed. He gave up and went to bed, thinking he might look in every nook and cranny of the present church.

It shouldn't take that long, and if the box had been hidden somewhere safe, he just might find it.

As he lay in bed, his mind filled with thoughts, he wondered if the old chest might be hidden away in one of the outbuildings that lay on the back side of the church's property—a shed that listed heavily to one side, which Elias had never ventured into, an old barn that was collapsing in on itself, and a rustic outhouse that had served the old church before its demise. The most likely candidate was the shed, and the least the outhouse, and he decided that tomorrow he'd dedicate some time to investigating them.

CHAPTER FORTY-ONE

From the church, Landry and Jack embarked on the most important task of the day—finding Jack's sister, Melody. The sky was a heavy gray, casting an oppressive pall over the desolate streets of Pendle. Jack had to find someone who could tell them where his sister was, so he began canvassing houses and businesses door-to-door.

Wary eyes peeped around drawn curtains each time they knocked, and most people didn't answer. Most who did seemed nervous and refused to help once they saw Landry. A handful claimed to have seen Melody recently and told him where she'd been, but their vague directions led Jack and Landry to abandoned buildings and dark alleys with no sign of the girl. It seemed the townsfolk were deliberately misleading them to save her from being found.

Frustrated, Jack told Landry he was going back to see Lydia Peel, the good witch whose arcane intervention had saved Landry from a dire fate. When Lydia answered the door, the warmth that had greeted them before was absent. Her eyes were cold and unreadable, and she stepped onto the porch rather than inviting them in.

"I need your help," Jack blurted. "I'm losing my mind here. Everyone's leading me in circles. Is my sister in on it too? Is she deliberately staying away from me?"

Lydia considered her response before speaking. "You must listen carefully. Things are not as they appear. It's possible that Melody is in danger, but not in the way you might think. She's ensnared in something far deeper than mere conspiracies or petty grievances. Most of her situation is of her own making, and regardless of what she said, she doesn't want to leave Pendle."

"I don't get it. Why would she call me after all these years? Why would she ask me to rescue her if she didn't want to leave?"

The old lady whispered, "Because Pendle is awash in ancient curses and malevolent forces. Melody is involved with dark magic. The secrets of this town have twisted her until she's become something other than the person you knew."

Jack's heart pounded as Lydia's words sank in. The notion that Melody might be complicit with the evil permeating Pendle was unbearable. Yet Lydia's words cut through his denial.

Landry replied, "I don't understand what you're saying. What's happened to her?"

"The enchantments here are potent; they can bend and corrupt the vulnerable. Melody's mind has been warped by the dark forces. She might be trying to divert you from a greater danger, or—"

A chill ran down Jack's spine as the implication crystallized. "Or she might be the bait to trap Landry."

Lydia's silence was a tacit confirmation. "You're beginning to understand. As you know, Mr. Drake, it's you the mayor wants, and you know why. Melody is ensnared by the darkness, although she might still be reaching out for help in her own twisted way. You cannot know what to expect if you confront her, and it's better for you both to leave. The mayor's attention is already focused on you, and the longer Mr. Drake is in Pendle, the greater danger to both you and your sister."

Jack shook his head. He had abandoned Mel once during his dark days of alcohol-induced self-destruction, and he wasn't about to forsake her now. "I can't believe she's involved in witchcraft. I'm not leaving this time until I find her. Will you help me or not?"

"I can help, but you won't like what you find, because Charity has reshaped her into something beyond your understanding. There's an old building a few blocks away." She gave him directions. "It was a library once, though now it's been left to ruin. Answers may lie within. But I warn you that the mayor knows you're here, and It may become impossible for you to leave if you delay."

Grateful yet apprehensive, they thanked Lydia for being their only ally in a town gripped by fear.

She shook her head. "Don't think of me as your ally. You and Landry are a means to an end. I want peace for Pendle. That's all." She turned, walked into her house, and closed the door.

The old library wasn't hard to find. It stood like a silent sentinel, its stone I weather-beaten and grim. Landry pushed against the heavy wooden door, and it swung open. Like most every other venue they'd seen in this spooky town, the air inside smelled of decay. Shadows clung to the corners, and the only sound was the echo of their footsteps against the cold floor. Wooden shelves crammed with books stood covered in dust, their once-proud spines now shrouded in neglect. It was as if time had frozen this place, and the eerie silence spoke of secrets waiting to be uncovered.

As they moved deeper into the library, the beam from Jack's iPhone cut through the darkness, revealing books bound in cracked leather. Landry directed his own light to the spines, brushing away dust to see the titles. "Some of these are books about witchcraft," he whispered, as though raising his voice in this old building would summon things he didn't want to see. "We might learn a lot from them."

"Yeah," Jack replied, "but there are thousands. Where would we even start? And would we even be allowed to look at them? You know how people in this town operate."

A cold draft swept through the aisles, carrying the light, tinkly sound of voices—voices that seemed to call Landry's name. *Drake. Drake. Drake,* they said, the whispers echoing about them. They came to an open space at the end of an aisle and listened as the voices grew louder, speaking at once but enough off-kilter to create a confusing, ear-splitting cacophony.

Landry stood still, waiting to see what would happen next, but Jack turned, the beam of his flashlight playing down another long aisle flanked by shelves. At the far end in the shadows, he saw a figure—pale and indistinct, standing between the shelves. He whispered to Landry, but his friend had walked away down another aisle.

Jack moved toward the figure, his muscles taut with tension. As he drew near, the figure slowly solidified into the familiar form of his sister, but in the shadows she looked different; her eyes were vacant, her skin as pale as snow.

"Mel?" Jack whispered.

She did not answer but extended a hand toward a particular shelf and pointed. He hesitated, asking if she was okay, and explaining once more that he wanted to take her home. But she stood like a statue, seemingly unable to understand his words, and kept her finger in place.

"Do you...do you want me to take that book?" he stammered, but the figure said nothing. At last he pulled it from the shelf, and Melody withdrew some distance away and waited. As Jack's fingers brushed against the cover, a sudden chill swept through the room, and the still-whispering voices rose to a deafening roar as though a crowd were cheering for a team.

Lan-dry Drake! Lan-dry Drake! Lan-dry Drake!

Mere feet from his sister now, Jack examined the book, which was very old and constructed like a modern diary—bound in leather with a strap and a lock that required a key. He called out to Melody, "Are you telling me to take this book?"

But she was gone. The library's deep silence returned, and Jack had a fleeting thought that they were running out of time. The book in his hands might save his sister and Landry—and perhaps even the town itself.

He looked for Landry and found him two aisles away, searching for the unseen things that had called his name. "I saw Mel," he said. "It was an apparition, but it was her. She guided me to this book, and then she vanished. Let's get out of here. This might help us figure everything out."

CHAPTER FORTY-TWO

Father Elias rose with the dawn, the first light of morning filtering through the worn curtains of his modest quarters. He began his morning rituals—prayer, a shave, a fresh cassock, and a steaming cup of coffee, its aroma rich and comforting, that offered a moment of solace as he prepared himself mentally for the search. He was determined to find that wooden box, and he had a feeling it remained on the property. But where?

After spending an hour vainly searching up and down inside the small church he served today, he set out towards the three outbuildings that lay behind the ruins of the stone church. The barn, a crumbling relic, presented the greatest challenge. Most of the roof had caved in, and the walls sagged as if losing a battle to hold themselves together. Inside was a chaotic jumble of fallen beams, making it a treacherous landscape to navigate. He'd keep the barn as a last resort. If God blessed him today, he might get lucky and not have to tackle an outbuilding crammed with memorabilia.

He turned to an old shed that stood like a relic of a bygone era, its weather-beaten wooden planks sagging under the weight of time. Although in better shape than the barn, it was a haphazard assemblage of rotting timbers and rusted nails, creaking and groaning with every gust of wind.

Inside, the air was heavy with the musty scent of decay and mildew. Dust motes floated lazily in the shafts of weak sunlight that filtered through the grime-encrusted windows, casting an eerie glow over the cluttered space. Few floorboards remained, and even they were on the verge of collapse. Every step had to be taken with care.

The shed was a jumbled repository of the church's cast-offs and forgotten relics. Piles of furniture were haphazardly stacked. He saw carved wooden pews coated in grime and heavy, dark mahogany chairs with cushions ravaged by insects. Near a corner stood an old altar, its once-gleaming brass fittings tarnished and dull, and its wooden surface scarred by scratches and stains.

Broken glassware lay strewn across the floor, jagged edges glinting in the light. Old paintings, their frames cracked and peeling, were propped against the walls or tossed in disarray. The images depicted saints and scenes of worship, their colors faded and smudged as though time itself had sought to erase them.

Elias pushed aside dust-covered cloths and sifted through the clutter. He untangled a jumble of disjointed altar pieces—candlesticks, brass communion cups, and faded vestments. His fingers traced the edges of old wooden boxes and crates, but a wooden chest was nowhere to be found.

Over several hours he examined every corner of the shed, moving aside stacks of unused hymnals and old Bibles, their pages yellowed and brittle. He had no idea how big the box he sought was, he only knew it had been a time capsule, so he had a vague idea of its likely size. He pried open an old cabinet, its doors groaning in protest, and found only dusty shelves filled with more relics that had been used and discarded.

As he worked, his mind toyed with thoughts of what he might find. He imagined the box when it was sealed within the stone walls, its contents a window into the lives and faith of those who had come before him. Perhaps it contained not only artifacts but also letters and prayers, a snapshot of a vanished world. The box—the time capsule—had been removed when the church burned in the 1930s, and as far as Father Elias knew, no one had heard of it since. The priest who'd served St. Margaret's in those days was long gone, and Father Matthew, who'd told Elias about the box and its contents, had forgotten to mention where.

Another hour of fruitless searching ensued. By now his hands were grimy and his cassock dusty, but he continued to dig through the refuse with unwavering determination. But despite his fervent efforts, the chest remained elusive, and at last he began to wonder if it had survived at all, or if it had been discarded on some trash heap years ago.

With a final, resigned sigh, Elias took a step back and decided he'd spent enough time in the shed. It was time to turn his efforts on the least desirable venue—the outhouse. At least it hadn't been used as such in decades, the priest thought to himself with a smile. Digging in someone else's shit might be okay as long as it wasn't from yesterday.

CHAPTER FORTY-THREE

Near the decrepit old shed stood the outhouse, its condition mirroring the shed's own state of neglect and decay. This humble structure was a relic of simpler times, a small wooden building that had seen better days. Its once-proud walls were now weathered and warped, with planks so splintered that they resembled the skeletal remains of some ancient beast. The paint, if it had ever been applied, had long since peeled away, leaving the wood exposed to the ravages of the elements. The remnants of its door lay half-buried in a tangle of brambles and overgrown grass.

The structure was a "two-holer"—a colloquial term for a toilet featuring a bench with two round openings cut into it. The bench, surprisingly still intact, had seen better days; its wood was scarred and weathered, with patches of rot that made it unstable. The holes, which once had a practical use, were overgrown with cobwebs and dust, and the space beneath the bench was a dark, cavernous dung heap.

When the stone church had been erected centuries ago, indoor plumbing was unknown, and the outhouse had served as an essential facility for staff and parishioners alike. It was a place where the sacred and the mundane intersected, a humble accommodation for the practical needs of those who came to worship. Its simple design reflected the utilitarian approach of the time—a functional necessity rather than a place of comfort.

The outhouse hadn't been used in decades, and the air around it was thick with the musty smell of old wood and damp earth, mingling with the faint odor of its former purpose. The wind whistled through the gaps in the walls, creating an eerie, mournful sound that seemed perfectly normal in Pendle.

Elias had almost talked himself out of searching the outhouse; although it hadn't been used in years, the thought of digging in the stuff at the bottom of the hole turned his stomach. Hoping neither sight nor smell would remind him of his task, he walked into the little building and took hold of the bench with two holes. It was loose and pulled off easily. Elias gazed down into the darkness, searching the bottom with his flashlight. There was a layer of decomposing refuse. Leaves, earth, and remnants of bygone use formed a thick mat beneath the bench, pressing down into the cold, earthen floor.

The area was too cramped for Elias to crawl inside, bend down and dig. Instead, he knelt on the wooden floor and leaned his upper torso into the space. *Thank you for sparing me the smell,* he prayed to himself. He had brought a shovel, and he used it to scrape away at the thick, foul-smelling layer of accumulated waste. After only a few minutes of digging, the blade struck something solid. Elias dug faster, removing more waste around what he realized was the top of a wooden box approximately eighteen inches square.

He became excited when he saw its tarnished, corroded hinges and hasp. The wood was rutted and caked with debris, but it appeared that having been submerged in dung had preserved it well. This had to be the time capsule he had been searching for. He leaned far into the hole, dug out the sides, and steadied himself so he wouldn't topple into the dung. Then he gripped the box with both hands and removed it. Its old hinges still held, but the padlock was no obstacle, as the rusty latch broke free from the wood the moment he touched it.

Elias carried the box to his kitchen in the back of the wooden church. He locked the door behind him and put it on his table, where he opened the lid reverently. Inside lay a collection of artifacts—yellowed papers and brittle parchments, faded pen-and-ink drawings, and small, intricately crafted items. There were English and French coins dating to the sixteen hundreds, small handcrafted ceramic figurines, and a leather-bound Bible. Each item was a fragment of history, a glimpse into the lives and faith of those who worshipped in the early days of Pendle's existence. The contents were preserved through decades of decay, their importance magnified by their long concealment. And some Anglican priest like him had supervised the concealment of a capsule that stayed hidden for centuries.

As he dug deeper in the box and removed layer after layer of items, he discovered the oldest relics—ancient pagan symbols, intricately carved stones, and remnants of rituals that had been performed long before the building became a church. Obviously long ago this had been a pagan building—a temple, perhaps, dedicated to the dark forces who guided Pendle's founding fathers.

I thought so! He paused a moment to consider why a priest would allow blasphemous things in a church's time capsule. Perhaps everyone peacefully coexisted back then, although for the life of him he didn't know how that could be.

He found accounts of rituals and the witches' deep connection to the natural world, with descriptions of ceremonies honoring Satan. But for some reason, the ancient pagans had abandoned the structure and allowed the impressive stone church to be erected around it.

As he read, Elias realized that some of the markings he'd seen on the walls of the old stone church were actually pagan symbols subtly incorporated into the Anglican church's design. He wondered if the witches forced the Christians to include them to preserve the site's ancient significance, or if it was another example of two diametrically opposite religions agreeing to coexist. Still, it was difficult to think of a church father agreeing to include pagan symbols and documents in a time capsule.

Elias gave everything he removed from the box at least a cursory look, but today one particular document caught his eye—a handwritten letter that mentioned a key—a powerful relic capable of breaking the pact the Pendle witches had secured. There was no description of the artifact or clues to its whereabouts, but the unsigned letter called it crucial to controlling the dark forces, and that gave the priest goosebumps.

A paragraph explained a question that had nagged at Father Elias—the reason why the Anglicans didn't use the key themselves long ago and break the pact with the dark forces. The author referred to the introduction of Christianity in Pendle as a steadying influence that had effectively neutralized the influence of the witch families.

An incredibly naive opinion, Elias thought as he considered that statement in light of Pendle in the twenty-first century. Nowadays the witches controlled everything and organized religion virtually nothing.

That control was addressed in the next sentences of the letter. Someday the witches might regain their power or seek control over Pendle and its inhabitants. The key would be a safeguard against the pact becoming a real threat again. It would be there for future generations if they needed it.

Another naïve opinion. The word was that the witches had sacrificed a child to the devil every fifty years since the town was formed. Did those well-meaning Anglican priests turn away when those lives were taken, and why hadn't they used the key to stop the barbarism? So far, Elias hadn't had to witness the gruesome ceremony. But the time would come if he stayed at St. Margaret's long enough.

He took the remaining items from the box and added them to the assortment that filled his table, but when he picked up the box to set it aside, his eyes caught a glimpse of something at the bottom. Barely visible in the scarred, dark wood was a faint outline—a square plug in the center of the box's floor. It matched the other wood exactly, and but for the outline, Elias would never have noticed it. He ran his fingers over it before slipping the blade of a kitchen knife around all four sides. As he gingerly pried, he saw the square piece of wood rise a fraction. He continued, and in less than a minute he had removed the plug.

In the hole where it had been lay a tarnished metal key. He retrieved it and held it in his hand, considering the ramifications of the object he'd found. The key, if it was truly as powerful as described, might break the pact that had plagued Pendle since its inception.

As he turned the key over and over, an unfamiliar sensation crept into Elias's mind. A mortal sin—one of the seven deadly ones that believers thought separated them from God. Avarice, a sin no priest should allow. A priest's life was a simple one, free from greed. At least that was the idea.

But right now, in the privacy of his home and with no other people around, Elias allowed himself to wonder how different his life might be if he used the powers of the key he held.

CHAPTER FORTY-FOUR

Father Elias sat in his kitchen, the door still bolted shut behind him. His gaze drifted repeatedly to the key in his hand. He knew of the opposing sides who would want it. Jack Blair and Landry Drake had made their intentions clear. They saw the key as a means to stopping the witches for good—breaking the pact that required Landry's death, future child sacrifices, and eliminating the town of the witches and their stronghold. Jack also hoped to find his missing sister and hoped the key might provide answers.

But he had to consider the witches. Most likely Charity Device knew the key existed, and perhaps that it was hidden somewhere in the old ruins. But the sanctity of the church grounds prevented them from finding it. Regardless, he couldn't afford a misstep; they would stop at nothing to reclaim it and maintain the powers they had possessed for centuries.

Elias looked at the documents and relics spread upon his kitchen table, fingered the key lightly, and considered his two options. In the hour or so that had elapsed since his discovery of the key, its existence had shaken the very foundation of Elias's world. He knew its potential to break the witch pact that had bound Pendle in torment for centuries. Yet as he held the powerful object, Elias found himself caught in a moral tempest unlike anything he had ever faced.

The witches' influence over the town had led to unspeakable suffering, and now, the key offered a glimmer of hope. But as he considered that hope, Elias's thoughts wandered into a realm of fantasies—how his life would change if he were to use the power of the key for his own purposes.

Although Elias knew nothing about what the key was about, he closed his eyes and envisioned using it to create a life vastly different from the austere existence he led as a priest. The picture was vivid and alluring: he would leave the church behind and escape to a sun-drenched island paradise. Ocean waves would lap gently against sandy shores, and the air would be filled with the scent of tropical flowers. He imagined himself surrounded by opulence and indulgence.

He would live in a sprawling estate, a mansion with marble floors and sweeping balconies that overlooked the sparkling ocean. The home would be adorned with the finest furnishings, every room a testament to his wealth and taste. He would entertain guests in grand halls filled with laughter, music and flowers, and sumptuous feasts would be laid out on tables laden with exotic delicacies.

In this imagined paradise, Elias would indulge in every pleasure he had ever denied himself. Beautiful women would surround him, their companionship a delight. He would experience the finest things the world had to offer: luxurious cars, rare wines, and the latest in fashion and technology. The allure of such a life was tantalizing, a vision that seemed to promise fulfillment of every desire he had suppressed in his years of service. It was a life of hedonistic pleasure and boundless freedom, one in stark contrast to the constraints of priesthood.

Yet, as he allowed himself to dream, a wave of guilt and conflict swept over him. *Why are you allowing such thoughts into your mind?* The vow he had taken to the church—promises of poverty, chastity, and obedience—suddenly felt like chains binding him to a life of self-denial and duty. Elias had willingly dedicated his life to serving others, to forsaking personal desires and pursuing God's will. The prospect of breaking these vows for the sake of personal gain felt like a betrayal of every principle he had upheld.

Elias understood that his sudden yearning for a life of luxury was a fleeting thought, not a course of action he craved. These thoughts were mere daydreams; he would never cast aside his lifelong mission to live a life like that. Furthermore, he had no idea if the key could give people wealth and happiness. Money certainly didn't.

Each time a fantasy crept back into his mind, he focused on the consequences—how his abandoning the priesthood and embracing wealth would lead to a profound sense of emptiness and regret. Could he truly find satisfaction in a life of luxury if it meant living with the constant awareness of having broken his vows and betrayed his principles?

Elias took a deep breath, the fantasy of opulence fading as he returned to the reality of his kitchen. The decision he faced was not just about choosing between wealth and duty but about confronting the essence of his own values and purpose. The key symbolized not only a potential escape from his fears but also a moral dilemma—a crossroads where he had to choose between the fleeting allure of personal gratification and the enduring commitment to the priesthood.

As he gazed once more at the key, Elias knew that the path he chose would define not just his future but the legacy of his life's work. With a heavy heart and a mind tormented by doubt, he knew he needed to seek clarity beyond his own conflicted desires—guidance that could illuminate the right course of action and reaffirm his true purpose.

Elias believed Landry and Jack were good men, but his own desires and fears twisted his judgment. If he were to assist them, it would not only mean the potential end of the witches' curse but also expose him to their wrath. A priest's faith should be rooted in God's protection, but he feared for his safety, as any mortal would.

A knock on the door interrupted his thoughts, and Elias's heart quickened. "Who is it?" he called.

"Landry and Jack. Can we come in? We need to talk to you."

Father Elias glanced around his kitchen. The chest sat on the table, and a slew of artifacts was lined up next to it. He glanced around the room, frantically trying to find something to cover the table with. At last he grabbed a kitchen towel and draped it over the box. It was almost nothing, but selfishly he wanted to enjoy his find a bit longer before sharing it.

He opened the door. "Come in," he said, slipping the key into a pocket of his cassock. As they entered, their eyes immediately fixated on the table. The towel hid the chest, but old papers, artifacts and relics lay strewn about.

Landry's eyes brightened with excitement. "Look at this! Did you find these after we left?"

Elias paused, thinking of how many years he had dealt with the devil in his community, and understood that now he was dealing with the devil inside his head. "Yes, and I also found the key," he said at last, removing it from his pocket and showing it to them. "From what you've read, this key can break the witches' pact. It could free Landry from the family curse and end Charity Device's stronghold over the town. But there's the risk of incurring their wrath and unleashing further chaos. If it doesn't work as you think it will, it could be the end of this town and its God-fearing people."

Landry said, "We understand the dangers, Father. We're prepared to face them, and the people deserve to be freed. But we need the key to break Charity's power."

Elias closed his eyes and spoke. "The decision is not an easy one. The key could bring great change, but it must be wielded with utmost care."

Landry replied, "The mayor knows what we're up to, Father. She's going to use everything in her arsenal to stop us. Join with us. Use the power of your faith to help us win this fight."

"Come back in an hour," the old priest replied. "I must pray about the move I'm about to make; I must feel a peace about giving you the key. If something goes wrong and you create a confrontation with the dark forces, it will likely mean the destruction of every good person in Pendle."

CHAPTER FORTY-FIVE

Exactly one hour later, Landry and Jack returned to the sanctuary, explaining that they had spent the time exploring the ruins of the old church. "You told us we'd be safe on the grounds, so we took your advice. And now we're hoping you'll give us the key. Please, Father."

Elias's voice was firm yet weary. "All right, the key is yours. I doubt you comprehend the danger you're going to face by using it. Charity will muster every dark entity she can to stop you."

Landry's eyes lit up with a mixture of gratitude and urgency. "Thank you, Father. We won't waste this chance. I promise. Will you help us?"

"Yes, I will," he replied, feeling a pang of sorrow. After today, things would never be the same. But it had to be done this way. He had a tacit understanding with Charity and the others in her coven, he wouldn't stir their pot, and they wouldn't stir his. He felt safe when he left the grounds to go to the grocery or visit a parishioner. But the moment he removed the key from its hiding place, the rules had changed. The three of them wouldn't be safe anywhere off church property.

Jack told Father Elias about the apparition of his sister and the book she guided him to. It was made of leather, he added, describing how it was bound with a simple strap, but when he tried to cut it, the strap and the binding turned out to be as strong as steel. Nothing but a key would open the book, and Jack asked if Father Elias would allow him to bring the book here to open it.

Elias considered the request. It made sense to keep the book's power and the key's effects under the church's protection. But there was one consideration—one dangerous obstacle. "Where is the book now?" he asked. "You know the witches would take it if they could."

Jack nodded. "We thought of that. After the spirit pointed out the book, we brought it straight here. It was of no use to us until we had the key, so we hid it among the ruins. We'll go get it now."

"Bring it into the sanctuary through the front door," the priest instructed. "I'll bless the book before we try to open it."

He watched as the men left his kitchen and walked toward the old church, his heart heavy with a mixture of relief and dread. He knew that his own safety was now precarious, but he had made the right decision. Now he resolved to face whatever came with courage and faith. Would the book explain what they had to do? There was only one way to find out.

There must be a blessing before we begin the ritual, Elias had decided. He walked into the sanctuary, arranged several candles on the altar, and lit them. He glanced out through an open window, the street just past the church grounds seemed quiet and empty, and he brushed away a shiver as he thought what the witches might be planning even as he prepared the blessing. He knew they were out there somewhere, just waiting for a mistake.

Within moments, Landry and Jack were back. They handed over the book, and Father Elias compared the key to the hole, calling it a perfect fit. Elias grasped the book with shaky hands and carefully placed it on the altar, surrounded by the flickering candles casting eerie shadows on the walls.

"Before we open it," Elias began, "let's consider what we'll do with what we find. If there are detailed instructions about breaking the curse, I believe we should perform that rite as quickly as possible to avoid interference from Charity Device and her kin." They agreed, and the priest took a deep breath and began.

He dipped his fingers in a small bowl and sprinkled water on the book. "Let us pray," he said, and as Landry and Jack bowed their heads, he raised both hands high into the air and prayed for guidance, protection, and understanding. He prayed for victory over the dark forces that held the town captive, for release from ancient curses and pacts, and for a future free from those who practiced witchcraft. When he finished, he lowered his hands and said, "Let us open the book."

He placed the key into the lock and turned it with a deliberate motion. The lock clicked open.

As soon as the key turned, the ancient symbol embossed on the cover began to glow with a pale light. The illumination was faint at first but grew stronger, casting a greenish hue over the room. The symbol began to pulsate with a heartbeat of its own, as if the book was alive and breathing with dark energy. Landry and Jack glanced at each other apprehensively.

Simultaneously with the turning of the key, there came a frightening shift in the weather. What had been a sunlit morning suddenly transformed into darkness. The sky, once a clear expanse of blue, darkened in an instant as black thunderheads filled the heavens. Heavy, roiling clouds gathered swiftly, tumbling over each other with unsettling speed.

Thunder crashed from everywhere at once, a low growl that swelled into a deafening roar echoing through the empty streets of Pendle. In a stunning display of fury, a massive bolt of lightning lit the sky and struck a tall tree just beyond the church grounds. The tree splintered with a blinding flash, its trunk shattered into splinters. The impact was so powerful that it sent a shockwave through the air, rattling the windows and doors of the church.

"Charity's work has begun," the priest said. "She knows what we are about to do, and she can't attack us herself, but she can harness the power of a storm. It's no longer safe for you to leave the grounds until this is over." As the storm's fury unleashed its wrath, raindrops began to fall, quickly escalating into a torrential downpour. The rain hammered against the ground with a relentless intensity, pooling in gutters and cascading off eaves in torrents. They paused for a moment to look outside, watching as the wind picked up, howling through the streets with a wail. It buffeted the church and its surroundings as if the fury of the gods were against them. And perhaps that was exactly what was happening.

Elias, Landry, and Jack returned to the altar, their faces illuminated now by both candles and the frequent flashes of lightning. Outside, it was as dark as night, but they could see that the real fury was taking place beyond the church grounds. From their position, the only effects were relentless rain and wind. Once again, the sanctity of the church seemed to protect them, but the heightening storm increased the urgency of their task, and Father Elias slowly opened the book.

They turned pages filled with intricate diagrams and arcane symbols, difficult to make out in the dim light. Jack and Landry retrieved their phones, directing more light on the book. Elias's hands shook as he turned the pages, the words and symbols becoming more vivid and menacing under the book's eerie illumination. "Look at this page," he said to them. "What's happening is fascinating. The words are in a language I cannot decipher, and the symbols mean nothing, but as I look at each line, my mind translates them as I go. How is that possible? Does the same thing happen to you?"

Landry peered at the page. "Yes." He gulped, his scalp tingling as the instructions for preparing a ritual became clear in his mind. It worked for Jack as well.

"That's impossible, you know," Landry said, and the priest agreed. Whatever the reason, it would allow them to perform the ritual.

"We must follow the instructions precisely," the priest said, raising his voice to counter the racket from the storm. "Are you prepared to take these steps, knowing that we may not be able to backtrack once we've begun?"

"Let's do it," Jack said as Elias tossed him a pad and pencil. "I'll call out the items we need for the ritual. You make a list."

Landry, pacing the length of the sanctuary, raised a valid concern. "Where do you plan to get that stuff? I'm sure the things we need aren't something you'd find in a Christian church or a little village, so where can you get it?"

"Getting the materials is the easy part. I'm confident the Peel sisters will have everything we require. They practice white magic—so-called good witchcraft—or so they claim. As a priest, I don't believe any witchcraft is good, but I know them, and if I can make it to their house without Charity stopping me, I can get everything."

"We know them too," Landry said. "They've helped us several times. Could we call and ask them to bring the things over?"

The old priest shook his head. "We have no phones in Pendle. You and Jack have cellphones, and they should work when you call someone outside of town. For this, I must go myself, and we're running out of time. I've always been free to move about town without interference, but I wonder if that luxury is still available to me. After seeing this bizarre rainstorm, I'm sure Charity knows what we're up to."

Landry disagreed. "You can't go. If they capture you, we lose everything."

"There's no alternative. She'll kill you and Jack if you go, but at least I have a chance based on past history. And no matter what, I'll get the things back to you so that you can perform the ritual yourself."

"Me? I don't know anything about—"

Elias pointed to a page in the book. "But you can do it. The preparation begins here"—he flipped to another page—"and the ritual itself starts here. Translate the instructions in your mind, and do exactly, precisely what it tells you to do. Don't let anything distract you once you begin."

Jack and Father Elias cross-checked the list of items once more. There was no time for error; they had one chance only to get this right. As he stood next to them, Landry began to hear things inside his mind and realized he wasn't safe inside the church at all. Charity might not be able to physically invade the sanctity of the church grounds, but she had other means such as inserting her sinister presence into his thoughts. As he listened to Jack and the priest talking softly, he suddenly reeled, unable to concentrate. He felt Charity's presence as strongly as if she were standing beside him.

"Landry," her voice whispered, "you think you can defy me? You've found the book and the key. But know this: if you do not give them to me, I will kill every soul in this town. Melody Blair will be the first."

Landry's face paled, and he clutched the altar to keep from falling.

"Landry!" Jack shouted, taking hold of his arm to steady him. "Are you all right? What's going on?"

"What's wrong?" Elias cried as Landry staggered back, trying to block out the tormenting whispers that created a whirlwind of terror in his mind. He tried to answer, but in his eyes they saw the torment he was experiencing.

"Turn yourself over to me," she taunted. "Walk out with the book and key, or watch as I destroy everything and everyone in this wretched town. The blood of hundreds of innocents will be on your hands."

As Landry struggled to stay upright, the storm outside intensified, fueled by Charity's rage. Lightning split the sky with blinding flashes, and the thunder roared like a beast awakened. The winds howled with a mournful fury as if echoing the torment Charity inflicted upon Landry.

In moments, Charity's invasion of his mind abated, and Landry revealed what had happened. Father Elias wasn't surprised, and braced Landry for more to come. Jack was concerned about her threat but said, "I know she said she'd kill Melody, and all I can do is hope to stop this somehow. For now, we have a mission to complete."

But Landry's resolve wavered. The weight of Charity's threats and the apocalyptic storm outside were almost too much to bear. He imagined the wails of the townspeople, their suffering a stark reminder of what his actions had caused.

Elias was deeply concerned but kept his thoughts to himself. He believed she had far more weapons in her infernal arsenal than mind control, but he could not allow this setback to thwart the mission. He had promised to help end the curse, and he could not falter now. With grim resolve, he raised a crucifix high into the air and said, "Lord God, arrest the dark one until we finish this ritual. Cast out the demons who seek to stop us. And if it is your will, lead me safely to procure the items necessary to perform the ritual."

As Landry heard Elias's prayer, a rush of stillness enveloped him. The voice was gone, and he returned to the table, knowing that Charity was far from finished. Outside, the storm raged on, an unholy maelstrom of destruction and despair. Pendle was in the grip of Charity's wrath, and the fate of the town—and Landry's soul—hung precariously in the balance. The key, the book, and the ritual inside it were the town's last hope, and they must act swiftly and decisively to end the nightmare that had been unleashed.

CHAPTER FORTY-SIX

Elias put the list in his pocket, donned a poncho, and set out in the storm. They watched him leave the grounds and walk down the sidewalk without incident. In minutes they could no longer see him. And they thought back to his earlier comment—if he didn't return, he'd get the things they needed to them. How would that be possible?

As they waited, fearful thoughts ran through Landry's mind. He might have to face the witches and perform a ritual that would undo their power. How would they react? Would the sanctity of the church really protect him, or had Charity been biding her time, making them think they were safe, and striking when their guard was down?

Landry thought about Cate, knowing the situation he faced now was exactly the thing she had left him over. Unnecessary risk-taking, she called it. But to him, it was everything this time. He was the subject of a curse, and so was an entire town. Jack's sister might be a captive here too.

I must finish this, Cate. Please understand, he said to himself, wishing he'd called her earlier. Now there was no time left, so Landry turned his focus to the ritual ahead.

As Landry and Jack pored over every word of the ritual's requirements—rare herbs, sacred symbols, and tools—Elias was walking through the maelstrom to the house of the Peel sisters. Although he had seen no one since leaving the church, he felt he was being followed, and that came as no surprise. Shortly he could see the house, and despite his uneasy feeling, he arrived at the Peel residence unharmed. Lydia opened the door and let him in.

Ten minutes later he stepped back onto their porch and put a cloth sack under his poncho. Then he started out, retracing his steps, but he had only gone a block when he saw Charity Device standing up ahead, blocking his way. As he had feared, the leeway the witches had given him was gone. As she approached, he began to pray.

Back at the church, Landry and Jack waited for what seemed like an eternity. The sky began to lighten as the intensity of the storm decreased. Fifteen minutes passed, then twenty, and they knew something must have happened to the priest.

"What do we do now?" Jack asked. "We can't do the ritual without the things it requires."

Landry's heart pounded, but he took the old book into his hands, listening in his mind to the initial instructions. Jack watched closely; they were both engrossed in the book when they heard someone rapping at the church's front door.

Surprised that Elias would knock, Jack flung open the door and saw Lydia Peel standing in the rain. She held out a cloth bag and said, "These are what you will need. Good luck." She turned to leave, but Landry cried, "Wait! How did you get here, and where's Father Elias?"

"Charity has Elias," she replied without emotion. "We were both afraid that would happen when he started back to the church. At his insistence, I gave him a sack filled with useless things, and I brought the real items to you. There's nothing of value in his sack. And I got here by walking, of course. I told you she has no power over me."

"Can you please stay and help us?" Landry asked. "We could really use a person accustomed to performing rituals and using these ingredients."

She shook her head. "That isn't possible because I cannot cross the threshold. I have no use for churches or your religion. I have faith in you, Landry Drake. You can make the ritual work if you follow the instructions precisely."

"Father Elias said the same thing—follow the instructions exactly. I get it. One mistake and I blow the whole thing."

Lydia looked him in the eyes. "Yes, Landry. Hopefully at last you understand the gravity of what you face."

When she left, Jack emptied the contents of the sack onto the altar. Landry consulted a diagram in the book and placed each item where it went. Lydia had marked everything for easy identification, which was helpful since many were things Jack and Landry had never seen.

As Landry prepared the altar, a faint humming sound filled the room. It seemed as if the church itself was waiting in anticipation. At last everything was ready, and Landry turned to the proper place in the book. He was ready to start the ritual.

CHAPTER FORTY-SEVEN

An hour earlier, the mayor had joined members of her coven on the sidewalk outside St. Margaret's Church. They couldn't go any closer, but watchers stationed around the perimeter of the grounds confirmed to her that the priest, Landry and Jack were still inside.

She wondered why Landry and Jack had gone to the church. She knew that Jack had been in contact with his sister, Melody, that unpredictable, naïve woman who had sold her soul for a pittance. Charity had used the girl to lure Jack to Pendle, hoping he would bring along his friend Landry Drake, and she had been pleased when her plan worked. Landry was her prey and the others merely pawns, but now she had to rein Melody in. Today the girl had helped her brother by guiding him to the book of spells, and she would pay a dear price for that lapse of judgment.

The book contained valuable secrets, but Charity was certain no one could interpret its ancient words and symbols. It existed because it was a means to exert power over the other covens in Pendle. If another coven attempted to wrest control from the Device family, everything could be unwound in an instant.

An o256minous thought swept through Charity's mind. Although diminished these days, her powers of perception still existed, and suddenly she had an overwhelming feeling that the lost key was lost no more. As much as she concentrated, the details wouldn't come together for her, but she knew it was no coincidence that Landry was here at the same time the key surfaced.

She stood behind a tree, watching Landry and Jack emerge from the back of the church and walk across the grounds to the ruins behind. Soon they returned, and she saw Jack carrying the book of spells. This time they entered the sanctuary through the front doors.

As they disappeared inside, she realized they now had everything they needed—the key and the book—and that Father Elias must be helping them. Still, she believed the secrets in the book would remain just that. Regardless, Landry now had the key, the object that could unravel centuries of dark enchantments. Though her powers could not breach the sanctity of the church property, she had options. If she could not reach Landry directly, she would unleash a tempest of terror upon the town itself.

While Father Elias, Landry and Jack prepared the ritual, Charity began her assault. The sky erupted in a violent cacophony of thunder and lightning, the heavens cracking open as if in fury. Within seconds, gale-force winds roared through Pendle, uprooting trees and sending debris hurtling through the streets. Mobile homes, a dangerous choice of housing in storm-ravaged areas, were torn from their foundations and flung about like discarded toys.

The storm's fury was relentless. In the midst of this chaos, Charity reached into the minds of the hapless townspeople, sowing confusion and fear. Her voice, a sinister echo, reverberated through their thoughts. They scrambled for safety, their screams mingling with the howling wind. A few would die—not the witches, of course, but some of the others.

CHAPTER FORTY-EIGHT

Landry's face was set in grim determination. The instructions detailed every aspect of the ritual, from the exact arrangement of the elements to the precise wording of the incantations. He was hopeful he could perform the task, but he wished the leader were Father Elias, a man of the cloth, instead of him.

The storm intensified again, becoming a virtual hurricane, the winds and rain pressing against the walls of the church as though it intended to squeeze them to death. The raging storm was a fitting backdrop to their incantations, and every flash of lightning and roaring peal of thunder underscored the gravity of their mission. The book lay open on the altar, its pages emitting a soft glow that allowed Landry to see the instructions without issue.

"We begin by making a ring on the floor around the altar with salt, mixed with these herbs"—he held up vials of powder—"and draw these symbols around the perimeter. You do the salt and herbs, and I'll start drawing." As they began their preparations, the room seemed to grow colder, and the windows rattled sharply. The eerie light from the book flickered ominously, casting long, sinister shadows throughout the sanctuary. Landry shivered, thinking that unseen forces knew what they were getting ready to do.

With careful precision, they laid out the circle of salt and inscribed the runes as instructed. Landry's hands trembled as he saw each symbol pulse with light as it was drawn. He could feel a growing sense of unease, as if the very air was thickening with malevolent intent.

"Okay, the circle is done," Jack said, wiping sweat from his brow. "What's next?"

Landry flipped through the book, his eyes following the text as his mind translated the words. "Place these candles at specific points around the circle," he said, indicating a diagram that showed the precise arrangement. "Then we recite the incantations."

Jack arranged the candles as instructed, their flames flickering nervously as if aware of the ritual's significance. The final step involved using the rune embedded in the book's cover. It was a delicate process, requiring them to trace the symbol with a special ink, which they found among the things Lydia had provided.

As they began the incantations, the room's temperature dropped further. The flickering candlelight cast strange, moving shadows on the walls, and they could hear screams in the wind outside that might be real or not. The book's glow became almost blinding, and the markings on the page seemed to writhe in the light.

Landry felt a presence, something dark and menacing pressing against the edges of the sanctified circle. The storm outside escalated into a full-blown tempest, the thunder shaking the house with deafening roars. Lightning illuminated the room with blinding flashes, casting grotesque, shifting shapes on the walls and revealing the presence of one twisting, undulating black blob—one of the same that had dogged them every visit.

How did it get in here? Jack wondered to himself. Instead of interrupting Landry, he said, "Just concentrate. Make sure everything you do is correct."

Landry was aware something else was in the sanctuary with them, but he couldn't lose his focus. He shouted incantations, filling the room with a haunting resonance as he cleared his mind of anything but the ritual. It required total concentration, but the storm and whatever was in the shadows threatened to distract him.

As Landry chanted, the candles flickered even more, their flames stretching toward the ceiling as if reaching for something unseen. His heart raced as he turned a page and continued to intone the words he saw in his mind.

Suddenly he commanded, "Jack! Raise the key as high as you can."

Jack held the key high over his head. The metal began to glow with a beautiful golden light that throbbed in sync with Landry's words.

Suddenly, the book that contained the ritual instructions reacted violently. Its brittle pages flipped on their own, whipping through the air as if possessed by some invisible force. Page after page, faster and faster, until the book abruptly stopped on its final page. The words on it blazed with fire, not burning but glowing with a fierce, unearthly heat.

Landry's eyes widened, and he staggered back, momentarily blinded by the fiery script. The words, though written in an ancient tongue, again resounded clearly in his mind, guiding him.

This is the final instruction. From here, there can be no turning back.

Gritting his teeth, Landry nodded to Jack, who was clutching the key tightly. "Channel the light from the key into the rune," Landry instructed as he closed the book.

Jack pointed the key toward the book's cover. As the glowing metal hovered near the rune etched into the ancient leather, a surge of electricity jumped from the key and connected with the relic. The entire sanctuary trembled; waves of power rippled through the air, the force reverberating like a massive, slow-beating heart.

Landry felt the ground beneath him quake, but he held his focus. The energy intensified, the pulsating rhythm growing louder, almost deafening. From the key a beam of pure, blinding light erupted, flying toward the ceiling like a bolt of lightning.

A bloodcurdling scream pierced the air—high-pitched, shrill, and agonized. The dark presence that had been lurking in the room, unseen but deeply felt, was now visible. The blob writhed and twisted in the beam of light, its shadowy form distorting as it tried to escape the searing power. Its howls echoed off the walls, shaking the sanctuary to its core.

But things weren't only happening inside the church. From outside, more screams rang out—this time human. Alarmed, Jack rushed to the window and peered out into the storm. Just beyond the church grounds, he saw the coven. Charity and her witches, once so terrifying in their dark majesty, clutched their heads, hands pressed tightly to their ears, their faces contorted in sheer agony. They fell to the ground, writhing, staggering and screaming in unison with the blob inside the church, proving their bond to the dark side.

"Landry!" Jack shouted, his voice filled with both astonishment and fear. "The witches…they're—they're in pain!"

Landry didn't need to see. He felt it. The energy coursing through the sanctuary, the light radiating from the key, was undoing them—ripping apart the evil that had taken root in Pendle for centuries.

As the final words of the ritual were spoken, the book flew open; its eerie light flared violently, casting a searing crimson glow that appeared to coat the room in blood. A blinding light and a deafening roar erupted from the middle of the circle, as though the heart of the storm was converging with the ritual's dark energy.

Landry and Jack held their ground, their bodies shaking as the power of the ritual surged around them. The runes and symbols on the book's cover glowed fiercely, and the circle of salt seemed to shimmer with a protective aura. The energy was almost too intense to bear, and for a moment, Landry wondered if they'd be consumed by the darkness.

The dark blob in the room let out one final, deafening scream before dissolving into the beam of light, vanishing as if it had never existed. At that moment the room fell silent, the walls stopped shaking, and the pulsating waves of energy ended. The key and the rune were mere objects once again, leaving only dim light from the candles behind.

Landry collapsed to his knees, gasping for breath. He glanced up at Jack, who was still staring out the window in disbelief. "It's over," he whispered, the weight of it all finally hitting him. "The ritual is finished."

Through the windows, rays of sunlight flooded the room as the oppressive weight of darkness lifted, leaving the sanctuary in eerie silence.

Landry mustered enough strength to stand, and he said, "Did we do enough to break the curse and the pact against my family? Did I say the words right? Do the witches still have power? We have to find out."

"And I have to find my sister," Jack whispered.

CHAPTER FORTY-NINE

The ritual was over, but the weight of its aftermath hung heavy in the air. Landry felt as though he'd gone twelve rounds in a prizefight, his body drained of every ounce of energy. Jack stood by the window, trying to process everything he saw and felt—Charity Device and the screaming witches outside, the dark entity vanquished, and the eerie stillness that blanketed the sanctuary.

Jack flung open the church doors. Outside, the air felt clean, as if the weight it had carried for years had been lifted. The storm that battered the village was gone now, leaving only a cool breeze in its wake. The clouds parted, revealing a sky so blue it seemed unnatural after weeks and months of darkness and dread.

Stretching his aching body, Landry stood at the church doors for a moment. He couldn't shake the image of Father Elias selflessly agreeing to go into the town in hopes the witches wouldn't harm him.

"We need to go to Lydia's house and find out what happened to Elias," Landry said.

Jack, still pale and shaken by the events that had unfolded, nodded silently. His eyes were distant, lost somewhere between relief and shock. The memory of the dark forces they had confronted was too fresh, too vivid. But despite their exhaustion, they had to learn whether the ritual had worked.

They walked out of the church into a world that no longer felt haunted. The town had changed. The people had changed. Where there had been fear and suspicion, now there was curiosity, even tentative joy. Neighbors who had long shut themselves away were standing outside, chatting in low voices as if unsure of whether it was safe to believe in this new reality. The townspeople knew something monumental had occurred, they felt the palpable change, the lifting of a shroud, but they were hesitant to believe it could last.

Children who for years had been hushed indoors now stood in their yards, their eyes wide with wonder. Dogs barked happily in the distance, freed from the eerie silence that had long blanketed the town. On a bright afternoon, Pendle was waking up.

"These people don't even know," Jack muttered. "Most of them have no idea what just happened."

"Not specifically, but they understand everything has changed, and the word will spread quickly," Landry replied. "All that matters is that they're free. But we're not done yet."

Jack nodded, though his thoughts were elsewhere. He knew what Landry was thinking: Father Elias had been the one to guide them, to risk everything for the town's salvation. And now, after the storm had passed, there was no sign of him. No word.

Lydia's house came into view; its old Victorian style suddenly looking out of place in the now-bright and hopeful

Pendle. Its weathered boards seemed to groan with the weight of secrets, and its shadow stretched across the street like a lingering reminder of the darkness that had so recently lifted.

They reached the front door, and Landry knocked. A few moments later, the door creaked open. As always, Lydia's face was unreadable, but she nodded when she saw them both. "Come in. I know why you're here," she said, stepping aside to let them enter. "You've come about Elias."

Landry's stomach twisted. The way she said it, the finality in her tone, made his heart sink.

Lydia led them into the parlor, where her sister Rose sat in a rocker. Lydia took a chair, motioning for them to do the same. For several moments, no one spoke.

"Is he...is he alive?" Landry asked at last, choking on the words.

"Father Elias did something wonderful for this town," she said slowly, her voice carrying an unexpected softness. "He knew the cost, and he accepted it."

"What are you saying?" Landry felt his hands clenching into fists. "What happened to him?"

Lydia's eyes met his, and he saw a deep sadness and a resigned acceptance in her face. "When I brought the things for the ritual, I told you Charity had him. He left my house with a bag to make them think he had the supplies you needed. He sprang a trap to save the town. But Charity was waiting for him. They killed him, Landry."

Landry felt as if someone had punched him in the gut. Elias, dead? This was what he had feared, the man who had guided them, who had yearned to free the town from its curse, slaughtered by the evil forces he sought to defeat.

"He gave his life," Lydia continued, her voice steady. "He did it to sever the town's connection to the witches, to free you"—she looked directly at Landry—"and to free the town from the pact that had bound us to the dark forces."

Landry's head spun. His sacrifice...the pact...was it really broken? Could he truly be free from the fate that had doomed him?

"Elias made sure the witches can never return here," Lydia said, her voice growing firmer. "The curse is broken. The devil no longer has any claim on Pendle—or on you. You're free, Landry."

He felt a rush of relief wash over him, but he grieved because his freedom cost a man's life.

Jack asked, "Are the witches dead?"

"No, but they no longer have power in Pendle, thanks to the ritual you performed. They've retreated deep into the bayous, beyond the reach of this town. They'll lick their wounds and plot their next move. And trust me, Landry, they haven't forgotten who caused all this trouble for them."

"They'll come after me," Landry said.

Lydia nodded gravely. "They will, but not here. They can't touch Pendle anymore. The power they had here is gone. The land is free from their influence, thanks to you and Jack—and Father Elias as well. But that doesn't mean they're powerless. They'll regroup in the bayous, biding their time. Charity will do everything she can to track you down and kill you. You must always be aware of your surroundings, Landry. She'll strike when you least suspect it."

Landry clenched his fists, anger bubbling beneath the surface. "I'm not afraid of her, and I'm not going to change my life because she's still out there somewhere."

"Don't be foolish," Lydia warned. "You *should* be afraid. You've wounded her pride, and that's a dangerous thing. She's patient, Landry. She'll wait for the right moment—months, perhaps years—and when she strikes, she'll aim to destroy everything you hold dear."

Jack had waited as long as he could. "And Melody? What about my sister?"

Lydia's face softened with a kind of pity. "She's with them now, Jack. She's one of them."

The room fell into a heavy silence, the weight of the truth settling over them like a shroud.

Landry felt defeated; although he and Jack had just completed the ritual, Father Elias was dead. The witches had been banished for the moment. But would he spend the rest of his life looking over his shoulder because of what he did today?

"Thank you, Lydia," Landry said, rising from his chair. "For everything."

Lydia gave a small nod. "You've done a great thing here, Landry. Don't forget that. But be careful. The witches may be powerless here, but they're still dangerous."

As they turned to leave, Jack said, "I have one more question. There was one of those black blobs in the church while Landry was performing the ritual. I thought sanctity offered protection against the dark forces."

The old woman thought a moment. "That is unusual, but it proves only one thing. You cannot assume the church grounds will repel anything and everything that strikes. Charity and her coven have much more power than the blobs, and that means it would be harder for them to breach the church grounds. In my opinion, the blobs are formless shapes that do the bidding of the dark side. One of them somehow penetrated into the church, but the ritual was too powerful to allow it to do any harm."

As Landry and Jack stepped outside into the twilight, the oppression that had once suffocated Pendle was gone. The air felt lighter and the shadows less menacing. But a chill lingered in Landry's bones.

"We should get out of here before nightfall," Jack said, his voice breaking the silence.

Landry nodded, his mind already turning to the future. He had broken the devil's pact, but the witches weren't finished with him. They'd be waiting in the bayous, plotting their revenge.

As they walked away from Lydia Peel's house and the town of Pendle, Landry knew this battle was over, but the war was far from won.

CHAPTER FIFTY

In the days since the curse over Pendle had been broken, everyone seemed to have breathed a collective sigh of relief. Everyone except for Jack Blair, who continued his quest to find Melody.

Today he stood on the outskirts of the town, leaning against his SUV, watching the life that had returned to Pendle. His heart, however, remained heavy. No amount of sunshine or cheerfulness could penetrate the darkness that clung to his soul. While everyone else celebrated the town's deliverance, Jack was consumed by a grief that weighed on him like an anchor.

It was Melody and her embrace of witchcraft. He couldn't accept it. He couldn't wrap his mind around the fact that the bright, loving girl he had grown up with had willingly joined a coven. Years ago, he'd abandoned her when he left home and succumbed to the ravages of alcoholism, never caring about her welfare. For six years he'd lost touch. Then came the phone call from Pendle that led him to where he was today. He had left her behind once, and now she was lost in a world of darkness.

Jack felt an overwhelming sense of obligation to save her. He couldn't just walk away, not again. Not now that he knew how far she had fallen. He had to give it one more shot. He owed her that much.

The people of Pendle had no answers for him when he asked where she might be. Lydia said the witches had retreated, banished from the town's borders, and were now lurking somewhere deep in the swamps. She also said they were licking their wounds, waiting for the right moment to take Landry down.

He drove through Pendle and into the swamps, where the roads became mere trails. Out here the bayou was dark, mist-covered, and desolate—perfect for hiding those who still wished to cling to their magic.

It was dangerous to look for Melody, but he had to try. He remembered her as his little sister, her soft laugh, the way she'd grab his hand and pull him along on their adventures through the woods behind their house. She had always been braver than he was, always more daring. But she had also been kind and loving. Maybe he could help her find that again.

He tried first one road, then the next. They all dead-ended at Bayou Dularge in groves of trees heavy with moss that dripped down like a veil over the murky waters. Alligators lazed in shallow water, their watchful eyes just above the surface, waiting for something to come near.

A third road brought him where he wanted to be, but he had second thoughts about having come.

Here the swamp was dark, a thick canopy of trees blocking out what little light there was. The air was humid and thick, almost suffocating, and Jack inched his way further along in his SUV despite the growing sense of dread that gnawed at him.

He stopped when he heard a sound—a rustling in the distance. Was it them? The witches? Or was it something else, something darker that still lurked in the shadows?

"Mel," he whispered, though his voice barely carried in the oppressive silence. "Please, if you're out there…"

But there was no answer, only the steady buzz of insects and the rustling of leaves in a light breeze. Jack swallowed hard, pushing forward. He had come this far. He couldn't turn back now.

Suddenly, he saw it—movement in the distance. A figure up ahead, standing in the middle of the rutted trail. His heart leaped into his throat. Was it her?

He jumped out of the car and ran toward it, and as he came near, the trees seemed to close in, their branches reaching for his sleeve, touching his skin, as if pulling him into some dark place.

The figure had vanished, and he began shouting. "Melody! Mel, are you here?"

For a long moment, there was nothing but silence. The swamp held its breath, as though waiting. Then, from the shadows between the trees, she stepped out in front of him.

She looked different—her hair wild, her skin pale and shadowed with dark smudges beneath her eyes. There was an emptiness in her gaze, a hollow reflection of the sister he had once known. She stepped closer, and though her face was calm, her words were ice.

"Stop trying to save me. You need to let me go."

"I can't do that. I won't let them take you. Come back with me. I'll help you start over."

She shook her head slowly, a sad smile curling her lips. "There's no life left for me, Jack. Not the one you want me to have. I'm not your sister anymore. I'm theirs."

"No," Jack said firmly, stepping forward. "I don't believe that. You're stronger than this. We can fix it—we can—"

"Stop it!" Melody's voice cut through the air like a whip. Her face twisted into fury, and for the first time, Jack saw the true darkness inside her. "You don't get it, do you? You and Landry saved the town. Hurrah for you. You banished us to the swamps, but you can't save me. Not anymore."

Jack reached out for her, but she slapped his hand away, her eyes wild with rage. "I'll kill you," she hissed.

His heart raced, but he kept his voice steady. "But you won't."

For a moment, it seemed like his words had struck something in her. Melody's face flickered with uncertainty, her lips quivering as if she was holding something back. But then her expression hardened again.

Her hand moved quickly, and before Jack could react, she pulled a knife from her belt, the blade gleaming in the dim light. She lunged at him with it, her scream echoing through the trees. Jack stumbled back, his mind reeling as he tried to process what was happening.

"Stop!" he shouted, his hands grabbing her arm and struggling to keep the blade away from his body.

But she was stronger than he remembered, her movements frantic and desperate. "You can't save me, Jack! You never could!" she screamed, her voice raw with rage and sorrow.

Falling to the ground, they wrestled for control of the knife, their bodies thrashing in the muddy swamp. Jack felt his strength waning, his heart pounding in his chest as Melody pushed harder. His mind raced—this was his sister. He couldn't hurt her. But she was trying to kill him.

And then, in one terrible instant, the knife slipped from her hand, spinning between them. Jack reached for it, but as his fingers closed around the handle, she jerked it back, and the blade plunged deep into her own chest.

Everything stopped.

The swamp seemed to go silent, the world shrinking to just the two of them. Melody gasped, her eyes wide with shock as she looked down at the blood blossoming across her shirt. Her body collapsed against Jack's, her hands clutching at him as though trying to hold on.

"No," Jack whispered, his voice choked with grief. "No, no, no…"

Melody's breaths came in shallow, ragged gasps. Her eyes, once filled with rage, softened for just a moment as she looked at her brother. "I told you…why couldn't you…just let me go?" she whispered, her voice barely audible.

Tears streamed down Jack's face as he held her in his arms, the weight of her body heavy and cold. He couldn't speak, couldn't move. All he could do was watch as the life drained from her, the sister he had loved, lost forever to the darkness.

As Melody's body went limp, Jack heard something—faint at first but growing louder. Cries, low and guttural, came from the direction of the witches' encampment. Dark shapes began to form in the trees, their eyes glowing with a malevolent light. The witches had sensed what had happened, and they were coming.

Jack's heart raced. He had to leave. He had to get out of there before they reached him.

With one last look at Melody, Jack gently laid her down in the mud, the knife still buried in her chest. His hands shook as he rose to his feet, his legs barely able to support him as he stumbled back toward his car. The cries grew louder, closer, the dark shapes moving through the trees like predators.

He ran.

His feet pounded against the ground, his breath coming in ragged gasps as he reached the car and fumbled with the keys. The engine roared to life, and without looking back, Jack tore away from the swamp, the tires kicking up mud and gravel as he fled the darkness.

Tears blurred his vision as he drove, his mind a whirlwind of grief and terror. Melody was gone. She had been gone long before this day, and he had been too blind to see it. Now, all he could do was escape the witches' wrath and live with the weight of what had happened—the sister he couldn't save, the darkness that had claimed her, and the curse that would never leave him.

As the sun began to set, casting long shadows across the road, Jack turned onto Interstate 10, the highway back to New Orleans. Tears rolled down his cheeks as he realized he'd tried and failed at the most important task of his life. But at least he had tried. He had done that much for his sister, but that was all he could do.

CHAPTER FIFTY-ONE

One Year After Pendle
The Town

Pendle, now bathed in the light of freedom and renewal, stood like a phoenix rising from the ashes of its dark past. Twelve months after the banishment of the witches, the town had transformed in ways the residents could scarcely believe. Where there had once been shadows and fear, there was now hope and laughter. The yoke of oppression that had held Pendle in its grasp for four hundred years had finally been lifted, and with it, the town was reborn.

The first sign of change came with the election of a new mayor, a man named Thomas Reilly. He was not descended from the family who had ruled Pendle for generations, nor did he bear the weight of their secrets. Reilly was a retired postal inspector who had moved to Pendle years ago and stayed despite the town's oddities. He had always seen its potential, the beauty beneath the darkness, and for years he tried to help. With the witches gone, Reilly became a symbol of the town's fresh start. His first order of business was simple: rebuild, reconnect, and revitalize.

Gone were the old symbols of control and fear. The town square, once a place where Charity Device had hoped to hang Landry Drake from the gallows, had playground equipment and new sidewalks. City hall was in the midst of a renovation, and merchants and residents alike had taken it upon themselves to spiff up their properties. On one corner now stood a weekly farmers' market that sold everything from locally sourced produce to artisan crafts.

For the first time in centuries, people gathered in the town square for events. The annual harvest festival, which had always been a somber affair marked by the weight of unspoken fear, had transformed into a celebration of life. Children danced around a maypole, families picnicked on the grass, and musicians played well into the night. The oppressive presence that had once lurked at the edges of every gathering was gone. Instead there was joy—real, unbridled joy.

New families were settling in Pendle. The once deserted streets bustled with life, as young couples and old alike moved into the beautiful, affordable homes that dotted the town. With the bayou in the distance and the rolling green hills on the outskirts, Pendle was fast becoming a destination for those seeking peace and a slower pace of life. It was country living, while being only a short commute to New Orleans and other smaller cities. The real estate market, once stagnant, was robust. An art gallery and a small restaurant were among the newest retail venues, the latter offering fresh local seafood.

The bookstore, one of the last remnants of the old town, still stood, though it too had undergone a transformation. It had always been a place of arcane knowledge, filled with dark manuscripts and hidden secrets, run by a crony of mayor Charity Device. But with the witches gone, the bookstore had found new life in the hands of a retired couple who took it upon themselves to preserve its history while adding shelves of modern books—mysteries, romances, historical novels, and bestsellers. The old manuscripts remained, but now they were treated as relics of a forgotten time, no longer filled with the power they once held.

But despite the bright future Pendle was carving for itself, not everyone believed the past was completely vanquished.

Lydia Peel and her sister, Rose, remained ever watchful. Though they were witches themselves, their magic had always been for good—healing, protection, and knowledge—and they had not been driven away with the others. They had worked tirelessly to break the hold of the darker forces that had ruled Pendle for so long, but even though the coven was banished to the bayous, their work wasn't finished. There was a sense of unease that lingered in the air, a subtle shift in the wind that only those sensitive to magic could feel.

The witches, led by the vicious Charity Device, were dormant but not beaten. Though their power was diminished, and they had been forced to build new lives deep in the swamps, their hatred burned bright. They'd lost everything—their power, their homes, their grip on Pendle—and they would not forget the one who had vanquished them. They were biding their time, watching from the shadows.

Although the ritual had freed Pendle from witchcraft, as an additional protection, Lydia and Rose Peel regularly cast powerful spells around the town to keep the dark magic at bay. The witches' hatred was immense, and someday they might test the spell that protected Pendle.

The townspeople lived their lives, free from things they had long been denied. They believed the worst was over—that the darkness had been vanquished for good. And for now, it was. But Lydia and Rose knew that could change. They would protect Pendle for as long as they could, but they had to remain vigilant. For while Pendle had entered a new era of prosperity, the witches of the bayou were still out there.

And the true test of Lydia and Rose's power would be the protection of one who had not returned to Pendle for a year. Landry Drake.

CHAPTER FIFTY-TWO

One Year After Pendle
Melody Blair

One year had passed since the witches had been banished from Pendle, but for Jack Blair, the dark shadows of that once-cursed town still invaded his mind. He'd lost his only sibling, his little sister. He loved New Orleans, with its vibrant streets and swirling sounds of jazz, and he had immersed himself in his work in an attempt to heal and forget. But a week ago, as the setting sun bathed the French Quarter in gold and crimson, the past had found its way back to him.

It started with a call from the receptionist, summoning Jack to the lobby to greet a visitor. He had arrived to find Melody—the sister he thought was dead—waiting for him. She smiled as she saw the shock on his face. His mind raced, recalling carefully placing her lifeless body on the ground before he fled. But somehow, here she was. She looked different from when he last saw her. Gone was the deathly pallor of her skin, the hollow look in her eyes. She was not just alive, but glowing with a vitality that stunned him. Jack could barely believe his eyes. He had watched his sister die—felt the bitter sting of loss as her blood stained his hands, taken by the dark forces she had aligned with.

"Mel," Jack whispered as he grabbed the reception desk to steady himself. "Is it really you? How can this be happening?"

She smiled, but somehow it didn't reach her eyes. "I'm free, Jack," she said softly. "I'm free of them. Is there a place we can talk?"

Unable to process what he was seeing, he stared at her dumbly for an instant, then led her into a nearby conference room. He closed the door, and they sat. Doubt gnawed at the corners of his mind; this didn't make sense. Lydia Peel had told Jack that Melody was lost forever, choosing to cast her lot with those in the netherworld of witchcraft. Her soul had been twisted beyond salvation. There was no coming back. And then she'd died. She'd truly died—he'd held her as it happened. But here she was, sitting beside him as though she'd been away on vacation.

Jack's heart pounded in his chest as he struggled to make sense of this. She looked like Mel—his sister's face, her hair, the same eyes that once held so much light before she lost herself to Pendle's dark forces. But something in her gaze, an unsettling coldness, made his skin crawl.

"You...you died," he stammered, the words choking in his throat. "I watched you die."

"I did die," Mel said quietly, her voice hauntingly familiar but edged with a chilling distance. "I was gone, Jack. But they brought me back."

"The witches?" Jack asked, his voice barely above a whisper. He couldn't comprehend how any of this was possible, even though from his time in Pendle, he'd learned that things weren't as simple as he once believed.

She nodded, a flicker of regret passing over her features. "They needed me for something else, something bigger. But I was tired, Jack. I couldn't do it anymore. The darkness takes everything from you. Even your soul."

"Then why are you here? Why come back now?"

Melody looked down at her hands, as though unsure herself. "At first, I thought it was to finish what they started. But something changed. I began remembering who I was before...before Pendle. And it hurt. I missed you. I missed everything I gave up." She looked up at him, her eyes shimmering with emotion. "I came back to find myself, Jack. To get out of their grasp. I can't be part of that world anymore."

Jack wanted to believe her, but something about her was different. "Why now? How can I trust that you're truly free from them? After everything you've done, how do I know this isn't another trick?"

A shadow passed over her face. "You don't. The witches brought me back, but I wasn't theirs anymore. I'm something else now. I'm evolving—neither fully theirs, nor entirely me. I hope you can understand that I chose to leave that life behind. I chose to come back to you, to try to mend our relationship."

Jack could see the pain in her expression, but there was an undeniable difference about her. "Why now?" he repeated, his voice firmer. "Why did you wait a year to come back?"

"I was trapped; they still controlled me. It took everything I had to break free. It wasn't just about the witches—it was the power they used to bring me back to life that day. I'm not like I was before." She hesitated a moment. "There's a darkness inside me still, one I can't fully control. That's why I stayed away; I didn't want to hurt you. But I had to see you, to tell you that I'm still fighting. Can I keep it at bay forever? I don't know, Jack. I just don't know. But I want to try. For me...and for you."

Jack's heart clenched. This wasn't the reunion he had dreamed of. She was back, but not entirely. Her body was alive, but her mind might never let her stay in this world.

"Do you really want to come back for good?" he asked, watching her facial expression closely.

She met his gaze, and for a moment, he saw a flicker of his sister—the real Melody. But it was fleeting, like a flame about to be snuffed out. "I think so," she whispered. "I'm willing to try. That's why I came to you. I need help if I'm going to overcome what they did to me."

"Okay. I can't say I trust you, but I'm willing to do what I can."

He took a few days off, trying to help Melody readjust to life in New Orleans. He fixed up the tiny spare bedroom in his apartment, telling her it was available until she got on her feet and found a job. She seemed genuinely grateful, repeatedly telling him how sorry she was for everything that had happened before. But she refused to talk about Pendle, her involvement with witchcraft, how she had cheated death, and what she'd been up to for twelve months. She told him she wanted to concentrate on the future, not the past.

"I didn't choose that life, Jack," she said one evening as they walked along the Mississippi River. "Charity Device manipulated me. But I've left them for good. I'm so glad to be part of your life again. I want to be your sister, the way we were when we were a family in Memphis."

Jack wanted to believe her. He truly did. Often he would catch a glimpse of the old Melody—the girl who had been his little sis growing up. Often, but not always.

He had deliberately avoided telling Landry his sister was back. It wasn't that hard; now that Cate was home again, Landry was spending all his free time with her and Simba. He hadn't heard from Landry in a week, but at last he decided it was time to let his friend know about Melody. He called and arranged to meet Cate and him for coffee at Fleur de Lis, a restaurant close to Landry's studio. He didn't mention his sister, preferring to make it a surprise.

And what a surprise it turned out to be.

Landry waved from a back table, and Jack led the way. "This is my sister, Melody," Jack announced as they sat.

In a flash, Melody's entire demeanor changed. Landry froze, his eyes locked onto the girl, and Jack could see doubt and concern in his face. He stared at her with a mixture of shock and disbelief. He had seen many things in his line of work, but the sight of Melody, once thought dead and lost to the dark forces, left a pit in his stomach. There was something wrong about her—something unnatural that his instincts told him to avoid. And yet here she was, supposedly alive but undeniably touched by the shadows.

He looked at Jack. "What's going on? Who is this?"

"What do you mean? It's my sister," Jack snapped. He knew what Landry was thinking, because he'd thought it himself every day since her return. Something was very wrong.

After years of investigating the paranormal, Landry had developed a sort of sixth sense about things that weren't what they should be, and his brain was pounding out messages as the girl sat across the table from him. He dropped any pretense at civility. "I don't know what's going on here, but she's…something about her isn't right."

Jack's eyes darted between Landry and Mel as he struggled for something to say. Landry never said things like this to a person's face. But Jack understood exactly what he was talking about.

In an instant, Melody changed. Her smile twisted into something dark as her eyes flashed with a cold, malevolent gleam. "You've caused us enough trouble, Landry Drake," she hissed, her voice losing all its softness. "You may think it's over, but it will never be over while you're alive. The witches will have their revenge."

Before anyone could react, Melody began to chant, her words laced with a curse, venomous and filled with hatred. But her voice faltered, and Landry sensed she didn't have the powers she claimed.

Cate cried out in alarm, but Landry never flinched. He looked her in the eyes and asked, "Why did you come here? Why did they send an emissary with no powers?"

Other patrons turned to stare at the unfolding scene, watching Melody's face twist in frustration and fury. She bolted from her chair, knocking it to the floor, rushed through the crowded restaurant and disappeared out the door. Jack and Cate sat in stunned silence until Landry said, "She's lost, Jack. They cast a spell on her—something that made her appear to be alive, but she's theirs and always will be. Chasing her will cost you your sanity…maybe more."

Jack's heart was shattered once more. "Surely there's something I can do," he muttered, his voice breaking.

Landry shook his head. "No, there isn't, and deep inside you know that. Look how far we've come in a year. Don't throw it away. If you keep at this, you may not survive."

Without saying a word, Jack rose from the table and shuffled out. He walked back to his apartment, found the door standing wide open, and called out her name. She didn't reply, but he heard movement in her bedroom. He walked to the open door and looked in. Melody stood over a small table, staring intently at a bowl of water. She was muttering something under her breath, her hand hovering over the surface of the water as if she were casting a spell. His heart sank.

He slammed the door shut, and a few minutes later, she emerged. "I don't know what got into me at that restaurant," she said with a feeble laugh.

"I want to know what you were doing in the bedroom," he replied.

"Practicing a meditation technique that helps me relax. You still believe in me, don't you, Jack?"

He couldn't form the words to reply, so he walked out and went back to work. He didn't reach out to Landry and was thankful Landry hadn't either. He needed time to process all this. Deep in his heart, he knew there was no hope, but he couldn't give up trying.

Then something else happened that same afternoon. A custodian found a small bundle of twigs, tied together with a crimson thread, hidden in the conference room where they had talked. Jack was the paranormal expert at Channel Nine, so the man took the twigs to him. "Looks like witchcraft," he quipped, but Jack knew there was nothing funny about it. When he confronted Melody, she claimed to have no idea what he was talking about, but he knew she was lying.

Lydia Peel's words echoed in his mind: *"The witches have claimed her, and there's no bringing her back."* He had tried to push those words aside, to convince himself that Melody had somehow broken free of the coven's influence.

But the evidence was overwhelming, and Jack couldn't ignore it any longer.

The final straw came that evening after he returned from work. He passed her bedroom on the way to his. Something told him to knock; when she didn't answer, he opened the door. She sat on the floor with a circle of candles lit around her, black smoke curling in the air, whispering in a language he didn't understand, but the scene left no question about what she was doing.

"Mel!" he shouted, stepping into the room. She jumped, startled, but the look in her eyes was cold and distant—nothing like the sister he knew.

"What are you doing?" he demanded.

Her expression hardened, any softness and vulnerability she had shown him over the past few days vanishing in an instant. "You wouldn't understand, Jack," she said, standing up slowly, the shadows from the candles casting eerie patterns on her face. "This is for us, for you and me. I want power, Jack. The witches are just a stepping stone. I want to move beyond them."

Jack's heart sank. She hadn't left the darkness behind. If anything, she had embraced it fully.

"What do you want?" he asked, his voice barely more than a whisper.

"You, Jack. I want you to help me. Together we can have immense power."

He shouted, "To do what? Turn Landry over to Charity Device? I'll never help you. All I wanted to do was help, but now you've shown me what you really are."

Melody's smile faded, and something darker replaced it—a cold fury that sent a shiver down Jack's spine.

"Then you can die with your friend Landry, for all I care," she hissed, her voice dripping with venom. The candles flared, their flames growing taller and more intense, casting long shadows that seemed to move on their own.

"Melody, please," he said, his voice cracking with desperation. "Please don't say that."

Her eyes were cold, devoid of any trace of the girl he had known. She took him by the arm, led him out the door, and slammed it behind him.

With that, Jack turned and ran, his heart pounding in his chest. The power his sister was after would allow her to work magic in awful ways, and he had to stop her. There was only one person he could think of who could make it happen.

CHAPTER FIFTY-THREE

One Year After Pendle
Jack Blair

Jack ignored the revelry in the French Quarter as he hurried down the cobbled streets, his breath coming in ragged gasps. The memory of Melody's cold, merciless eyes haunted him, the way the shadows had danced unnaturally around her as she embraced the darkness that had consumed her soul. His heart ached—this wasn't how it was supposed to end. But he had no choice now.

He needed Lydia Peel.

After the witches left Pendle, modern amenities had been adopted quickly, and although Lydia and her sister didn't go so far as to purchase a cellphone, Jack knew they had a landline now, and he had the number. In breathless gasps he explained everything, and the good witch told him to remain calm. He gave her the address of the TV studio, and she promised to be in New Orleans as quickly as she could.

"How?" he asked, doubting either of the spinster sisters had ever driven a car, but the call had ended. Two hours later she met him at Channel Nine. He attempted to take her back to his office, but she demanded to see Melody at once, saying there was no time to waste, and he walked her over to his apartment just outside the Quarter.

When they were inside, Lydia said, "Oh my, things are not good in this house. She wants to kill you and Landry. Are you prepared to let her go this time, because once this begins, it cannot stop."

Jack nodded, unable to speak. The weight of what they had to do pressed heavily on his chest.

"Where is she?" Lydia whispered, and Jack pointed to the closed bedroom door.

She dropped a satchel to the floor, took out a thick book, placed it on the table, and opened it to a page near the back.

Lydia's fingers traced the words on the page. "I'm so sorry this happened, But now that Melody has fully embraced the darkness, there's only one way to stop her."

Jack swallowed hard. "You mean…?"

Lydia nodded, her face grim. "She must be removed, permanently. Not to die, you understand, but to be divested of her power. You were there when she died earlier, when the knife went into her chest. And that was real. The mortal who was your sister died that day. Now she's returned, but she isn't alive; she appears to be only because the witches conjured up a spell, one with which I have some familiarity. The magic that brought her back is powerful, but it comes with a price. Unless I counteract that spell, she'll keep coming back. The only way to end this is to destroy the source of that magic."

Jack felt a knot tighten in his stomach. "How do you do that?"

She flipped to the page she wanted in the old book. "By using a counter-curse. I came prepared; I brought everything I'll need." She began unpacking the satchel, arranging stones and relics and powders on the coffee table. She brought out a tall gold candlestick and inserted a black taper, which she lit.

"We must hurry," Lydia muttered to herself. "She will be aware I'm here soon, and I must be ready for her." As Jack watched from across the room, she consulted the book, chanted in an unfamiliar language, then repeated the steps. It seemed surreal to Jack that a magic ceremony was taking place in his apartment, but what more appropriate place than New Orleans for such a rite, he thought.

"She's coming out soon," Lydia whispered, her voice trembling. "We don't have much time, but I only need a few more minutes." She began to chant once again, raising her voice this time. The air in the small flat crackled with energy, the floor shaking as the magic in the curse resisted her attempt to stem it. And now it attracted the attention of the one against whom it was aimed.

The door to Melody's bedroom flew open, and she stepped into the room. Her eyes glowed with an unnatural light, her face twisted in fury. "You hag!" she screamed. "Your magic won't stop me! I am eternal!"

Jack shouted one last time. "Mel, please! Don't make her do this!"

But there was no reasoning with her now. She was too far gone.

With a scream of rage, Melody lunged at Jack, her hands crackling with dark magic. Jack braced himself for the impact, but Lydia's spell was already taking effect. Before she could reach her brother, Mel screamed, her body writhing in agony as the magic that had sustained her was ripped away. Her form began to flicker, like a candle flame about to be snuffed out.

"No!" she shrieked, her voice filled with desperation. "You can't do this! I won't let you!"

But it was too late.

With one final, earth-shattering crash, a bolt of energy rose from the runes on the coffee table, enveloping Melody in flames for a lingering second, then extinguishing itself.

And with the last flicker of candlelight, his sister vanished.

Jack stood there, breathing heavily, his heart aching. He muttered, "That wasn't her. She would never…but did it work? Is she gone for good?"

Lydia placed a hand on his shoulder, her voice soft. "What you saw, and what I stopped, was not your sister. It was the demon in her. It's over, Jack. She's at peace now, and I hope you can find peace as well."

Jack nodded; even after seeing her true side, the pain of loss still weighed heavy on him. He had lost his little sister to the darkness.

As the evils of Pendle were eliminated one by one, Jack knew that not only his life, but also Landry's, might become normal again at last.

And so it would be for Jack, but only for him.

CHAPTER FIFTY-FOUR

One Year After Pendle
Landry Drake

Landry sat in the third-floor studio at the Paranormal Network, his fingers dancing over a keyboard as he edited the final audio and video feeds for "The Bayou Witches," the latest episode of *Bayou Hauntings*. The glow of the screen bathed his face in pale light as eerie music swelled through his headphones, complementing the chilling retelling of the events in Pendle. He was a master at transforming real-life horrors into stories that people could savor from the safety of their couches, all while keeping the darkest secrets of the paranormal world hidden in plain sight.

Henri, the creative mind behind the visuals, stood beside him, watching the footage on a separate monitor. Although they had been working together for more than three years, the bond between them had grown significantly stronger since Pendle. So far, Landry had kept his promise to Cate: no more dangerous investigations, no more diving headfirst into the unknown. He'd taken a step back, not from his fascination with the supernatural but from the reckless pursuits that had once put him and those he loved at risk.

Cautiously optimistic while afraid to believe him at first, Cate had watched him change. After all, how many times had Landry sworn he would pull back, only to rush headlong into another investigation that had her fearing for his life? But this time really did seem different. He seemed committed to something more meaningful than his work.

Their little family, including their beloved dog Simba, was flourishing. In the evenings, the three of them would sit on the patio with their drinks, Simba curled at their feet, and watch the sunset. They would laugh about simple things, share meals, and plan for the future, all with a warmth Cate thought might have been lost a year ago.

She loved him deeply, and she knew he loved her too. Perhaps more than anything else, he had proved that by stepping back from the risks he loved to take.

"Looks good," Henri said, breaking Landry's concentration as the final cut of the episode played out. "You've got the pacing down perfectly. That final scene where you talk about the curse over Pendle gives me chills every time."

Landry chuckled, removing his headphones. "Yeah, it's weird how after a year, it all still feels too close."

"You've earned a break," Henri said, standing up and stretching. "This is a wrap. How about taking a couple of weeks off to spend some time with Cate and Simba. You've earned it."

Landry nodded. He saved the project and shut down his computer. Cate was waiting at home, as always, and he couldn't wait to be with her.

Later that evening, Landry sat on the patio, cradling a cold drink in his hand. The warm Louisiana air settled around him like a familiar blanket, thick and humid. The distant sound of partying on Bourbon Street provided a familiar backdrop, and through the double doors, he could hear Simba's playful growls as he played with Cate in the bedroom.

It had been a good year—maybe the best of his life. No risks, no battles with dark forces, no sleepless nights wondering if something unseen was lurking just out of sight. For once, everything felt normal. He loved Cate more than he could ever put into words, and for her, he'd agreed to leave the darkest parts of his past behind. He wanted to believe he could do it. He *needed* to believe it. And so far, it was working.

He sat there nursing his drink, thinking of nothing, and gazing down the dimly lit street. Just then, something stirred in the corner of his vision. A shadow passed under the streetlamp at the far end of the block, barely visible in the half-darkness. His breath caught in his throat. He looked more closely, thinking it might be a trick of the light, or perhaps one of the stray dogs that roamed the Quarter. But then he saw it again. In the shadows at the end of his block stood a figure.

His senses sharpening, Landry watched closely as the figure moved slowly but deliberately, as though it knew exactly where it was going. And although he couldn't see the features, couldn't make out the details, a deep, gut-wrenching certainty settled over him.

It was *her*.

Charity Device.

And she was coming for him.

He hadn't seen her since that fateful day in Pendle, and as time passed, she never entered his thoughts any longer. He had defeated her, at least for a time. But as he'd been warned, she and her coven weren't dead—they were merely waiting. She had borne a grudge against Landry that remained unfulfilled. She was an embodiment of hatred, of vengeance, of the centuries-old evil that had cursed Pendle. And now, she was back.

Landry gripped the arms of the patio chair, his knuckles turning white. His heart raced, pounding in his chest like a drum. He wanted to run inside and tell Cate, to warn her. But he couldn't. Not after everything they had been through, not after he had sworn to her that he would leave that world behind, and not after things were going so well. He couldn't drag her back into the nightmare.

Instead, he forced himself to stay calm, to act as though nothing had happened. The figure at the end of the block faded into the shadows now, but Landry knew she wasn't gone. She was out there somewhere, watching him.

He took a deep breath to calm himself and stood, wiping his palms on his jeans as he walked inside to where Cate was sitting on the couch with Simba curled up beside her. She looked up and smiled, her eyes soft and filled with love.

"Hey," she said, patting the cushion next to her. "Come sit with us."

Landry double-checked the patio door locks and sat next to her on the couch, wrapping his arm around her shoulders and pulling her close. He could feel her warmth, her presence grounding him, reminding him of what he had to protect. Simba shifted, let out a contented sigh, and rolled onto his back, stretching his paws in the air, clearly pleased to be in the safety of their home.

For a time they sat in silence, the flicker of their muted television casting soft light across the room. Cate rested her head on Landry's chest, her breath slow and steady. She was happy. And that was all that mattered.

But in the quiet moments, when the world outside their window grew still and the darkness thickened, Landry's thoughts turned to his foe. He sensed this time she wasn't just after revenge. She was after something much deeper, something he couldn't yet understand.

He kissed the top of Cate's head, lingering there for a moment, inhaling the faint scent of her shampoo. She stirred slightly, looking up at him.

"You okay?" she asked, sensing something was off.

"Yeah," he lied, forcing a smile. "Just thinking about work. We wrapped the 'Bayou Witches' episode today. It's going to be a good one."

She studied him for a moment, and then she said, "You've been working too hard. You need to relax. Let's plan a trip. Where shall we go? Europe? Mexico? The Caribbean?"

He laughed. "Have you been talking to Henri? He thinks I need some time off too. So I'll go anywhere you want. Do you think we should find dog-friendly hotels or leave our baby with a sitter?" They both laughed, and she snuggled closer to him.

He held her close while guilt gnawed in his mind. He couldn't tell her about the figure he had seen—about Charity Device and the nightmare that was creeping back into their lives. Cate had trusted him, and for her sake, he had to pretend he deserved that trust.

But as he sat there enjoying the comfortable feeling of her head on his shoulder, Landry knew that certain parts of his past were far from closed. There would come a day when he would be forced to renege on his promises to Cate for the sake of them both.

That night Landry lay awake, staring at the ceiling as moonlight filtered through the windows. Cate was asleep beside him, her breathing soft and even. But Landry's mind stirred with fear.

He couldn't push that shadowy image in the street from his thoughts. What did she want? His soul, or was there something more she was after now? Something told him that this time it wasn't just about him. There was something deeper, darker—something that threatened much more than him.

Landry had faced many supernatural horrors in his time, but nothing had ever felt this personal. He could never erase the memory of the horrors he'd faced in Pendle. And Cate had been thrown into it as well. The thought of losing her, of her getting caught in the crossfire, terrified him more than any ghost or demon ever could. He would do anything to protect her. But what did that mean, when something evil had lurked in the shadows a block away?

He glanced over at her, watching the way the moonlight softened her features. She was everything to him. He wouldn't let Charity Device take that away. But deep down, he knew that facing her again was inevitable. The darkness that had haunted him for so long was rising once more.

And this time, it wasn't going to let him go.

WAIT A MOMENT!

THERE'S MORE TO THIS STORY!

Here's a preview of the next book

The Witches' Revenge

Available in paperback
or e-book

Summer 2025

THE WITCHES' REVENGE
Bayou Hauntings 11

CHAPTER ONE

Charity Device, the last of a long line of witches who founded and had until recently ruled Pendle, Louisiana, now commanded her coven from a crude assortment of shacks and structures deep in the swamps near Bayou Dularge. It was a far cry from the power she once exerted over the townspeople. She had reveled in he way they trembled when she was nearby, and with that gone, anger seethed and burned inside her.

Exiled from their dark throne in Pendle after paranormal investigator Landry Drake lifted an ancient curse, Charity and her followers bided their time until they could exact retribution from him. For centuries, her family had ruled the town unchallenged, bending its will and feeding off the darkness that festered beneath its surface. Now, almost a year since their banishment, Charity grew restless, her once-unchecked power now confined to a small coven of followers hiding out in the bayou.

From her swampy lair, for months Charity waited for the perfect moment to strike. Her desire for revenge was fierce and personal—Landry's interference cost her everything. As the days passed, her patience broke at last. She could wait no longer. She convened the others to a spot under the twisted cypress trees where she prepared a ritual steeped in blood and shadows that would summon the dark forces older than Pendle itself to aid her in locating her quarry. There had been a time when Charity could have found him on her own, but even before leaving Pendle, she had noticed a change in her supernatural abilities. She was aging, and her powers were slowly diminishing. Then and now she managed to keep that fact to herself, knowing that any sign of weakness would surely lead to her leadership being snatched away from her. The others respected and feared her, but she had no friends, no one who would stand with her in times of need.

Now, under the dense, moss-laden cypress trees of Bayou Dularge, Charity Device stood surrounded by her coven, the embers of their anger and bitterness smoldering in their hollow eyes. The murky swamp ripples around them, the beady eyes of alligators watch from the water, and a thick fog rolls in as they prepare for a summoning far darker than any they had ever attempted. Charity, draped in tattered robes that once shimmered with the power of Pendle's twisted magic, raised her arms, her fingers clawing toward the sky. With her voice low and dripping with malice, she began the incantation, summoning a force as old as the shadows lurking everywhere in the bayou.

She was apprehensive about performing the ritual today after resisting doing it for months. She had never controlled the dark forces; in fact, they had done as they wished in Pendle, and when Landry Drake overpowered her and banished the witches from Pendle, Charity wondered if the devil's henchmen would remain her allies or turn against her for being weak and helpless against a mortal. For better or worse, today she would have her answer, because she could no longer wait to exact revenge against her enemy.

Following her instructions, the coven formed a tight circle, their fingers slick with a mixture of blood and swamp mud as they traced symbols into the ground. Charity's voice grew louder, stronger, each word laced with venom as she called on entities older than Pendle, older than the earth they stood upon.

"O spirits of the forgotten depths, dwellers of endless night," she intoned, her voice a guttural growl, "I summon thee forth. Come, creatures of shadow and smoke, bind thyself to my cause. Bring me the one who has undone us, that I might reclaim what was stolen. Deliver Landry Drake to me."

The witches glanced around themselves as the air thickened and a fetid wind swirled around the circle, filling their nostrils with the scent of decay and sulfur. Now all chanted in unison, voices melding with the swamp's heartbeat. The ground trembled beneath them, and slowly, a shadow began to rise from the damp earth, twisting and coiling as it took form.

A black mist arose, seething and shifting, until a figure solidified within it—a creature with skin like charred bark, fissured with veins of glowing crimson. Its face was a horrifying amalgam of man and beast, with eyes that burned like hot coals and a mouth stretched in a sneer that revealed razor-sharp, glistening teeth. Around its horns, dark smoke curled, and its elongated fingers, each tipped with claws dripping a thick, oily substance, reached out, hovering just above the coven's circle.

The younger members of Charity's coven drew back in fear; they practiced witchcraft, but none had experienced anything like what was unfolding before them. Even the older witches, those who had used spells and incantations to achieve their desires, bowed their heads in reverence to the creature their leader had brought forth from the beyond.

Drawing a deep breath, Charity stepped forward and met the creature's fiery gaze. "Moloch," she breathed. "You came." The creature's name hung in the air, sending a tremor through her followers as they stared in terrified awe at the demon before them. Moloch, an ancient harbinger of torment who once fed on the souls of entire villages, hovered before them, summoned from the depths of hell itself.

"What do you seek, woman?" Moloch's voice rumbled like thunder, dripping with mockery. "You who once tasted power but now cower in the swamps, hollow and beaten, dare to summon me." His tone was laced with mocking contempt, but a glimmer of amusement flickered in his blazing eyes, a sign that he was intrigued by her desperation.

Charity steeled herself, swallowing her pride as she forced her voice to remain steady. "I want Landry Drake. He is the one who broke our hold on Pendle, who undid the spell that bound the town to my family for centuries. I want him brought here, his strength sapped, his spirit broken. For the pain he caused us, I want to cause him to suffer miserably before I kill him."

Moloch's mouth twisted into a grin as his eyes narrowed to snakelike slits. "Ah, revenge. You witches always hunger for such delights. But what will you offer in return for my assistance?" His voice dripped with cunning, each word laced with ancient cruelty.

Anticipating the demon's requirement for payment, Charity knew what to offer that would entice him to help. She hesitated for only a heartbeat before lifting her chin. "A soul," she whispered, nodding toward the youngest of her coven, a teenaged girl who stood with her mother's arm around her shoulders. Both understood the child's fate, and as the girl began to weep, the mother remained stoic.

The demon let out a low, rumbling laugh, the sound vibrating through the swamp like the sound of an approaching storm. "Very well, Charity Device," Moloch said, extending a clawed hand that pierced the fog. Smoke and spells swirled in the humid air as her followers chanted, their eyes flickering with an unnatural light. Soon, a vision began to form: a grand old sternwheeler sailing along the Mississippi River. Figures on the upper deck came into focus, and Charity recognized Landry and his girlfriend Cate. Her heart jumped with excitement as she considered how close she might be to exacting revenge on her archenemy.

The demonic creature spoke. "Your quarry will soon be taking a vacation—a riverboat cruise. His guard will be down, his senses dulled by relaxation—a perfect opportunity. At the appointed time, my power will ensure that his fate will be sealed within these swamps. I shall bring him to you—but know this: his suffering shall nourish me, just as his capture will satisfy you. The darkness binds us both."

He lingered as the swamp lay in an unnatural stillness, as if every creature lurking in its murky depths knew better than to stir while the demon remained there. As Moloch's eyes fell on the child, Charity's followers instinctively took a step back, sensing an unspoken danger. The girl, barely thirteen, stood pale and trembling at the edge of the coven's circle, her wide eyes darting between the monstrous figure and her mother, silently pleading for mercy. Now the mother wept as well, and Moloch's expression twisted into a gruesome sneer. His eyes flared like embers in a dying fire as he advanced toward the girl, his footsteps silent but with a weight that seemed to sink into the very earth.

Charity, despite her resolve, found herself transfixed, unable to look away as the creature stretched one long, spindly claw toward the girl. He paused, glancing back at Charity with a glint of wickedness in his eyes, a silent confirmation that this was his price. The witches gasped— they had never seen a ritual such as this. They stood transfixed as they watched the demon seize the girl by her shoulders, his hand tightening with a strange, almost tender grip. In that moment, the swamp was silent, the air thick and stifling, as though the entire bayou held its breath.

Without a word, Moloch leaned in close to the girl's face, his gaze consuming her with an intensity that seemed to pull her essence from within. The girl's lips parted, her mouth forming a silent scream as her eyes widened, emptying of all life and color. Her spirit was drawn out in a wisp of silvery light, a glimmer of innocence lost as it twined around Moloch's clawed fingers. Her body went rigid, her head tilting back, mouth agape, as her soul was devoured by the creature's insatiable hunger.

The witches watched in horror as Moloch's form flickered, momentarily swelling with dark power, absorbing the stolen essence like a thirst quenched. The girl's empty, lifeless body crumpled to the ground, her skin already taking on the pallor of death. A wave of dread settled over the coven as they stared down at her fragile form, now nothing more than a husk discarded at their feet. Charity swallowed hard, steeling herself as she looked into Moloch's eyes, now glowing with renewed energy, as if the soul had rekindled his ancient, monstrous power.

Before he vanished into the shadows, Moloch fixed his gaze on Charity, a low, gravelly chuckle rumbling from his chest. "Your payment is received," he whispered, his voice barely more than a hiss, sending chills through everyone gathered. "I will bring you Landry Drake, broken and bound as you desire." His eyes narrowed, a dark promise lingering in the air and he dissipated into thick, curling smoke that lingered in the air before sinking into the soil, leaving the swamp heavy with his presence. Only the girl's body remained as evidence of their dark transaction.

The silence that followed was deafening. The witches shifted uneasily, casting glances at Charity, their eyes questioning if their leader had made a pact too horrific even for their standards. But Charity straightened her shoulders, masking her unease with a smile that didn't reach her eyes. She had to maintain control after the horrific act she'd caused. She put an arm around the mother of the dead girl, a gesture of kindness none of the witches had ever seen from her.

"We will never be free as long as Landry Drake is alive," she told them. "Thanks to him, we lost the power to seize him ourselves, and I had no choice but to summon Moloch and pay him what he demanded."

Charity knew Moloch would not fail her. The trap had been set, and Landry Drake would soon be hers to punish— his suffering a payment long overdue.

Thank you for reading *The Bayou Witches*.

If you enjoyed it, I'd appreciate a review on Amazon.
Reviews allow other readers to find books they might
like, so thanks in advance for your help.

Please join me on:
Facebook
http://on.fb.me/187NRRP
Twitter
@BThompsonBooks

This is book 10 of the Bayou Hauntings series.
The others are available on my website and Amazon.
Go to billthompsonbooks.com to purchase ebooks, and
to Amazon.com to buy paperback or ebook versions.

MAY WE OFFER YOU A FREE BOOK?
Bill Thompson's award-winning first novel,
The Bethlehem Scroll, can be yours free.
Just go to
billthompsonbooks.com
and click "Subscribe."

Once you're on the list, you'll receive advance notice
of future book releases and our newsletter.